Fractures

A Detectives Seagate and Miner Mystery

Volume 5

MIKE MARKEL

Fractures

A Detectives Seagate and Miner Mystery

Volume 5

ISBN-13: 978-0692387535
ISBN-10: 0692387536

Prologue

Lee Rossman shut off the lights as he exited the reception area of his office in the New Century Building. Locking the door behind him, he walked down the carpeted hall toward the elevator. The faint sounds of Mexican pop music drifted into the hall from the open door of the title-company office a few steps ahead. As he stepped around the cleaning cart that protruded into the hall, he glanced inside but didn't see anyone. He would have said hello. He was comfortable with Hispanics from his years in Houston, and he mixed easily with people who came from nothing, as he had.

The elevator, smooth and almost silent, delivered him to the basement parking garage. The click of his leather soles on the concrete floor echoed in the silent garage. There were only eight or nine cars left. He recognized a midnight-blue Lexus, a dark green Jaguar, and a silver Audi that seemed to be there when he arrived every morning around seven and were still there when he left, twelve or fourteen hours later. As he walked toward his BMW 7 series in parking spot 96, he glanced at his watch: 9:25.

He often thought of what his father had told him, his father who quit high school to work the oil fields for a buck-and-a-half an hour: "You got time or you got money. Nobody got both."

He tossed his wool topcoat onto the passenger seat and started the BMW, the running lights throwing two white circles on the grey concrete wall, just below "Rossman Mining" painted in maroon letters four inches high. He had been so successful for so many years he no longer thought about how far he had come in his forty-five-year career.

Lee Rossman eased the car toward the exit, tripping the mechanism for the steel gate, which clanged and shuddered as it rose. He saw the blue light flash and heard the buzzer sound out on the sidewalk as he steered the car onto Main Street. Red and green Christmas decorations on the light poles swayed in the wind. After dark here in central Montana, when the gusts picked up, the squat old brick and stone commercial buildings provided intermittent windbreak; but when he crossed each side street he heard a muffled whoosh and felt his heavy BMW tilt for a moment as the wind barreled through the tiny commercial center of Rawlings.

He drove six blocks, past the holiday lights and decorations on the stores and offices, now closed for the night. He passed a handful of people huddled in their heavy coats, hunched over in the frigid night air. A digital sign on the bank display read 3 degrees. The movie theatre, its bright bulbs illuminating the lobby posters and the V-shaped white marquee extending out over the sidewalk, offered the only attraction in the frozen purple night.

Lee Rossman turned left on Harrison and drove slowly toward the grittier section of downtown, where the storefronts cowered behind steel accordion gates. He slowed down as he approached Johnny's Lounge and put on his blinker. Above the gouged, dirty wooden door, the bar's name was spelled out in cursive letters, garish blue and red neon. To the left of the name was a huge neon top hat; to the right, a giant cocktail glass, tilted slightly.

From the door emerged a tall, thin young guy wearing matching denim jeans and jacket and a white cowboy hat. He pulled a cigarette from his jacket pocket and, cupping his hands, lit it with a butane lighter.

Sizing up the young man's clothing, Lee Rossman concluded

he wouldn't be walking, certainly not more than a few steps. The young man moved slowly and deliberately, concentrating as each boot hit the sidewalk, as if he were rehearsing walking a straight line in case the police stopped him. Rossman scanned the line of parked cars and pickups, trying to guess which one belonged to the young man, before settling on a new black F-150, its sides streaked with mud.

The young man stepped off the curb, momentarily losing his balance, and steadied himself on the hood of the black pickup. Lee Rossman smiled as the roughneck walked over to the driver's door and struggled to retrieve his keys from the pocket of his tight jeans. He was out on the town in his new denim and his new truck.

Rossman pulled up behind the truck and waited while its big block engine turned over. The pickup shook and let out a rumble, and the young man steered out of the parking spot slowly and drove off.

Rossman carefully parked his BMW in the empty spot thirty feet from the entrance to Johnny's Lounge. He let the engine idle for a few moments, his fingers gripping the heated, leather-wrapped steering wheel. Warm air blasted from the vents on either side of the wheel, filling the cabin. He felt the warmth from the leather seat penetrating his wool slacks, which were designed in London and tailored in Hong Kong but never intended to be worn in Rawlings, Montana, in late November.

What did it mean, Lee Rossman thought, that he was summoned here? At nine-thirty on a Sunday night?

He shut down the engine and held his palms over the heat vents. He looked up as two girls in their mid-twenties approached the heavy wooden door to Johnny's Lounge. They were wearing thick down jackets, blue jeans with rhinestones on the back pockets, and cowboy boots with two-inch heels. One of the girls pulled at the door, then flashed a big smile as a beefy guy, obscured by the shadows inside the bar, helped them pull it open.

Lee Rossman didn't recognize these girls, but he knew they were at Johnny's for the first shift. Until about midnight, there was live music from a country band that had both a male and a female singer and therefore could play any of the popular songs on the two country radio stations in town. Some of the girls on the first shift were there for the line dancing, some for the free drinks from any of a couple of dozen guys who walked in with two or three crisp hundred-dollar bills in their jeans pockets and left without a penny. After midnight—after the girls in denim and cowboy boots had selected their guys and left—another set of girls started to work the pole on the platform behind the bar, and the professionals in tight skirts started to work the guys who hadn't come for the line dancing.

He got out of the BMW and slipped into his topcoat. He slid his hands deep into the coat pockets and walked toward the bar. The battered door opened, and a couple stepped out into the frigid air. Lee Rossman felt the vibration from the bass guitar. He heard the crack of the snare drum, as sharp as a gunshot, and the metallic tinkling of women's voices competing with the amplified music. He felt the humidity coming off the young bodies inside and smelled the spilled beer and the cheap, sweet perfume mingled with sweat.

Lee Rossman said "Excuse me" as the young couple, laughing and oblivious to the old man in the charcoal wool topcoat, stumbled into him. He kept walking, past the window with the big neon Coors sign, toward the spot where he had been instructed to appear. He turned into the alley that ran along the wall of Johnny's Lounge. He walked toward the floodlight mounted above two heavy steel basement doors in the pavement. He stood there, as he had been directed.

It took him some time to make out the objects in the alley outside the cone of light in which he stood. The moon was hidden behind fast-rushing clouds, and there were no other lights to push back the darkness. On one side of the steel doors were a dozen empty beer kegs lined up alongside the concrete-block wall. On the other side was a stack of three wooden shipping pallets and a big green dumpster on wheels, with trash and cardboard boxes propping open its lid. Across the alley was a three-story brick building, probably a hundred years old, with ornamental stone-framed windows now bricked in, a vestige of a time when the alley was a through street.

Lee Rossman felt the cold penetrating the soles of his shoes. He glanced down at his feet. The alley, its surface rippled, broken, and patched in various shades of grey and black, was covered with dirty ice, crushed paper beer cups, broken glass, cigarette butts, and condom wrappers. Off to the side he saw a frozen starburst of vomit. He caught a faint smell of urine.

He stood there, under the light in the alley next to Johnny's Lounge, waiting as he had been instructed. He glanced to his right when he heard footsteps.

They looked at each other for a long moment. "Why here?" Lee Rossman said.

His killer did not respond.

"You owe me an explanation," Rossman said.

The killer paused. "You don't want to talk about what we owe each other."

"What do you want?" he said.

"I want your answer."

"I considered what you said."

"And are you done considering?"

"Yes." His tone was strong but full of regret. "I am."

"What is your decision?"

"My answer is no. I will not do it."

His killer was silent.

"I'm going to go now," Lee Rossman said. "I expect that you

will not mention this to me again. Ever." He started to turn.

"You know it's the only way."

He stopped and turned to face his killer. "There's always another way."

"I'm afraid you've made the wrong decision." His killer walked toward him.

Lee Rossman did not realize what was happening when the killer pushed aside his open topcoat. Only when he felt the knife slide into his abdomen and the pain radiate out in all directions like electric charges did he understand.

His eyes were open wide in disbelief. His knees began to buckle, and he sank to the pavement, his head hitting hard and coming to rest near a patch of ice in which a candy wrapper was frozen.

The killer bent down and reached into Lee Rossman's suit jacket pocket and removed his wallet, then lifted the velvet cuff of the victim's topcoat sleeve, unbuckled the clasp on his heavy gold watch, slipped it off his wrist, and let his arm fall to the pavement. Lee Rossman appeared to be breathing, but his skin was beginning to pale and his eyes were glassy and unfocused. The killer turned to walk away, then stopped and returned and, pushing Rossman's topcoat and suit jacket aside, lowered the zipper on his impeccably tailored black wool slacks.

Chapter 1

The alley full of the usual alley shit, including swirling garbage, frozen puke, a dirty grey sock, a used condom with dried blood streaked on it, and actual shit from at least two different species, I decided not to bother putting on my paper booties.

I stepped under the yellow tape that spanned the alley next to Johnny's Lounge and followed Barlow, the first officer on scene, toward the body of a sixty-something-year-old whiter-than-white guy. He was Caucasian, like almost everyone here in Montana, with long, thick white hair, recently trimmed. His skin was the color of bleached ivory, except his nose, his ears, and all ten fingers, which were dark gray from frostbite.

I glanced down the alley. A big blue garbage truck was parked up against the brick wall. "The garbage guy called it in?" I said to Barlow.

"Yeah. He'd already emptied the dumpster. I told him to shut the truck down and leave it here."

"Good thinking," I said. "Thanks."

I crouched down next to the body and pulled back the unbuttoned black topcoat. Beneath it was a black suit jacket, which I pulled back, too. The blood spot on the pale blue shirt was about six inches across. The slice in the shirt was about an inch across. With that little amount of blood, I figured he was killed outside, last night, and the cold closed up the wound.

My partner, Ryan, who had been scoping out the buildings to see if there was anyone to canvass, came over. "Just that one wound?"

"That's all I can see." I looked up at Barlow, who nodded his head. "Any residences that have a line of sight on the alley?" I said to Ryan.

"No."

"Any businesses would've been open last night?"

"Just this one." His chin pointed toward the wall of Johnny's Lounge.

I looked up at Barlow. "Wallet? ID?"

He shook his head. "No wallet or ID."

"Car keys?"

Barlow opened the paper evidence bag he was holding, pulled out a set of eight keys gathered in a tooled leather holder, and handed it to me.

Ryan crouched down close to the body. "Whoever he was, he had some money."

"The clothes?" I looked at the vic's topcoat, then at Ryan's. "His is nicer than yours, right?"

Ryan already had his latex gloves on. He lifted the coat and looked at the label. "Burberry. About two thousand dollars nicer."

"You're shitting me."

"The horn buttons, the velvet on the collar. This is the real deal." He paused a moment. "We're going to want to figure out what he was doing here."

"You don't know what he was doing here?" I looked at him. "It's a tittie bar. You buy a girl a twenty-dollar whiskey, she rubs her tits in your face."

"Yes, Karen," he said, offering me a small smile. "I'm aware of what happens *inside* a tittie bar. But you'll notice we're *outside* this particular tittie bar, on what could be the most disgusting piece of real estate in the great state of Montana."

"He wants to fuck the girl. She's not allowed to fuck him inside. They go out in the alley. He pushes her up against the wall."

Ryan was shaking his head. "This guy can afford to take her wherever he wants."

"Come on. That's a pain in the ass. He'd need a half-hour to get there, get her into the room. Someone could see him. He just wants to bend her over, grunt a few times, and zip up. This place is perfect," I said. "Where's your sense of romance?"

Ryan raised his eyebrows. "Well, you've certainly convinced me."

"You see a watch on him?"

Ryan held up one of his cuffs, then the other. He leaned in closer. "He was wearing a heavy watch on this wrist," he said. "See the hair? How it's matted. And some of the hairs are broken off. I'd say a metal bracelet, not a leather band."

I couldn't see well enough to confirm what Ryan was talking about, but I was willing to take his word for it. "So they grabbed his wallet and watch but left that ring?" I pointed to a thick gold ring with a big black stone on his right hand.

Ryan tried pulling on the ring, but it didn't budge. "The guy was probably just smash-and-grab, not the kind who'd chop off a finger to get the ring."

"Yet willing to stab the guy in the alley and not phone it in, so the vic would die in the street in the cold?"

Ryan stood up and faced me. "Maybe the guy was just trying to take the easy stuff. The vic puts up a fight, starts screaming. The guy panics, stabs him, runs away."

I shrugged. At this stage, I wouldn't rule out anything this side of vampires. And with the right puncture marks in the neck, I'd be fine with vampires.

I looked down at the key ring Barlow had handed me. One of the keys was a fat one, obviously a car key. "You recognize this?" I held it up for Ryan to see.

"Barlow, you want to stick your head out there," Ryan said,

pointing to Harrison Street, "see if you can spot a BMW with frost on the windows?"

Barlow nodded and walked off toward the street.

"If I were a sixty-year-old guy, with money," Ryan said, "I'd feel awfully disappointed with myself if I had to come out to a place like this to look at naked girls."

I'm only forty-three, but I've got so many disappointments I can line them up in alphabetical order. If I make it to sixty and want to go see naked girls or naked guys—or do anything, really, other than piss my diaper—I'd consider that a small triumph.

The shrink the department assigned me after some bad shit happened last year blabbed all the time about seeing simple accomplishments as triumphs and victories. Every few sentences there was a "celebration," which made me want to read him his Miranda rights. But I guess I'm coming around to his point of view, a little bit, at least.

I won't say it to Ryan because he's only twenty-nine and therefore shouldn't have to hear stuff like this, but I think the trick to getting older is to ask for less out of life. Right now, although I've lost most of the feeling in my toes standing out here in the alley, I've got bladder and bowel control, I've got a job and a car, the bank hasn't thrown me out of my house, and nobody's shooting at me. This is me celebrating.

Barlow came back and nodded his head.

"What model?" Ryan said.

"A 7 series," Barlow said.

"Knew it," Ryan said, and the two boys turned to go check out the car. I followed.

It was a beauty. Black paint that seemed to be 3-D, with little gold flecks in it. And clean, too, which is pretty rare here in Montana, where the air is mostly dust and the wind howls so bad the tumbleweed flies more than it tumbles. I shielded my eyes from the new sun coming up and peered through the tinted windows. The inside was all black leather, with a dashboard full of swirly burled walnut and enough gauges to outfit a jet cockpit.

"Want me to open it up?" Ryan said.

"No," I said. "I want to let Robin check the door handles for prints."

"Let me just see if we've got the right car." He pressed the remote control on the key ring, and the four knobs rose silently. "Okay, this is it."

"Call Robin, tell her she'll want to arrange to have the car brought in."

Ryan nodded, handing the key ring back to Barlow and pulling his phone out of his inside jacket pocket.

A beat-up old green minivan rolled up slowly toward the three of us. Harold Breen put down his window. "Can I park at the end of the alley?"

I nodded, and Barlow started walking to the spot to show Harold where to park.

"Robin's on her way." Ryan put his phone away. "Three or four minutes."

"All right," I said. "Let's go see what Harold says."

We made it over to the minivan as Harold was starting to get out of the driver's seat. Harold weighs something north of three-fifty—I don't think anyone knows the exact number—and with his bulky down coat pushing up hard against the steering wheel, it took him a little while to wrestle himself free, the seat groaning all the while. The van rose a couple inches, and Harold shifted his feet on the pavement to get his balance.

Ryan and I led him over to the crime-scene tape. "No booties?" he said.

"Don't bother." I lifted the tape high for him. He doesn't bend well.

"Jesus Christ," he said, looking down at his feet as he lumbered over toward the body.

I squatted next to the body and pulled the coat back to reveal the knife wound. "Would this be enough?" I said to the medical examiner.

"Sure." He was breathing hard from the walk. "If the blade hit the liver or a kidney and he wasn't on the table within a half-hour, he'd be gone."

"So the cold wouldn't have saved him? You know, shut down his systems?"

He shook his head. "All the temperature's done is give him frostbite. If he starts out at room temperature and cools down over an hour, the internal bleeding would have killed him before he got cold enough to prevent tissue death."

"Can you call a time of death?"

"Not really," Harold said. "I can't test for rigor in this temperature. I might be able to figure it out back at the lab, but at the moment I'll have to say sometime before now."

I nodded. "Okay, that's good."

"Unless you've got a knife with some sticky stuff on the blade. That would help me."

"I'll be sure to let you know if we find something like that."

"I'll see you later." He turned and headed back to his minivan.

I turned to Ryan. "Barlow already looked for a weapon, right?"

"Yeah," he said. "In the alley, but not yet in the dumpster or in the garbage truck."

"Call in to headquarters, will you, and request a team for that?"

"Two uniforms?"

"Ask for four. Hope for two."

Ryan was taking out his phone when Robin came walking up to us. She was wearing a red wool ski hat, a powder-blue, tight-fitting ski jacket, and black spandex pants that showed off her long legs and her young ass. "Look at all this shit," she said, giving me a cheerful smile.

"There's no shortage of shit, that's for sure," I said.

"Excellent." She pushed a strand of blond hair back behind her ear. "This'll take me a couple of hours, easy."

"Well, good," I said. "I'm glad you're looking forward to it."

She walked over to the body. "Robbery?"

"Maybe," I said. "Wallet and watch are gone."

Robin looked around and pointed toward the wall of Johnny's Lounge. "He could've been buying himself a blowjob."

"Blowjob. Robbery." I shrugged my shoulders. "Blowjob, then robbery."

"Great," she said. "I'll get started with the photos."

"How much of this shit you gonna collect?"

She looked around a little bit, then paused. "I think I'll leave the shit. But I'll grab anything that isn't frozen to the ground. Except for all the used rubbers and the wrappers. I'll chip them out if I need to."

I followed her as she walked over toward the wall of Johnny's Lounge and bent down to study a used condom. "That frozen cum down there?" She pointed. "That could be our guy's. And the blood and the pubes on the outside? That could be his killer."

"All right, then." I nodded my approval. "So you're gonna call me with the killer's name in, what, forty-eight hours?"

"I'm going to shoot for thirty-six."

"I'll catch up with you later, okay?" I said, but she was already trotting off to get the cones and the camera.

I have very mixed feelings about young people.

Chapter 2

"The John Doe from this morning?" Robert Murtaugh took his seat behind his desk and motioned for me and Ryan to sit in the two upholstered chairs facing his desk. As usual, he was wearing a dark suit, this one navy, pinstriped, an ivory button-down and a dark green tie with a small gold tie tack holding it in place.

His expression was noncommittal. He wasn't broken up that a guy bit it, but he wasn't excited, either. He's been a cop for three decades. For Chief Murtaugh, the job was all about procedure. There was a right way and a wrong way to do everything. You do it the right way, good chance you'll clear the case.

"Yeah," I said. "We identified him."

"Close the door, will you, Ryan?"

One thing I really like about the chief is he doesn't make you stand so you know he's more important than you, and when you talk to him he actually listens. He never sneaks a look at his computer screen or takes a phone call.

"Guy's name is Lee Rossman, age sixty-five." I looked up from my notebook.

The color drained from the chief's face. He didn't say anything for the longest while. "You sure on that?"

I didn't quite understand where he was going. "Well, not DNA sure, but he was driving Lee Rossman's car, and when we pulled up his driver's license, it looked just like him." I glanced at Ryan, who shrugged his shoulders, then back at Murtaugh. "What are we missing, Chief?"

Murtaugh turned to Ryan. "You think it's Rossman?"

Ryan nodded. "Absolutely. I did a Web search. Must have seen twenty photos of him. It's him."

"Shit," the chief said. He put his elbows on his desk, his fingers tented underneath his chin.

I'd never heard the chief curse. He's very big on setting the right example for his cops. That starts with important stuff—how we can't shake down drug dealers, can't plant evidence, can't lie on the stand—which I agree with, in principle, anyway. But it extends all the way down to trivial stuff, including dressing and talking like professionals.

So he leaves his suit jacket on all day at headquarters. Once Ryan and I and a bunch of uniforms were putting on our gear before heading out on a meth-house raid. Murtaugh wanted to come with us. He took off his jacket, buckled himself into his tactical vest, then slipped the jacket back on.

I wasn't sure exactly why he's so anal retentive about the rules, but I would guess it has to do with being a recovering drunk, like me and half the other detectives. Of all of us, he's wound the tightest, which might explain why he's been sober for nineteen years. Me, it's been more than a year, except for a few episodes when I curled up to relax in a bottle of Jack Daniel's.

"Lee Rossman was the main reason I took this job." The chief ran his hand through his thick salt-and-pepper hair and exhaled. "He was a very good man." He shook his head. "Damn it."

"You knew him from California?" I said. Murtaugh was assistant to the chief in Sacramento before coming here.

He shook his head. "I met him during the hiring process. The mining business in eastern Montana was taking off at the time, and he told me he understood how it was going to introduce all sorts of challenges for law enforcement. He was a big supporter of the department. Donated money for training, equipment, for the Benevolent Association." He looked at me like I should have known this. "You didn't hear about that from Chief Arnold?"

This guy Arnold was the chief's predecessor. "He wasn't really that into communicating with cops."

"Remember that human-trafficking bill that was introduced last year?"

"Yeah," I said. Ryan nodded. The chief was referring to the law that would overturn prostitution convictions if the girls could show they were coerced into hooking.

The chief nodded. "Lee offered to donate a hundred thousand dollars to set up training and counseling for the girls, statewide." He paused and looked down at his desk. Then he lifted his gaze and looked at me. "What do we know?"

"It was a homicide. Stabbed once, outside a bar, then left to die overnight in the cold." I paused. "Harold's not sure yet which killed him. His face and hands were all frostbitten, and his abdomen near the stabbing wound was bright pink, which is hypothermia, but he says Rossman probably died from internal bleeding from the stabbing. There was a bump on his head, probably from when he went down, but not big enough to have done any real damage."

"Harold hasn't done the autopsy yet?"

"We talked to him a few minutes ago," I said. "He can get to him this afternoon or tomorrow morning."

"You said outside a bar?"

The chief liking Rossman, I knew he wasn't going to like this answer. "On Harrison, Chief. In the alley next to Johnny's Lounge."

The Chief's eyes closed slowly and stayed shut for a few seconds. "We know what he was doing there?"

"Not yet," I said. "Harold said he didn't see any defensive wounds on Rossman's hands. And one other thing."

"What's that?"

"His zipper was down."

"We have any evidence of sexual activity in the alley?"

"There's lots of evidence that people are into all kinds of shit in the alley. There's condoms, wrappers, baggies, a couple needles. Robin's still cataloging it all. But nothing to say Rossman was doing any of that. Nothing that would put a girl there with him— or a guy or anything."

"So it could've been a robbery that went bad."

I shrugged my shoulders. "Could've been. Wallet and watch are gone."

"Have you made contact with the bar manager?"

Ryan looked down at his notebook. "We got a name off the liquor license. Philip Vinson. We put in a call to him at home. We're going to meet up with him a little later this morning."

"Have you canvassed the scene?"

"Not yet, Chief," Ryan said. "I didn't see any businesses or residences that overlook the alleyway, but we'll give it a try."

"I'll assign you whatever manpower you need."

"That would be great, Chief," I said. "There's a dumpster right near where the victim was recovered. The garbage truck— the driver had already emptied the dumpster this morning when he saw the body."

"The truck's been locked down?"

I nodded. "If we could get a few uniforms out there, that would really help Robin out."

The chief was making notes on his legal pad. "Have you notified his wife?"

"Not yet," I said.

"Did she ever file a missing person?"

"No," Ryan said. "We checked on that."

The chief looked puzzled. "That's odd."

"We thought so," I said. The chief didn't respond. "You know anything about the wife?"

"Her name is Florence. She's quite a bit younger than Lee. Not his first wife."

"You met her?"

"Once or twice." He shook his head. "But I don't know her well enough to tell you anything."

"We're gonna start with Mrs. Rossman, then interview the bar owner. That sound all right to you?"

The chief was gazing over my shoulder. Suddenly, he caught himself and focused on me. "Yeah, that's good."

"And you're going to work on getting us a couple of officers to help Robin?"

"You got it," the chief said, standing up.

"We'll keep you in the loop."

He nodded. "See if you can …" Then he stopped.

I waited a few beats. "Chief?"

He shook his head. "Nothing," he said. "Let it go where it goes."

Ryan and I stood up and left the chief's office. Out past Margaret, the gatekeeper, back down the hall to the detective's bullpen.

We sat down at our desks, arranged head-to-head in the middle of the bullpen.

Ryan said, "What do you think he meant?"

"When he said, 'See if you can'?"

"Yeah. You ever hear him say anything like that?"

I thought a second. "We haven't had a case where he knew the vic, have we?"

"Not that I can think of."

"I think he wanted to say, 'See if you can make it so Rossman wasn't getting his dick sucked by a twenty-year-old Russian girl when her boyfriend stepped out of the shadows, stabbed him, and took his wallet and watch."

Ryan smiled. "Well, can't blame him for not wanting to finish that sentence." He paused. "What do you want to do about it—I mean, that the chief knew Rossman?"

"Nothing. Except enjoy the fact that he's authorizing the uniforms we need to sort through the shit in the garbage truck."

"And do the canvass, too."

"Now you're thinking like a detective, Ryan."

"But you don't think he's going try to manipulate the investigation."

"No," I said. "I don't. He wants to keep Rossman out of that alley. That's understandable. But we haven't seen anything makes me think he's gonna try to rig the case. Besides, if he does, he'll probably do it so well we won't even know about it."

"So there's no problem," Ryan said.

"I'm planning to keep my head down, follow the evidence, and—what did he say we should do?"

"'Let it go where it goes.'"

"That's it. Just work the case. On the other hand," I said, "you find out that while Rossman was getting a blowjob from that Russian girl the chief was at Rossman's house nailing Florence, and when we interview her this morning she's got a bloody knife on her coffee table, then we'll talk some more about whether the chief might want to rig the case."

Chapter 3

"What are we talking here?" I said. Rossman's place flickered in and out of view behind the brush and the boulders as we snaked along the road that clung to the bluff a few hundred yards above the reservoir on the Rawlings River.

"Between one point five and two mill," Ryan said. He can eyeball real-estate prices, although I have no idea why he even bothers, what with his cop salary and a wife who plans to stay at home not only with their two current kids but also with the next three.

We were a few miles east of town, winding our way along the hairpin turns. The last of the big estates set on a couple of acres was in my rearview mirror. The paved road turned into rutted dirt and gravel flanked by bedrock, scrubby bushes that stayed brown all year long, and the occasional stunted pine or spruce trying to survive on the dry hillside.

A small metal sign announced the end of the public road, which transitioned into what must have been Rossman's driveway. Another sign said "Private Property," but nothing about who owned it, and no obnoxious threats about how you'd better not drive up. The roadway was made of some kind of round stones set in concrete, which made the wide tires on our Charger hum.

We continued on for another three- or four-hundred yards. As we got closer, I could see the house was one story, built right into the bedrock, with a flat roof pitched up at an angle as it emerged from the hillside. The whole place was hanging out over the bluff, balanced on what looked like cross-braced steel poles, with a wide deck extending out another fifteen feet. If you decided to take a flyer off the deck, you'd have a good three or four seconds to consider your decision before you became one with the rock.

I had phoned Florence Rossman as soon as we finished up with the chief. She sounded surprised and a little concerned getting a call from a detective—a reasonable reaction—but gracious and suave. She offered to talk to me on the phone so we wouldn't have to go to the trouble of driving out to her place. I told her it was no trouble. A sophisticated forty-something women talking to an unsophisticated one, both of them working hard to communicate but using different codes.

When I gave her the standard line about how it was in regard to a case we were working on, she must have realized we were going to drive out to her place whether she liked it or not, so she said the only thing a smooth talker can say: that she looked forward to meeting us. Great, I said, trying to keep up, we'd be there in ten, fifteen minutes.

I parked on the driveway in front of the four-car garage built into the rock. The formal entryway to the house was along the side, the double-wide doors flanked by local stone. To the right of the door, the wall was glass, and I could see down the hall the whole length of the house, through the glass walls on the other side, out to the unbroken steel-grey sky.

Ryan rang the bell. A few seconds later, a fifty-year-old Hispanic woman wearing a housekeeper's uniform opened the door. "Are you detectives?" she said in a thin, reedy voice.

"Yes," I said. "We're here to see Ms. Rossman."

"Here, please," she said, inviting us into the foyer. "I get her." She turned and walked down the hallway, the light streaming in through the glass walls overlooking the reservoir.

"You ever seen a place like this?" I said as we looked out over the rock face and the gray-green water rippled by the winds.

Ryan shook his head. "I need to log more overtime."

I turned as I heard footsteps approaching from the interior of the house.

"Detective Seagate?" Florence Rossman said, giving me a wide, friendly smile. Except for the crow's feet around her wide-set gray eyes, I would have put her at thirty-five. She was my height, about five-ten, with long, fine chestnut hair tied back. She wore a beige linen no-close jacket with turnback cuffs. A white silk V-neck blouse and a string of what looked like real pearls. Pearl earrings. Chocolate linen wide-leg pants and beige suede flats that matched her jacket.

I wondered if I'd mistakenly told her I was from *Vogue* and my photographer and I would be stopping by for a shoot. She extended her right hand, a couple of thin gold bracelets jangling lightly.

"Detective Karen Seagate," I said as we shook hands. "This is my partner, Detective Ryan Miner." The two of them shook.

"Shall we?" she said, turning to head into the main part of the house.

"That would be lovely," I said, stupidly. The "shall" threw me off. I was trying to remember when I last heard someone say it. I wasn't sure, but I think I was looking forward to my first training bra.

I felt a little wobbly as I followed her along the glass wall. The floor was polished concrete, but being a few hundred feet over the ground, high enough to touch the clouds and the brown hawk gliding past the windows on an updraft, was disconcerting.

Florence Rossman looked back at me and smiled. "It takes a little getting used to," she said as we passed the kitchen and dining area and entered the great room. "Follow me." She slid one of the glass doors open and walked out onto the deck.

It took me a few seconds to see the clear plastic posts and railings that were the only barrier that would keep you from walking right off the deck. The wind whistled, and the strip of turbulent white water feeding the river from the edge of the reservoir produced a faint hum. The tiny automobiles on the two-lane below were silent.

"When Lee and I saw this, we knew we had to build here."

"It's really something," I said.

She let us stand silently there for a half-minute. "Let's go back inside," she said.

The great room was full of brown leather couches, loveseats, and arm chairs arranged into three sitting areas. The hill side of the wall was filled with built-in red oak bookshelves surrounding an oversized gas fireplace. The ceiling was narrow-planked red oak and massive oak beams that supported the roof, with tiny pendant lights separating the beams. The dark walls, almost charcoal, were weathered, unpainted siding, like you might see on a hundred-year old barn, highlighted by three massive oil paintings: a crow against snow, a hawk in flight, and a bald eagle perched on a tree branch. The grey concrete floor was punctuated by three brightly colored throw rugs in Native American patterns.

"This is a beautiful house, Ms. Rossman," Ryan said. He gave her a muted smile.

"You're very kind," she said, bowing her head slightly. "Won't you both take a seat?" She gestured to a sofa and sat in an armchair facing us. When we were all settled in, she interlaced her fingers in her lap, leaned forward, and put on a serious face, which meant the house tour was over.

"When did you last see Mr. Rossman?" I said.

She tilted her head slightly upward, and her eyes half-closed. She paused before answering. "Yesterday morning, at breakfast." She nodded her head, confirming the accuracy of what she had just said. "May I know why you're asking that? Did something happen to Lee?"

"And when did you last speak with him?"

Her face was cloudy now. She still looked terrific. Worried but still terrific. "He called me yesterday afternoon. Between three and four. He usually calls at that time." She leaned forward toward me. "Why are you asking me this? You're scaring me."

"He didn't come home last night?"

"No, he didn't." Florence Rossman shifted in her seat.

"You didn't file a missing-person report, is that right?"

"Lee often stays out overnight."

"Where does he stay when he's out overnight?"

"He's got a trailer at the man camp, as well as a bed and a bathroom in his office downtown—in a little storage room near his office."

"Wouldn't it be just as easy for him to come home as stay in his office?"

"You don't understand my husband," Florence Rossman's features relaxed a bit, as if she had momentarily shaken off the fear that something had happened to him. "He grew up in drilling, and he likes to stay close to the rigs. I can't tell you how many times I've gotten a call during the middle of a fund-raiser—here in our own house—to tell me there's a problem at the rigs, or he's meeting with his landmen or the workers. I used to believe him," she said with an indulgent smile, "but then I just came to accept the fact that he'd rather be out with his men than making small talk with a bunch of rich people." She paused, worry clouding her expression again. "Now, Detective, I've answered your questions patiently, but I have a right to know what this is about. Has something happened to Lee?"

"Ms. Rossman," I said, my voice low, "a body of a man was recovered early this morning. We're going to show you a photograph, and we'd like you to tell us whether you think this might be Mr. Rossman."

"Oh, my God." Her hands came up and covered her nose and mouth.

Ryan slid a photograph out of his black leather briefcase and walked over to her. She looked at it for a moment, then let out a long scream. She seemed to sink into the leather of her chair, her head bowed. She began crying loudly.

I heard footsteps coming toward us rapidly. I turned. It was the housekeeper. I put up my hand and shook my head no to tell her not to come into the room. She stood there, confused. I waved her off, and she turned and walked away, down the long hall.

After the longest while, Florence Rossman's crying trailed off. She reached into her pants pocket and pulled out a handkerchief and started drying her eyes and dabbing at her nose.

"A heart attack?" She started crying again. "I knew this was going to happen."

"We don't have all the details yet, Ms. Rossman, but no. It was homicide."

She let out another scream and then began to breathe again. "Was it out at the rigs?"

"We don't know exactly where it happened, but his body was found here in town. In an alley next to Johnny's Lounge, on Harrison."

"In an alley?" Like that was unbelievable. "What would he be doing in an alley?"

"We were hoping you could help us with that." I paused a moment. "Did he go out to bars?"

She waved her hand and sighed loudly. "He was an oilman. He practically grew up in bars. But now? He never talked about that. I guess it's possible he was having a drink with a couple of the roughnecks from the rigs."

"So when he talked to you yesterday afternoon, he didn't say anything about how he was going to go meet some guys downtown?"

"No." She shook her head. "Nothing like that. He said he was going to drive out to the rigs."

"And did he say he was going to stay out there overnight or come back to town?"

"He didn't really say."

A gust of wind shook the floor-to-ceiling window overlooking the deck. I jumped a little. "And that was the way you would leave it?"

"Yes." She dabbed at her eyes. "Excuse me." She paused. "He would go out there—and if he was too tired to drive back, or there was weather, or something he needed to do there the next morning, he'd stay at the man camp. He had a room there, just for that purpose." She paused. "Do you know what time he was at the bar?"

"No, ma'am, we don't even know if he ever went into the bar last night."

She put her head into her hands and started to cry again. In a moment she raised her head and said softly, "How did he die?"

"We know he was stabbed once. But we don't know whether that wound was fatal."

"What do you mean?"

"We believe he was in the alley for a number of hours last night. Hypothermia might have played a role."

She folded her arms across her stomach and leaned forward. "I can't believe what you're telling me."

"We understand, Ms. Rossman. It's a terrible shock to learn something like this." I waited a few seconds. "Can you help us with anyone who would want to hurt Mr. Rossman? Anyone he was having a feud with? Personal or business?"

"Personal?" Her brows furrowed. "No, nothing. He never mentioned anything like that." She swept her arm, taking in the house. "We don't even have any neighbors. Lee was well-liked. I mean, he donated money to so many causes around town—you must have discovered that already—no, I can't think of any personal enemies. Business? Obviously, it's a rough business. There are competitors, and some people don't like oil drilling, but I can't imagine anyone would do something … do something like that."

"Mr. Rossman never mentioned receiving any threats? Anything from other people in the oil business? From activists?"

"No." She shook her head.

"And he never said anything about any of his own employees? Anyone who might be having a dispute with him about something on the job?"

She closed her eyes and shook her head.

"Ms. Rossman, I need to ask you a difficult question now."

She looked up. Her mascara was smudged below her eyes.

"Could you tell us where you were last night? Yesterday, from around three in the afternoon until this morning."

"You don't think … I might have had something to do with this." She leaned back in her chair.

"It's a question we need to ask, ma'am. We have to ask all his associates."

Anger flashed across her face. "I'm not an associate. I'm his wife, and I loved him completely."

"I'm not saying you didn't, Ms. Rossman. It's just a question I have to ask."

She took a deep breath. "I was out shopping. At the mall. I got home around five in the afternoon. I ate dinner here, alone. I was in all night. I didn't leave the house from five yesterday until now."

"Your housekeeper, what is her name?"

"Imelda. Imelda Hidalgo."

"Is she live-in?"

"No, she comes in the morning. Does some cleaning, some

cooking. Sometimes I have her do some errands. Dry cleaning, some shopping, things like that."

"Do you know what time she left last night?"

Florence Rossman titled her head back and looked up. "She cooked last night. I usually eat around six-thirty. So she probably finished cleaning up around seven-thirty, then left for the night."

"And you say you were alone in the house after that."

"Yes, that's right. I was doing some e-mail. Some other things on the computer for a few of the organizations I work with. Watched a little TV. Went to bed, around eleven-thirty, like I usually do."

Ryan said, "Did you make or receive any phone calls after you got home from the mall?"

"I'm sure I did." She paused. "I must be on the phone ten times a day."

"Someone from the Police Department will get in touch with you soon to arrange for you to come in and identify Mr. Rossman's body." She stood. Ryan and I did, too. "I want to tell you how sorry we are to give you this terrible news."

"We're very sorry for your loss, Ms. Rossman," Ryan said.

She nodded her thanks. "I have to notify Bill now."

"Bill?"

"My stepson. Bill. Lee's son."

"Does he live here in town?"

"Sometimes here, sometimes out at the rigs. He's a student at the university some semesters. Other times he's at the rigs. He's out there now."

"He's going into the oil business?"

"He's already in it." Florence Rossman tried to smile. "It's all he's ever wanted to do."

"Are you two close?"

"It's a work in progress. He's a very good young man. But, you understand. His father marries a woman who's a generation younger. That mustn't have been easy."

"I do understand." We turned to leave. I paused. "Again, Ms. Rossman, our condolences."

She nodded. "Let me get Imelda to show you out," Florence Rossman said.

"That won't be nec—" I started to say. Ryan put his hand on my arm.

"Thank you," he said to Florence Rossman, giving her an official smile.

Florence Rossman left the room. A moment later, the housekeeper came in. "This way, please," she said. Her expression was wary. She knew something bad had happened, but didn't understand exactly what. She led us out the way we had come in, over the concrete floor, the big wall of windows full of grey sky.

I'm not sure I could get used to living in a place like this. But I'd like to try.

Imelda opened the door and gave us a little bow.

"Actually, Imelda," Ryan said, "can we talk to you for just a moment before we go?"

"Yes, of course." She closed the door. She looked confused, as if none of the Rossman's guests had ever wanted to talk with her. "There is problem with Ms. Rossman?"

"We just wanted to check with you on something. Mr. Rossman—sometimes he didn't come home at night, is that correct?"

"That's right. Sometimes he stay in his office or out at oil well. Yes."

"Did anything unusual happen yesterday?"

"Unusual?"

"Did anyone stop by the house here who you didn't know? Did Ms. Rossman get any phone calls that upset her? Anything at all unusual?"

"No, nothing. She get phone calls, but not upset."

"And was she home here all day?"

Imelda took a moment to think. "No, she went out in afternoon. Shopping, I think. Came home for dinner."

"Okay, and you cooked dinner for Ms. Rossman, cleaned up, and went home. About what time was that?"

"It was around seven-thirty."

"And she didn't call you after you left?"

"No, no call."

"So the next time you saw her was when you got here this morning, is that right?"

"Yes, this morning."

"Did anything seem unusual this morning? Was she acting different in any way?"

"Ms. Rossman always very polite to me. Very nice to work for Ms. Rossman."

"Okay, Imelda," Ryan said, smiling. "Thank you very much."

"Something bad happen to Mr. Rossman?"

"Ms. Rossman will talk to you," I said. "Thank you, Imelda," and Ryan and I left. Yes, indeed, something very bad happen to Mr. Rossman.

Chapter 4

"Thanks for coming in, Mr. Vinson," I said. "This is my partner, Detective Miner."

The three of us were sitting in Interview 2, which is the less scary of our two interview rooms. The tiles on the walls are dirty and cracked, and there's a one-way mirror that even the lamest of the lame-brain criminals know is so the prosecutor and other cops can look in from the outside and figure out how long they can put them away for. The surface of the steel table, scratched and dimpled, is missing quite a bit of its original paint, and the plastic chairs have got some permanent stains on them, not all of them from spilled soda pop.

But the one thing makes Interview 2 less scary than Interview 1 is that the handcuffs in 2 are attached under the table and therefore not so obvious, whereas in 1 they're attached to a rail on top of the table. Staring at the cuffs in 1 makes it harder for most of our suspects to lie to our faces. Not all. Most.

So we use Interview 1 for interrogations and Interview 2 for interviews. And Philip Vinson, the owner of Johnny's Lounge, was just an interview. At this point, anyway.

Mr. Vinson didn't look at ease. All I told him when I spoke to him a couple hours ago was that I wanted him to bring in a list with contact information of the bartenders, strippers, and bouncers working last night. He had asked why we wanted this— a reasonable enough question. In fact, we could even spin the question positive, like he wanted to know so he could volunteer to bring in any other stuff that would help us with whatever our problem was. I've seen it happen, though not that often.

But I've learned that the best answer to that kind of question is the vague kind: We're hoping you can help us with a case we're working on. That way, if the guy has damp temples or a shiny forehead or he can't stop tapping his fingers or toes for even a second, it helps us figure out how hard we ought to look at him. After all, who knows better than he does what kind of shit he's into?

It's true we get a lot of false positives, guys who look super nervous just because police stations creep them out. These are guys who think we're going to start out by me leaving the room, then Ryan locking the door and beating the crap out of them just because we can. That's television, not real life. Real life, people usually don't get beat up inside police stations. Too many closed-circuit cameras.

Philip Vinson was wearing a black suit. To be more precise, it was a black jacket from one suit, and a black pair of pants from another. He was short and doughy, somewhere between forty-five and sixty years old. There were a couple of food stains running down the front of the jacket. The gray mock turtleneck was a little grayer than it used to be. His hair, thin on top, was dyed an unconvincing auburn. He sported a thin gold loop in his fleshy left earlobe and had a new snow-white goatee, which for some reason he chose not to dye.

"I got ya that list of people working yesterday," he said. As he shifted his weight so he could pull a piece of paper out of a pants pocket, I could see his man boobs shift through his washed-out turtleneck. He slid the paper to me across the table.

"Thanks," I said as I unfolded it and scanned the information. It showed just the names of two bartenders, two bouncers, and three "girls." I shook my head, then looked up at him. "I asked for contact information."

"I don't have that on me," he said, shaking his head like I was asking for their mothers' maiden names and there was no way he could have foreseen that.

"By noon today. Fax, email, run a piece of paper over, whatever." I looked at him. "You understand me?"

He nodded. I could tell by the way he was pulling his shoulders in and bowing his head that he had some experience dealing with cops. "Can you tell me what this is about?"

I glanced down at the sheet of paper. "You got a girl listed as Natalya. No last name?"

He put his hands up. "I'm sorry. I don't have the records on her. My accountant has her full name. She's Russian or something. I got it written down somewhere."

"She got papers?"

"That what this is about? Because, absolutely, we do a thorough check. Absolutely everything. She told me her name. It was kind of long and complicated. I just don't know where that piece of paper is." He wiped at his forehead with a damp handkerchief. "But I'm saying, we only hire legit girls."

I sighed. "Like I said when I called you this morning, we're hoping you can help us with a case we're working on."

He nodded his head and put his arms out in a gesture of servility. "Of course, of course."

"That's great," I said. "We recovered a body in the alley next to your bar early this morning."

"Just to be sure, you understand the alley is not part of the bar. That's city property."

"You're not from Montana, are you, Mr. Vinson?"

He looked a little confused. "I know, I got a bit of an accent. New Jersey." He paused. "Why'd you say that?"

"Most people, they hear there's a body in the alley next to their place, they say, 'I'm sorry to hear that,' maybe "That's too bad.' They say something like that. You say, 'Don't blame me.'

See where I'm going?"

"You're right," he said, pushing his palms down to show he understood my point. "I'm very sorry to hear about that, I mean that someone died. It's just I don't usually get up this early. I'm up till three, four o'clock every night. And, to be perfectly frank with you, you bringing me here, I don't even know what it's about, it kind of shook me up. But your point is well taken. I shoulda said, 'I'm sorry to hear that.' So tell me what you need from me about that. Was it a cowboy passed out, froze or something along those lines? It wasn't a drunk-driving thing, am I right?"

"It wasn't drunk driving, and it wasn't a cowboy passing out and dying of hypothermia. It was a homicide."

"Holy shit." Philip Vinson's head pulled back. "I'm sorry. Didn't mean to use that language in front of a lady. But I had no idea we're talking about a murder. Are you thinking it had something to do with my bar?"

"Yeah, the thought did cross our minds, seeing as it wasn't all that likely that someone would want to hang out in that alley if he wasn't there because of Johnny's Lounge. That alley is a toilet. And not a clean toilet. Nobody would want to be there."

"I understand completely what you're saying." Philip Vinson nodded his head. "I've phoned the city about it I can't tell you how many times. They say they're gonna do something about it, but they don't. You'd think, with the taxes I pay, they'd be all over it." He took a breath, wiping a sleeve across his forehead. "I'm sorry, I'm getting off topic here. Did you want to ask me some questions about last night? Let me start by saying I don't know anything about someone getting killed there. You believe me about that, right? Personally, I got my hands full with things inside the bar. I don't ever go out there. But is there something you wanna ask me?"

"Were you at Johnny's last night?"

"The whole night. From maybe three in the afternoon till

after two."

"You didn't even go out for dinner?"

"I usually get some takeout. You know, Chinese, Thai, some pizza. I have this kid, he's maybe sixteen, seventeen, works for me. He picks it up."

"You ever seen this man?" I turned to Ryan, who pulled a picture of Lee Rossman out of a folder and slid it across the table to Philip Vinson. It was from *Montana!* magazine, a photo of Lee Rossman, standing outside his big house. He was wearing blue jeans and a camo jacket, a big smile on his face.

"Jesus." Vinson flinched. "I thought you were talking about a young guy, one of the oil workers, somebody like that." He looked at the photo some more. "Sorry, I don't think I've ever seen him in Johnny's." He tilted his head and paused, like he wanted to be sure he was telling me the exact truth—because I deserved nothing less. "Let me be absolutely honest with you. I'm not saying for a fact that he's never been in my place. We can gross fifty thou a night—that's a weeknight. Weekends, two or three times that. So I can't remember everyone comes in. You understand. I'm just saying I don't recognize this guy. This is the guy got murdered?"

"That's right, Mr. Vinson. Name of Lee Rossman. President of Rossman Mining. Got a bunch of rigs in the Bakken, out in the eastern part of the state. Most of your customers, the guys, they either work for him or know someone who does."

"I don't doubt you. I don't doubt you at all. I'm just saying I don't recognize this guy as being in my bar."

"All right," I said. "Do you remember any one of your employees—bartenders, strippers, bouncers—anybody telling you anything about a fight out there in the alley? Or any customers talking about how they're gonna take it outside? Any employees go outside to the alley to help with some deliveries? Anything like that?"

Vinson shook his head, looking disappointed because he really wanted to help. "We don't take any deliveries after business hours." He closed his eyes to think. "No, nothing about any fights in the alley."

"Do you know if any of your girls were involved with Lee Rossman—any of the waitresses, strippers? Any of the male employees?"

"Let me tell you my policy on 'involved.'" His face went all solemn. "We got an absolute, iron-clad rule. My waitresses carry the drinks, but they don't touch the customers. My dancers can take tips when they're dancing, and they do table dances—fifty bucks for five minutes—but it's completely out in the open. And there's no touching the girls when they're not on the stage. We got no private rooms, no VIP lounges, anything. I got an office upstairs, no couches, no mattresses. Nothing of the kind. My girls are not hooking out of my bar. Absolutely not. I find out they're even thinking of that, they're gone. That night."

"All right, Mr. Vinson, take a deep breath. No one's accusing you of running hookers out of your bar. I'm just asking whether you know if any of your girls were involved with Lee Rossman—prostitutes, girlfriends, nannies, housekeepers, whatever."

"I can't control what the girls do on their own time. I haven't heard of anything like that. Like I said, I can't swear it isn't going on, but I don't know anything about something like that. And I'm willing to swear to that."

"Okay, Mr. Vinson—"

"Look, I didn't put that money in those guys' pockets. I can't swear that there aren't some hookers come to my place, but most of the girls come for the dancing. They're not working girls. They're just there for the dancing. They want to leave with the oil guys—that's their legal right to do that. There's nothing illegal there. But any professionals come to my place, they're not on my payroll. That I can swear to on my mother's grave."

"All right, Mr. Vinson, we hear you. You're not running girls out of your bar. Here's what we need you to help us with." I picked up the sheet of paper with the five names. "My partner and I are gonna come over to Johnny's at one PM this afternoon. You get those people in there at one o'clock. Don't tell them what it's about. Just tell them to get in there. If there's any others you didn't list, call them, too. You hear me?"

"I don't know what their schedules are." He shook his head like this was a little more than he could promise. "Some of them might be off today."

"I understand that." I nodded. "But this is a murder investigation. If we don't see them all there at one o'clock, we're gonna come back tonight and start questioning everyone—all the employees, all the customers."

"You're gonna shut me down?"

"I didn't say that. I said we're gonna come over tonight. You can stay open. But we're gonna have to turn off the sound system, the DJ, whatever you got. So we can hear. And we're gonna turn the lights up bright so we can see. You know, to take notes. We'll have maybe eight or twelve officers with us. But we're not gonna shut you down. Do you understand me?"

He nodded. "One o'clock."

"That would be a good time to give me that list with the contact information."

And with that little interchange, Philip Vinson and I had reached an understanding.

Chapter 5

I parked the Dodge Charger in a metered spot a few doors down from the entrance to Johnny's Lounge. "I guess you've never been in Johnny's," I said to Ryan. He's Mormon and takes it seriously.

"Couple of times," he said, "when I was on patrol. Drunk and disorderlies."

I shut off the big engine and put down the visor with the Official Police Business sign on it. I glanced over at the alley, right beyond the bar. It was still taped off, a squad car blocking the entrance. Robin must not have finished scraping the various kinds of shit off the ground.

Walking up to the entrance of Johnny's Lounge, I recognized the big, heavy, scratched-up wooden door, cut in a crescent shape along the top. We walked in, and I felt that comforting warmth of a dimly lit bar at midday. It took me a few seconds to adjust to the darkness—no windows, only the red, yellow, and blue lights from the neon beer signs. Hanging from the ceiling was some kind of swoopy wood and metal fixture a good thirty feet across, filled with dozens of lights of all different sizes and shapes. Luckily, it was turned off. I imagined its purpose was to put out strobing light to amp up the Ecstasy when the DJ started thump-thumping around eight tonight. I breathed in the familiar smell of old beer, liquor, sweat, and drugstore perfume, but I didn't quite recognize the place.

A few years ago, when I was an active drunk, a shabby little place called Callahan's was my go-to, pass-out spot. Occasionally, I would hit other bars, part of my effort to remain well-rounded, well-travelled, and well-oiled. But Callahan's best fit my lifestyle: humble aspirations, underwhelming results. It was dark and generally quiet. There was an old-style TV, the kind that was deeper than it was wide, strapped to a thick metal arm sticking out of the wall over the bar. The volume was always off, with the subtitles misspelled to the point of gibberish at the bottom of the screen. A couple of cheesy little bookshelf speakers at the ends of the bar piped out white-people jazz at a low volume. There was one bartender, who lifted his chin a half-inch to welcome me and didn't need to be told to bring me a Jack Daniel's. No annoying lights, no dancing, no DJs, no live music, no strippers. Just alcohol and guys on business trips who wanted to nail a woman who wasn't all that into conversation.

Just then I remembered why I had crossed Johnny's Lounge off my list. It wasn't that it was too loud, which it was, or that it had strippers. I'm fine with strippers. I quit Johnny's when they started watering the Jack Daniel's, probably to pay for the stage and the lights and the sound system and the pole and the outfits and shit for the strippers. So, I guess it probably was because of the strippers.

We wiped our feet on the long carpet, which ran from the entrance right up to the bar. The carpet was red with black silhouettes of the woman with huge tits you see on truck mudflaps. Philip Vinson came rushing over, his boobs bouncing beneath his washed-out turtleneck. "Detectives, detectives," he said, his arms out in an ornate welcome gesture, his doughy face wearing a pained enthusiasm, "welcome to Johnny's Lounge. I've got most of my people here." He gestured to a group of young people with sour expressions, yawning, checking their phones, and talking listlessly over near the far end of the bar. He reached into an inside pocket on his stained black suit jacket and pulled out a sheet of paper. "Here's that contact information you needed," he said, an obedient student handing in his homework.

Right at the top of my list of things a cop can absolutely count on: If you want a bar owner to cooperate, tell him you're going to stop by tonight with a dozen uniforms and turn on all the lights.

"Thanks, Mr. Vinson." I scanned the sheet of paper he had given me. It listed two bouncers, two bartenders, and three strippers. "Appreciate it. You mind staying here a few minutes while we talk to your people?"

"Of course." He put his palms together and made a delicate suck-up bow. "Whatever you need." He turned and hurried off to an empty booth over in the corner.

"Okay, Ryan, you take the two bouncers—" I held the paper up close to read it in the dim light. "That's Billy and Ronnie. And the bartender named Rob." He wrote the names in his skinny notebook and headed over to the group.

I walked behind him, up to the group of employees. "Alison Parker?" I said. A woman of about twenty-five nodded. "Come over here, would you?" She followed me to a booth on the other side of the bar.

"My name is Detective Seagate." I gestured for her to sit across the table from me. "We're talking with employees who worked here last night. About a homicide we think took place out in the alley."

She was shifting in her seat but stopped. Her eyes got big. "Jesus."

I pulled a photo of Lee Rossman out of my big shoulder bag and slid it across the table to her.

She picked it up and held it close, brushing some strands of brown hair back behind her ear. "What's this guy's name?"

"Lee Rossman," I said. "He was the president of Rossman Mining, headquartered here in town."

"That's the company all the young guys work for, right?" She was pretty, with delicate eyebrows, brown eyes set wide, and a narrow jaw. "You said out in the alley?"

"Yeah."

"What was he doing there?"

"You should be a cop," I said. "That's what we're trying to figure out."

She shrugged her shoulders. "How can I help?"

"Did you see him last night?"

She shook her head. "I don't remember seeing him; can't say if he was here. We can have a couple hundred customers any given night." She pointed to the length of the bar. There was a section, about fifty feet long, with stools bolted to the floor, and another section, just as big, without stools. That section would be for the dancin' fools. "He could've been sitting at the bar for an hour—the other end from me—and I wouldn't have seen him."

"You don't remember a couple guys getting into fights, the security guys telling them to take it outside?"

She smiled. "There could be five or ten fights a night," she said. "Nothing out of the ordinary. But I didn't hear about anything involving an old guy."

"You didn't hear the security guys talking about anything they'd seen in the alley out there?" I pointed at the wall.

"No, nothing."

"How well do you know the dancers?"

She paused. "Not well," she said, sitting back a little. I couldn't get a read on her attitude one way or the other. "They've got a little dressing room. An old storage closet, actually. So they kind of know each other, but since I leave my clothes on, they don't hang with me."

"There's two dancers over there, right?" I said.

She squinted and reached into her bag for a pair of glasses.

"The blonde is Natalya."

"Got a last name?"

Alison Parker frowned and shook her head.

"What can you tell me about her?"

"I know she keeps to herself, doesn't speak much English, knows how to crawl around on a stage pretty good. The way she humps a pole, I'm surprised it doesn't cum and go limp."

"So she makes some money."

Alison's eyebrow went up a little. "Helluva lot more than I do."

"And the other one?" I gestured with my chin to the other dancer, a big-framed woman standing with her back to us.

"Name's Donna Hensley. Can't dance for shit."

"Why is she here?"

"Wait till she turns around."

I looked down at the list. "And the third dancer: Susan Warnock."

"Yeah, I know Susan a little. Older than the others. I think she's got a kid or something."

"She can dance?"

"Yeah, I guess, some. She's pretty. Does all right here."

"Let me ask you. The boss told us he's real strict on making sure the girls don't hook."

She smiled.

"What?" I said.

"Did he also say he's real strict about how you don't have to fuck him to keep your job?"

I looked at her. "If you want to talk about that, I'll put you onto some people who can help you."

Alison waved her hand. "We worked it out."

"Yeah?"

"I told him about how I grew up on a ranch with four brothers. How we'd use this big metal clamp to castrate the bulls. Things like that. I think I scared him."

I smiled. "He's a city boy."

"Yeah, it was all bullshit. I'm from Chicago. I don't know how to do any of that cowboy stuff. If he'd tried anything," she said, "I'd've just shot him."

"So you're good with Mr. Vinson," I said.

She nodded. "Yeah, we're fine."

"So the girls don't hook here in the bar."

"That's right," she said.

"If they do?"

"Couple times a year he catches a girl. She's gone."

"But hooking outside the bar?"

She exhaled and looked down at her hands on the Formica table. "That's kinda tough to call. A town this small, all of us have gone out with guys who're customers."

"I didn't say going out. I said hooking."

"I don't know that any of the girls are working. Do some of them have nice apartments, good clothes, you know? Better than their salary could pay for?" She raised her eyebrows.

"All right, Alison, thanks a lot," I said. "You mind sending Natalya over here?"

She nodded, took off her glasses, and put them back in her purse. She slid out of the booth and walked over to the group of employees. She said something to Natalya and pointed in my direction with her thumb.

Natalya started walking over to me. She was a thin woman, maybe a hundred pounds, with a model's gait. She was wearing blue jeans and a bone-colored knit turtleneck over what looked like a dark bra.

"Sit down, Natalya," I said when she made it over to my booth. "I only need a couple minutes."

She slid into the booth, no expression on her face. She had pale skin, dark brown eyes, and dark eyebrows. If she hadn't dyed her hair platinum, she would have been a really good-looking young woman. I hoped the platinum was a business decision.

"My name is Detective Seagate," I said. No response, so I kept going. "Do you know this man?" I showed her the photo of Lee Rossman.

She looked at it for a few seconds, then shook her head and slid back on the plastic seat, like that was all she was going to offer.

"Do you ever meet guys in the alley over there?"

"Why I meet them there?" she said with a thin, girlish voice. She had a thick accent.

"So sometimes you do meet guys outside the bar?"

She tapped the table twice with her index finger. "Dancer. No hooker."

Which I interpreted as dancer/hooker. "Can you tell me anything about last night? Anything about how a man was attacked in the alley?"

"A man attacked in alley?" Somewhere along the line, this girl had learned that the best way to deal with the authorities was to know nothing and deny everything.

"You didn't hear about that?"

She shook her head.

"Okay, thanks, Natalya," I said. "Would you mind asking Donna to come over here?"

"I go home?"

"Yeah, you go home," I said.

She nodded slightly, got up, and walked over to the group and said something to Donna.

Donna turned toward me and started walking over, with big loping strides. She was close to six feet, and right up against two-hundred pounds. I looked at her neck to check for an Adam's apple, but I concluded she was born female. She was wearing some kind of lime-green suit, which was a serious fashion mistake. It was a cheap poly, with a low-cut black blouse and a three-inch silver crucifix nestled in her cleavage. When she walked, each boob bounced separately, the flesh rippling in waves up toward her neck.

I glanced over at the guys leaning on the bar. All of them were looking at Donna walk, even though they must have seen her tits often enough.

"Thanks for coming in, Donna." I gestured for her to sit.

She squeezed in, her chest bumping up against the table, making it jump a couple inches toward me.

"You okay?" she said, giving me a concerned little smile. "I don't know how some of the guys fit in these little bitsy booths."

"I'm fine," I said, returning her smile. I introduced myself and started to run through my questions with her.

As I was talking to Donna, a woman rushed in, looking at her watch. She went over to the other employees at the bar, then hurried over to Philip Vinson at the booth in the corner of the room.

Big Donna leaned in, listening to my questions. I tried to ignore the two big boobs resting on the tabletop, like she'd just come back from the market with a couple cantaloupes. But I caught myself glancing down there when I realized they had swallowed up the crucifix. Donna answered my questions directly. She might have seen Lee Rossman before, but not last night. When she dances, she gets pretty caught up in the music and the guys whooping and hollering, so, no, she didn't notice him last night. Didn't know anything about why he might have been out in the alley.

When I was done, she smiled again. "Sorry I couldn't help you. And sorry about the old man."

"That woman who just came in?" I looked down at my list. "That's Susan Warnock?"

Donna shifted around, jostling the table again. "Yeah, that's her. Want me to send her over?"

"Yeah, thanks a lot. You've been a big help." Which wasn't even close to true.

Susan Warnock came over. She was wearing running shoes, baggy sweatpants, and a sweatshirt under a thick down jacket. No makeup. "Sorry I'm late," she said. "You know how sometimes things can get a little out of control at home?"

I nodded. "Yeah, I think I remember one or two times," I said. "I'm Detective Seagate—"

"You're here about Lee Rossman," she said.

She was the first one to admit knowing the vic's name. It must have made the news shows at noon. "Yeah, that's why we're here. See if anyone working last night remembers anything that can help us with his murder."

She shook her head. "I didn't see him here last night."

"You would have recognized him?"

"I think so. Very distinguished, you know."

I hadn't shown her his photo. They probably put it on the screen at noon. "Did he come in a lot?"

"I wouldn't say a lot. Every few weeks or so," she said.

"He sit at the bar when you danced?" I pointed to the separate bar ringing the stage with the poles.

She looked like she was thinking. She was a good-looking woman. Light brown hair pulled back in a ponytail. Big green eyes, slender nose. Thin lips. "No, that wasn't his style. He'd be in a booth, talking with other guys." She looked tired, grey bags starting under her eyes, and the beginnings of crow's feet.

"Were these young guys roughnecks? Older guys like himself?"

"Both, I'd say."

I looked at her. "You're a couple of years older than the other dancers …" I just let it hang out there.

She smiled. "I do all right. Dancing, that is."

"I didn't mean anything by that," I said. "Just wondering if some of the young guys, you know …"

"I can dance," she said. "I put on makeup, the boys don't see how old I am. Besides, they're not looking at my face. I think my tits've got another couple years. I hope so, anyway."

"You ever go out with Lee Rossman?"

The question startled her. It took her a second to process it. She frowned. "That's not why I'm here."

"Why are you here?"

"Money. I can make five times what I used to get ringing up groceries."

I nodded. "Okay, Susan," I put my palms on the table and she started to slide out of the booth. "I appreciate the information." I reached into my bag, pulled a card out of a little pocket, and slid it across the table. "In case you think of anything." I looked at her directly and held my gaze. "Anything."

She nodded and picked up the card. "Am I free to go?"

"Sure."

I looked over at the booth where Ryan was doing his interviews. He was still talking with one of the bouncers. Everyone else had already left.

I sat there and closed my eyes for a moment. I don't remember drifting off, but next thing I knew Ryan was standing in front of me. "You in there, Karen?"

I shook myself out of my sleep. "Yeah," I said. "Must've drifted off for a second."

"Learn anything?" he said to me as he slid into the booth.

"Let's see," I said, tapping my upper lip. "That Philip Vinson lets his female employees know that they don't have to sleep with him."

"But that it's okay if they're willing to?"

"Yeah," I said. "That's probably accurate."

"Anything about who killed Lee Rossman?"

"Uh, no. One of the three strippers knew his name and was

willing to admit she'd seen him before in the bar. The other two didn't know who he was, didn't know if he was ever in the bar, didn't know if anything happened to him last night. Didn't know, didn't know, didn't know." I sighed. "What'd you get?"

"The boys didn't know, didn't know, didn't know. Well, that's not exactly true. They were absolutely sure that they didn't break up any fights involving any old guys, including Lee Rossman."

"But nothing rules out Lee Rossman being in the alley getting his dick sucked by a freelance whore or one of the strippers."

"Got a particular one in mind?" Ryan said.

"I'd put my money on the platinum Russian girl."

"Why's that?"

"Because she made a big deal about how she was a dancer, not a hooker."

"Did she make a big deal about how she wasn't a murderer?"

"Shit," I said. "I knew there was something else I meant to ask her."

"I'll go thank Mr. Vinson for getting his people in here."

"Let me come along with you."

When he noticed us walking over toward him, Vinson squirmed out of the booth and put on a concerned face. "Did you get everything you needed, Detectives?"

Ryan said, "Yes, Mr. Vinson, thanks for bringing your people in."

"Absolutely," he said, with a bow. "Anything I can do to help."

"One other thing," I said. "Be careful when you explain the job requirements to your female employees."

He put out his hands to show his confusion. "I'm sorry, Detective?"

"When you tell the girls they don't have to fuck you, you want to make sure they don't misunderstand what you're saying—"

He was shaking his head in denial. "I don't know what you're talking about, Detective."

"Because that would be a crime: coercing them into giving you favors like that. And if we heard about that going on, we'd be down here in ten minutes with a warrant. You'd be in a shitload of trouble, Mr. Vinson," I said.

His forehead was getting shiny. "I would never say that to any of my girls."

"That's good to hear," I said. "So we understand each other."

"Absolutely," he said. "That would never happen."

"Goodbye, Mr. Vinson." And I sincerely hoped we'd never meet again.

Chapter 6

"You want to pursue it—what he says to his employees?" Ryan said as we got into the Charger.

I turned to him. "We get even a whiff of him running girls out of that bar, I'm gonna make it a personal mission to shut him down and arrest him for … what's that called?"

"*Quid pro quo* sexual harassment," Ryan said. "But I get the feeling he knows just how far he can go. Telling the girls they don't have to sleep with him—he's sending two messages at once."

I shook my head and pointed to the crime tape sealing off the alley next to Johnny's Lounge. "You think of anything else you want to do here?"

"Not until we hear from Robin or Harold."

I nodded. "Want to see what's going on at Rossman Mining?"

"Let me take a look around their site for a minute or two," he said, swiveling the computer to face him.

"I'm gonna grab a cup of coffee." I pointed at a small shop a few doors down from the bar. "You want something?"

"No, thanks." Ryan was already on the Rossman Mining site. "You go ahead."

Steel-grey clouds were settling in and the temperature was falling. I walked toward the little coffee shop with my head down, holding my coat tight against my body. We hadn't yet had any serious snow, but it was only a matter of time. Days or a week at most. It had hit zero every night the last couple of weeks. It was enough to remind me I was in for a good six months of hooking up the block warmer on my Honda at night, parking real careful so I didn't take out a parking meter under a snow drift, and sorting through how I would feel if I learned the planet had finally broken free of its orbit and was drifting off into black space, where it would ice over and die.

Inside the shop, I grabbed an insulated cup, pumped a black coffee out of the tall black carafe, put the lid on, and left a dollar bill on the counter. The cup was so hot I had to shift it from hand to hand. By the time I made it back to the Charger the coffee was cool enough for me to take a sip.

"They got anything on the site about Lee Rossman dying?" I said.

"No, not yet." Ryan shook his head. "Can't tell whether they've heard."

"I bet the chief contacted them."

"Or Rossman's wife."

"Who should we be talking to?" I sipped some more caffeine.

"I'd go with this woman." Ryan swiveled the computer to face me.

I read the caption on the photo. "Cheryl Garrity."

"She's the director of operations for the company. Plus, she oversees the wells here in Montana."

"They've got other wells?"

"Bunch down in Texas," Ryan said. "They're in the Marcellus Shale in Pennsylvania, and they're starting up in California, too."

"What do we need to know about Cheryl Garrity?"

"According to her bio, she's been with Rossman more than twenty years, since the early days in Texas."

"She's a techie?"

"No," Ryan said. "Her bio says she 'attended' Texas Tech."

"What's that mean?" I took a long sip of the coffee.

"Means she didn't get a degree. Anything from taking a single course to doing everything *except* getting a degree. Her bio says she runs all the operations in the Bakken Formation, which 'extends from eastern Montana, most of North Dakota, up into Saskatchewan and Manitoba.' For Rossman Mining, that's four-thousand employees, plus more than that many contractors."

"And she's based here at headquarters?"

"About a quarter mile away," Ryan said. "It's 7500 Montana Street. Suite 1450."

Montana Street was a main east-west artery through downtown, home to most of our business towers. At fifteen stories, the granite and glass tower at 7500 Montana was the tallest in town.

We parked in the basement garage and took the elevator to the fourteenth floor. Suite 1450 was at the end of the main hallway. Ryan held open the big glass door with Rossman Mining painted on it in fancy script. I fished into my shoulder bag for my shield and hung it around my neck.

Inside the reception area were a few leather couches and side chairs with end tables and tall, shiny brass lamps. There was a curved wooden reception desk with the company name painted on it in the same script as on the glass doors. There was nobody sitting at the reception desk.

Off to the side I counted seven employees huddled together in small groups. The women were hugging and crying. The men, hands in their pockets, were looking down at their shoes. Judging by the scene, I'd say Rossman's death was announced during the lunch hour.

A young woman, model-thin and wearing lots of makeup, separated from one of the groups and came up to me and Ryan. Drying her eyes with a tissue, she said, "Can I help you?"

"Detectives Seagate and Miner, Rawlings Police Department. Is Cheryl Garrity available?"

The woman took a breath and straightened up. "Let me see if

Ms. Garrity is available." She folded her tissue and put it into the pocket of her cranberry wool jacket. "Won't you please take a seat?" She pointed to the couch near the door. "I'll just be a moment."

Ryan remained standing, but I sat down. Our presence in the reception area seemed to throw the employees off. After the women finished up their hugging and the men tugged at their belts, looked at their watches, and in general did the meaningless gestures that men do, the employees started to disperse and wander toward the hallways on either side of the reception desk. They seemed confused. They weren't going to dive back into their spreadsheets, but they weren't able to stand around in the reception area, not with outsiders there. Not with cops there.

The receptionist appeared from the interior offices. "This way, please, Detectives." We followed her down a short hall with thick, blue-grey carpet and framed sepia-toned photographs of oil wells. At the bottom of each frame was a brass plate with a year from the 1930s and 1940s and the name of a Texas city.

In the doorway of one of the two large offices at the end of the hall stood Cheryl Garrity. She was a sturdy-looking woman in her fifties, with wavy salt-and-pepper hair carefully coiffed and plastic-framed half-glasses. She wore a loden-green wool skirt, below the knees, and a navy blazer over a cream silk blouse. No jewelry, no makeup except a little lip gloss. "This way," she said, without expression, without small talk. She led me and Ryan to a small conference room with a round table in the center. The lights came on automatically when the three of us entered the room.

"Tell me your names, please," she said.

"I'm Detective Karen Seagate. This is my partner, Detective Ryan Miner."

"I'm Cheryl Garrity. Director of Operations, Rossman Mining." She paused, still without showing us any expression. "Sit, please." She gestured toward the table and sat down. "This is about Lee," she said, as if she was announcing the topic for today's meeting.

"Yes, I'm afraid it is," I said. "Let me begin by expressing our condolences, Ms. Garrity. You and Mr. Rossman went back a long time."

She bowed her head slightly in acknowledgment. "Almost twenty-four years," she said.

"I'm a little surprised you're in the office now," I said.

She tilted her head. "Why is that?"

"Well," I said slowly, trying to give myself a chance to choose my words carefully, "you've just learned that the company president ... , your colleague for a quarter-century ..."

"Has died?" Cheryl Garrity said, raising her eyebrows.

"Yes." I nodded. "Has died."

"Where would you expect me to be?"

"I wouldn't have been surprised to learn you were at home now. Or with Florence Rossman."

Cheryl Garrity looked out over her half-glasses and nodded slightly, as if to concede my comment was not ridiculous. "As the Director of Operations—pending any changes announced by Florence—I am responsible for the business of Rossman Mining, and there is an enormous amount of business that must be attended to at this moment."

"Yes," I said. "I understand that." I tapped my chin with my index finger. "Are you expecting Ms. Rossman to make any changes?"

"Yes," Cheryl Garrity said. "When the founding president of a large, successful corporation departs, I think it's only prudent to expect changes."

"Do you expect those changes right away?"

"I was simply saying that the owner of Rossman Mining is now Florence Rossman."

"I see."

"How may I help you?" She reached for a yellow legal pad from a stack in the middle of the table. She held a pen, ready to start taking notes. I noticed there was a glass window built into the table in front of her. There probably was a computer or something under the glass.

"Let me begin by asking you what you've already heard about Mr. Rossman's death."

"Florence phoned me, soon after you informed her this morning, and told me what she knew at the time: that Lee's body was recovered this morning outside a bar downtown, and that you believe he was murdered." She paused. "Is that still your belief?"

"Yes, it is." I shifted in my chair. "We don't have a formal forensics report yet, and the autopsy hasn't been done, but, yes, that is what we told Ms. Rossman."

Cheryl Garrity didn't speak. Apparently, that was the prompt for me to answer her question about how she could help us. "Do you have any thoughts on who might have wanted to harm Mr. Rossman?"

"I do not know of anyone who would have wanted to harm Lee."

"I understand how, with his death being so recent, it must be difficult to talk about anyone who might've wanted to hurt him," I said. "But this was a man sixty-five years old, a man who'd made many millions of dollars in a very competitive industry, an industry a lot of people don't like. He had to have made some enemies along the way."

Cheryl Garrity lowered her head to look through the glass window in the table. She reached under the table, and the lights around the perimeter of the room dimmed to half-strength and a white projection screen began to descend from the ceiling.

In a moment, the Rossman Mining web page appeared on the screen. The cursor slid to a row of links at the top of the page, so quickly I couldn't tell what she was clicking. A page titled

Rossman Foundation appeared. The page was full of images of Lee Rossman smiling and shaking hands with various local bigwigs. There were pictures of Lee at groundbreaking ceremonies, Lee at dedications, Lee in front of a podium, addressing students in classrooms and adults in conference centers and auditoriums.

Cheryl Garrity spoke. "Lee Rossman was in negotiations with Central Montana State University to endow a professorship of petroleum engineering, which would have cost more than two-million dollars. In the last eight years, since we've been in Montana, he has donated more than one-and-a-half million dollars to other initiatives at the university—and not only in engineering. He was the largest donor to the new Arts and Humanities campaign. Ten ongoing four-year scholarships to Rossman Scholars, as they're called. In Rawlings, he supported job-training, the Ronald McDonald House, the Rawlings Regional Medical Center, the shelter for victims of domestic violence, Meals on Wheels. Little League, Pop Warner. Call the president of the university, call Mayor Rafferty. Call anyone who's deeply involved in the affairs of this city. I would be very surprised if they did not tell you the exact same thing: that Lee Rossman was the most generous and civic-minded resident of Rawlings, Montana."

Ryan spoke. "Tell us about his relationship with the environmental community."

She looked at him, her eyes briefly showing her annoyance. "You're referring to Nathan Kress. Rivers United."

Ryan nodded.

"Lee met with Mr. Kress on numerous occasions. I was present at some of those meetings. Obviously, Lee Rossman and Nathan Kress simply saw the issues differently. Lee believed—and of course I and everyone else at Rossman and everybody in the oil and gas industry still believe—that shale oil and gas represent our nation's best opportunity to free itself from dependence on foreign energy sources, because our nation is the Saudi Arabia of shale oil and gas." She glided through this little speech, like she had delivered it many times before. "That there have been no credible reports of significant environmental damage—or potential damage—from the extraction of shale oil and gas. And that the mining of shale oil and gas represents a significant source of secure, high-paying jobs for skilled laborers, now and for decades to come."

"And Mr. Kress?" Ryan looked at her directly. "What does he believe?"

"The opposite." She held up a finger and tilted her head slightly. "Excuse me. That's not completely accurate. Mr. Kress does not dispute that we are the Saudi Arabia of shale oil and gas. But he does dispute every other item I listed."

"But these differences between the two men, they're policy differences, correct?" Ryan said. "You don't believe that the dispute ever became personal, do you?"

"Not at all." Cheryl Garrity shook her head as if the idea was out of the question. "Lee and Nathan Kress did not socialize, at least as far as I know, but I believe they saw themselves as opponents, not enemies."

"Anyone else?" I said.

Cheryl Garrity turned to me. "Excuse me?"

"Anyone else in the environmental community we should be talking to?"

"The question of who you should be talking to, I leave that to you. But I know there was one other person from that community who Lee in particular did not care for."

"Who was that?"

"Lauren Wilcox. She's a professor—of ecology, I believe that's her title—at CMSU."

"Can you tell us what it was about her that Mr. Rossman

didn't care for?"

"Lee believed that she didn't play by the rules."

"The rules?"

"Lee and I and everyone else in the oil business, for a hundred years in this country, have acted according to the principle that both sides of the shale oil and gas debate are interested in the public good. We are all, in effect, patriots. We never question our opponent's motives. We believe in working hard, following the law, treating everyone fairly. I'm not saying we all love each other. But we would never cross the line by using illegitimate tactics to further our position."

"Illegitimate tactics?" I said.

"Intimidation, innuendo." Cheryl Garrity held my gaze. "Eco-terrorism."

"Are you saying Lauren Wilcox is associated with eco-terrorism?"

"I'm not saying that. I'm merely presenting examples of illegitimate tactics." She glanced at Ryan to be sure he was taking notes. "Let me just say this: Her name is spelled L-A-U-R-E-N W-I-L-C-O-X."

I glanced at Ryan. He looked up from his skinny notebook on the conference table. He looked at me, then at Cheryl Garrity, and nodded. "Got it." He smiled. "Lauren Wilcox."

"Ms. Garrity," I said, "what can you tell us about Mr. Rossman's wife and son?"

"Florence is Lee's second wife. His first wife, Helen, died of ovarian cancer about ten years ago. She was in her fifties. She was the mother of their son, Bill. He's a student here at CMSU, as well as a Rossman employee. Sometimes he puts in only a few hours, sometimes he works full-time. Lee was grooming him to take over the business."

"How did Mr. Rossman meet Florence?"

"Lee met her while he was on a business trip about three

years ago. They fell in love almost immediately and married within a couple of months. She was from St. Louis, had never been to Rawlings—or Montana, for that matter—as far as I know. But you met her this morning. She is a beautiful woman, very poised, quite charming. Lee relied on her as a representative of the company to the community."

"How has that gone?"

"The community is quite taken with her. Lee was an oilman, and while that served him very well within the industry, Florence has been the driving force behind his outreach and philanthropic activities."

"Any problems with that marriage?"

"I have no reason to think so."

"Any problems between Florence and the stepson, Bill?"

"I can't really say. I have no personal experience as a stepmother, but from watching them together on occasion I think these things take time. I'm not part of their social circle and therefore I can't give you much useful information, but my estimation is that while Bill isn't close to Florence, I don't believe that is a reflection of anything she has done. His mother died when he was about thirteen, which is a very vulnerable age. To this day, I'm not sure he has fully gotten over her death. But Bill has always understood how much his father loved Florence, and, to his credit, he never tried to stand in the way of their marriage. Given the awkward ages of the three of them, I think Bill has handled the situation admirably."

"You mean that Florence is much younger than Mr. Rossman was?"

"She is closer in age to Bill than she was to Lee."

I nodded. "Ms. Garrity, I'm going to ask you to forgive me in advance for this next question. I have to ask it—"

"I was home last night. I usually do some shopping Sunday afternoons. I returned home around five PM, but I was in the rest of the night. And no, there is nobody to corroborate that. I live alone at the Madison Condominiums. I believe they have CCTV in the lobby but not in the elevators or the garage."

I reached into my bag and pulled out a card. "Again, Ms. Garrity, my condolences." I walked over to her and handed her the card. "Please get in touch if you have any information you think might help us in our investigation."

As I turned to leave, I heard the hum of the screen disappearing back into the ceiling.

Chapter 7

"Interesting woman," I said as we got into the elevator.

Ryan pressed P. "You mean how she hears her boss has been killed? Her boss of more than twenty years? And she looks less upset than the receptionist?"

"Yeah, that's what I mean." The elevator hummed and swayed a little as we headed down. "Does she go to comfort her employees? Does she rush to be with Florence Rossman or Bill Rossman?"

"Apparently not."

"That's right. She stays in the office because there's a lot of work to do. With the boss dead and all, she has a lot of appointments to re-schedule."

"So she's interesting because she's a bot?" Ryan held the elevator door, and we started walking toward the Charger.

"I don't know what that means," I said. "She's interesting because she's so weird she doesn't realize how weird she is. Therefore, she doesn't even pretend to act like a human."

"Which could work in our favor," Ryan said. "Maybe it means she won't lie to us."

"That would be refreshing." I paused. "What did you get from her we should follow up?"

Ryan thought for a moment. "She's resentful. Lee's wife dies, he goes off and marries a young, attractive woman."

"In other words, not Cheryl."

"Then Lee makes the young wife co-owner of the company."

"In other words, not Cheryl." I eased the Charger out of the garage and started heading back toward headquarters. The sun low in the sky, I fished the sunglasses out of my big leather bag.

"She said Nathan Kress is on the wrong side of the fracking question but he's not a bad guy."

"So we shouldn't look at him?" I said.

"But she said L-A-U-R-E-N Wilcox is an eco-terrorist."

"Yeah, what do you make of that? You run across her name when you were reading about the company?"

"No, I didn't," Ryan said.

"It doesn't fit with the crime." I shook my head. "If Lauren Wilcox is an eco-terrorist—whatever the hell that means—I could maybe see her wanting to eliminate Lee Rossman. I could even see her stabbing him. But why is his fly down? No way he'd agree to meet her in an alley, even if she offered to suck him off."

"I'd like to see a picture of Lauren Wilcox before I conclude Lee Rossman wouldn't want to meet her in an alley."

"Good point." I nodded. "He could've been a horn dog, or he could've been so screwy he got his rocks off fucking a woman who hated him."

"But you don't buy it," Ryan said.

"No, I don't. And I don't see her killing him somewhere else and dumping him in the alley. If it's a political hit, she wants people to know why he had to die. So she wouldn't pull his fly down. She wants everyone to know he died because he's a polluter, not because he likes blowjobs."

I pulled the cruiser into the lot behind headquarters. Ryan slid his ID through the reader at the rear entrance, and we made our way to the detectives' bullpen. I put my stuff down next to my desk. "I'm gonna go check in with the chief. You figure out what you can about Nathan Kress and Lauren Wilcox."

Ryan nodded and I headed out to the chief's office. He okayed my plan for following up with the environmental guy and

the ecology professor. He asked if I'd heard from Harold or
Robin about forensics or the autopsy. "It just doesn't sound like
Lee Rossman …" The chief shook his head.

"You mean, in the alley with his fly down?"

"That's not him," he said.

I shrugged my shoulders, my way of saying I didn't know
Rossman, which was more polite than asking the chief how he
could possibly know the guy didn't spend a lot of evenings in the
alley with his fly down. I see it as a sign of my personal growth
that I no longer feel the need to tell everyone everything I think.

"Well," I said, "I'll get with Robin and Harold as soon as
they've got something." I thanked the chief and headed back to
the detectives' bullpen.

Ryan looked up from his screen when he heard me. "The
chief okay with what we're doing?"

"Yeah." I sat down in my chair. "He seems really hung up
about Rossman being in the alley."

"Did you explain your theory on how all men are pigs?"

"No, twerp, I think he's aware of my thoughts on the
subject."

Ryan smiled. "Rossman wouldn't be the first upstanding
citizen who gets caught with his pants down."

"Anyway, you learn anything?" I pointed to his computer.

"Nathan Kress was easy enough to track down. He founded
Rivers United six years ago. It's a general-purpose environmental
advocacy group, with an emphasis on water pollution. Since the
oil and gas boom, he's become higher profile, but from the look
of his site he's still pretty small scale. He's an attorney, so he
knows how to try to stop projects he doesn't like."

"He didn't stop the fracking, though, did he?" I said.

"He certainly did not stop the fracking."

"And Lauren Wilcox?"

"She's a professor, officially in the Biology Department.

Came here four years ago from University of Texas, where she was also a professor. Published four books and lots of articles on the politics of environmentalism. She runs this student ecology group on campus."

"See anything on her blowing up oil rigs?"

Ryan shook his head. "Apparently she chose not to put that on her CV."

"So why the hell was Cheryl Garrity calling her an eco-terrorist?"

"We might want to ask her that," Ryan said.

"Give me Nathan Kress's phone. You try Lauren Wilcox," I said. He slid a piece of paper across his desk to me.

A minute later, he said, "She's not in the office, and the cell went to voicemail. I left messages at both numbers." He put the phone back in its cradle. "Get through to Mr. Kress?"

"He'd love to talk with us," I said, standing and walking toward the coat rack.

"Please, Karen." Ryan followed me. "Nobody would love to talk with us."

We headed out toward 230 Sentinel, a mixed residential and commercial street just west of downtown. Back in the 1930s and 1940s, when the neighborhood used to be upper-class, people built three-story stone and brick houses with broad columns that didn't support anything heavy, ornate shutters that didn't shut, and other useless features that passed for class out here on the prairie. The houses were impressively large, with their five or six bedrooms, but what really dazzled was the indoor bathroom. Today, the bathroom situation, plus the fact that if you're over five-eleven you hit your damn head every time you clomp down the stairs, made the houses less practical for actually living in. So the places became offices for small businesspeople, like architects, accountants, graphic designers, and others who lived upstairs and eventually learned to keep their heads down as they moved from room to room.

In the middle of the scrubby front lawn at 230 Sentinel, the oak sign with the words "Rivers United" burned into it looked like a junior-high woodworking project. I parked out front and displayed the Official Police Business sign. Ryan and I walked up to the wooden gate in the picket fence. The fence was missing so many slats it looked like a grinning hockey player. The hardware on the gate was painted over so often the parts didn't move. I could have pushed the whole fence and gate over with the heel of my palm.

I climbed the concrete steps, crossed a creaky wooden porch, and rang the bell next to the smaller plaque screwed into the siding of the house announcing the name of the organization.

I heard footsteps approaching from inside the house. "Nathan Kress?" I said to the man who opened the door.

He was about fifty, with collar-length grey curly hair and a walrus moustache. He was a little below average height, with slender shoulders and the start of a pot belly. He wore a navy down vest over a plaid wool shirt and wrinkled chinos.

"Glad to meet you." He extended his hand first to me and then to Ryan after I introduced us. "Come in."

When we got inside, I understood the down vest. The temperature inside was pretty much the same as outside. I don't know if this guy objected to heat on philosophical grounds or he was broke, but the whole atmosphere screamed not-for-profit. He ushered us into what was originally a front parlor, filled with dark, heavy, mismatched Victorian furniture over a threadbare Persian carpet. Stained old black-and-white prints of birds and fish and other critters covered the walls.

"This is about Lee," he said after we all sat. He looked like he'd been crying.

"Yes, Mr. Kress." I nodded my head sympathetically. "I take it you've heard."

"It's been all over the Internet, all the places the environmental community hangs out."

"At this point, we're trying to understand whether the crime was personal or related to Mr. Rossman's business."

"My guess is it was business." Nathan Kress shifted his position in his overstuffed wing chair, stirring up the dust motes floating in a shaft of light coming in from a window behind him.

"Why is that?"

"You'd never met him?"

"No, never did," I said.

"Lee was quite a character. Big, outgoing, friendly."

"Even to you?"

Nathan Kress waved away my implication. "Lee didn't care what side you were on. If you were civil to him, he was friendly. We weren't friends, but we could talk. He knew who I was. Always greeted me by name, gave me a big slap on the back."

"Maybe he was being diplomatic?"

"Let me tell you a short story." He leaned forward in his chair. "Four years ago, my younger son, Arnie, was quite ill. He was in the hospital over three weeks. The bill was one hundred eighty-seven thousand dollars and change. Our insurance paid twenty. Couple of weeks later, we learned that the bill had been taken care of. We asked who paid it. They said he preferred to remain anonymous." Nathan Kress put up his hands in a sign of confusion. "Nobody I know has that kind of cash. I asked Lee if it was him. He squeezed my shoulder and said, 'Don't know what you're talking about. But glad your son's doing better.' It was Lee Rossman."

"That's quite something," I said.

"Lee was what was good and bad about the West. The good was what I mentioned. He came from a world where your neighbors lived too far away to see, but everyone had to rely on each other because the land and the weather were unforgiving—

and there wasn't a government to step in and fix things. That's why he paid for my son's medical bills. I didn't have the money; he did. To Lee, it was as simple as that."

"And the bad?" I said.

"The bad was that he had no sense of the interdependence of people and the environment. To Lee, there was oil and gas down there, and we needed it. So he figured out how to get it out and sell it."

"As simple as that?"

"I don't want to make him out to be a cartoon character. He understood that there were environmental dangers—especially when you have to send pressurized water and sand and chemicals down a mile or two and break up the shale to get the oil and gas. Lee was an extremely intelligent man, and I don't think there was anything about the geology of fracking that he didn't know. If he had his way, he'd have lived out there at the rigs."

"But ...?"

"But to him the environmental dangers were simply technical problems to be solved. If methane was escaping from the well heads and polluting the atmosphere, that was just another problem he needed to solve. If radioactive waste water from his rigs was leeching into the Yellowstone River upstream from the water-treatment facility—which didn't test for radioactivity and couldn't remove it anyway—well, just another technical problem."

"Aren't they technical problems? What's wrong with seeing them that way?"

"Nothing." He nodded his head and smiled. The smile said he'd heard the question often enough, not that the question was stupid. "You want to identify and fix the problems. But if you lack the humility to understand that some of the problems you've caused are going to lead to other, bigger problems that you didn't anticipate—and that you might not be able to solve—if you lack the imagination to understand that, well, you shouldn't be in the business of injecting millions of gallons of carcinogens into the Earth. The environment is a delicately balanced, interconnected ecosystem. It's not a toilet."

I turned to Ryan, to see if he wanted to ask something.

"Mr. Kress," Ryan said, "you mentioned Lee Rossman helped with your son's medical bills. Can you tell us how you know that?"

"A couple of weeks after Arnie came home from the hospital, I got a call from Florence Rossman. She asked how he was doing. We talked a few minutes. I told her how much it meant to me and my wife that Lee had done that. I asked her to tell him that, and she said she would."

Ryan nodded. "Do you know Lauren Wilcox, at the university?"

"Yes." His eyes brightened. "Of course."

"Can you tell us a little about her relationship with Lee Rossman?"

"I'm not sure I'd call it a relationship." He shifted in his chair. "She sees him—not just him, everyone in the extractive industries—as the enemy."

"Do you think she might have wanted to hurt him?"

"Oh, gosh, no." Nathan Kress half-laughed. "I meant only that she has no social relationship with Lee or Florence. They don't talk. To Lauren, Lee Rossman was not a person but a political opponent. Her focus is on helping students understand how to take effective political action against the oil industry— something, by the way, I wish I knew how to do a little more effectively."

Ryan said, "Would you describe her as an eco-terrorist?"

Nathan Kress's head jerked back in surprise and he laughed. "That's ridiculous. She's a scholar, a teacher. She organizes, she writes petitions, she testifies at state and federal hearings. An eco-terrorist? I'm going to be sure to mention that to her. She'll get a chuckle out of that." His expression became cloudy. "Did someone actually use that term in describing Lauren?"

I spoke. "Yes, someone did."

Surprisingly, Nathan Kress did not ask us who said it. He simply shook his head in disappointment. I wouldn't have told him.

"Mr. Kress." Ryan was looking down at his notebook. "In your September newsletter, you mentioned a rancher named Mark Middleton. Do you think he might have wanted to hurt Lee Rossman?"

Ryan was the kind of detective who did his research but didn't flaunt it. If he had a reason, he'd bring it up in an interview. I turned to Nathan Kress, wondering what he would say.

"That was a feature article about how a lot of landowners have been victimized by the leasing contracts. But no, I don't think Mark Middleton—or any other unhappy landowner, for that matter—would have hurt Lee."

"What was Mr. Middleton's grievance, specifically?" Ryan said.

Nathan Kress sighed. "His grievance was that he had methane infiltration into his water well, and he thought that Rossman Mining's solution was inadequate."

"Mr. Middleton didn't argue breach of contract by the company, did he?"

"No, he admits he signed the contract and that the company followed through on supplying him with potable water after the infiltration. He argued that the contract was weighted in favor of the company."

"The company that wrote the contract?" Ryan said.

Nathan Kress exhaled slowly and held up his hands in a gesture of exasperation. "Problem with the landowners is they don't know what they don't know. They don't bring the contract to an attorney first. They just look you in the eye and shake your hand. Then they say, 'Where do I sign?'"

"That kind of publicity can't be good for the company, right?"

"That's right. And I know Lee was furious when he found out some of his landmen were misleading the landowners. He read them the riot act."

"Did that fix the problem?"

"The way an exterminator fixes a cockroach problem."

"As in, pretty much, for a while?" Ryan said.

Nathan Kress smiled.

"Mr. Kress," I said. "I have to ask you a question. I hope you understand. Can you tell us where you were last night?"

He shook his head sadly. "We had a fundraiser here last night. For Rivers United. Unfortunately, not a very big turnout. Sixteen people. Three thousand dollars."

I stood up. "Thank you for your time, Mr. Kress."

"Would you let me know if there's anything I can do?" he said.

"You bet." But looking at him, in his dark, cold house, I couldn't imagine there'd be much he could do to help us. Or himself, or his family, or the polluted rivers of Montana.

Chapter 8

Back in the cruiser, I got a call. It was Lauren Wilcox. "Yes, Dr. Wilcox," I said. Ryan had taught me that almost all the full-time professors at Central Montana State University had a PhD. "Thanks for getting back to us." I hit Speaker.

"How can I help you?" she said.

"We want to talk with you a few minutes about Lee Rossman." Ryan touched my arm. I looked at him.

He put up his palm, shook his head, and mouthed the words, "Not now." I raised an eyebrow. He kept shaking his head.

"Would you be available tomorrow morning?" I said. Ryan nodded.

"I teach a seminar tomorrow afternoon …"

"We'll just need a few minutes. Promise."

"Can you stop by early?" she said.

"Eight-fifteen sound good?"

"That would be fine," she said. "Room 319 in the Sciences Building? On University?"

"See you then." I ended the call and glanced at my watch. A quarter to four. I turned to Ryan.

"Remember Nathan Kress said she's written four books?"

"I do remember that," I said. "You plan to read four books before the end of the shift?"

"Would you mind heading back to headquarters?" He smiled. "I'm going to need an hour."

I drove us there. Once we made it to our desks, Ryan hung

his suit jacket over the back of his chair and started hitting some keys. I walked into the break room and grabbed a beat-up donut half and a cup of murky coffee.

When I got back, Ryan was tapping his bottom lip with his finger, which he did when he was concentrating. He started writing in his skinny notebook. When he got in a zone like this, I didn't interrupt him. Half the time, he picked up on something that turned out to be important.

There wasn't any point in me offering to help him with the reading. It would have taken him five minutes to explain to me how to find the junk he was reading, and another fifteen to tell me how to understand it. No, the best thing for me to do was just stay out of the way. I was doing my part by finishing the donut.

A couple of minutes later, Ryan put down his pen, expelled a long breath, and looked up at me.

"She mention being an eco-terrorist?" I said.

"Not in so many words." He smiled. "But there's some interesting—"

Then it hit me. I held up my finger. "Wait a second." I opened up the contact list on my computer. I squinted at the list of names and dialed a number on my phone. I looked at my watch again as it went to voicemail. It would be 6:15 in D.C. "Hey, Allen. Karen Seagate in Rawlings, Montana. I got a long shot for you. There's this professor here in town: Lauren Wilcox." I spelled the name. "You guys keep a database on domestic terrorists? Not al Qaida types. Eco-terrorists. Could go back as early as the 1990s. Give me a call, would you?" I left a couple of numbers and hung up.

Ryan looked at me and nodded. "Very nice."

"Still got a half-dozen brain cells," I said. Off the Jack Daniel's more than a year now, with just a couple of blurry days here and there, I'd found I was in fact starting to think a little better. I'd never be as sharp as Ryan, but at least I wasn't slowing him down as much as I used to.

"The feds really cranked up the terror lists after 9/11—" he said.

"So if she was into any nasty shit after 2001, she might be in a database."

"Assuming she was Lauren Wilcox at the time."

"Most of today's terrorists are such pussies." I shook my head. "They're willing to blow things up, but they don't want to get caught."

"Yeah." Ryan put on a solemn expression. "That's the problem with terrorists: They're such pussies."

"So, anyway, you said you got something interesting on Lauren Wilcox?"

"Yeah, I'm going to read a little more of her stuff tonight, but the bottom line is, she's a situation ethicist."

I looked at him and held my gaze. Since he's been my partner for a couple of years, he understands why I stare at him when he uses college words.

"It's a Christian moral theory from the 1960s. You know Paul Tillich?"

My mouth went slack and I blinked a couple times.

"It says that love is the ultimate law. So you can violate other moral principles if doing so best serves love."

I blinked a few more times.

"A corrupt version of it is that the ends justify the means." He looked at me and smiled. "Comment?"

"I'm speechless."

"Actually, no." He gave me his big grin. "If you say 'I'm speechless,' the only thing we know for sure is that you're not."

"You realize it's been a long day, right?"

"You can do this, Karen. Lauren Wilcox believes that the ends justify the means."

I sighed and closed my eyes. "So if a company pollutes, it's okay to do some bad shit to them."

"That's right," he said. "One more step."

"I don't like you, Ryan."

"That's a feeling, not a step."

I paused a second. "And it's okay to play dirty because you can do more good by not getting caught."

He tilted his head, smiled, and put up his palms to show me I got it.

"I still don't like you."

He laughed. "The price I'll have to pay."

"So what you're saying is, she's a pussy."

"'Situation ethicist' will sound better when we bring the chief up to speed."

"I'm gonna head home," I said. "Need to stop at the liquor store first—"

He looked concerned. "You know you're not going to do that, Karen."

"Yes, I am. Because of you," I said, walking toward the coatrack in the corner of the detectives' bullpen. "Own it."

I didn't stop at the liquor store, of course. I headed home, ate dinner, and went to my eight o'clock AA meeting. When the chief re-hired me more than a year ago, he made me attend for ninety days. Now I was still going, almost every day. I'd never bought into the mumbo-jumbo about a higher power, but seeing some of my fellow losers there every day seemed to help. Made me feel I wasn't the biggest fuck-up in town. A lot of them drank themselves single, like I did, but since I'd never literally killed anyone from my drinking, I was among the less toxic of the drunks.

Back at home, I sat down at the computer and tried to smarten up about Lauren Wilcox. I couldn't understand any of the academic stuff she'd written, with all the footnotes and the references to dead scientists and philosophers. But after slogging through the opening pages of her books on Amazon and reading some of her op-ed pieces, I concluded that Ryan was, as usual, right. She never copped to any shit she might have done, her being such a pussy, but she did make it clear how chaining yourself to a tree was usually a waste of time, and pouring sand in the gas tank of the Caterpillar was amateur hour.

Unfortunately, she didn't get into whether it would be okay to kill a guy for doing stuff you didn't like.

I decided to pack it in for the day. I got into bed and tried to watch some TV, but I drifted off during the stupid singing and dancing contests. Ten o'clock news came on, and the chirpy twenty-five-year-old Barbie with the super-white teeth put on a frowny face as she ran through the career of Lee Rossman. There were lots of photos of him in tuxedos, and Florence in ball gowns, hanging with the mayor, then the file footage of the oil rigs bobbing up and down out in the Bakken. Barbie pointed out that fracking was controversial because it creates jobs but some people think it can cause pollution, which was what passes for an in-depth, balanced analysis of an important public-policy issue on the crappy local station. But since the station's motto is "We're there for you!" maybe it was me looking for the right thing in the wrong place.

I turned the TV off and drifted into a dreamless sleep. A few weeks ago I'd stopped taking the over-the-counter sleeping pills I'd been using forever. I was glad to be done with the morning grogginess, but I did miss how the fog floated in and put me out, most nights, in ten minutes.

Then I became aware of the sounds. At first there was a thump, then some tiny, tentative squeaks. I couldn't make out what they were, except that they were solid surfaces rubbing against each other. Because I can dream anytime, even before I'm really out, I assumed the sounds were part of a dream.

I noticed how the sounds started to get louder, although idiot that I am it never occurred to me that they were getting closer. I just assumed the dream was starting to form into a story. And then they formed into a pattern, and over the next few seconds I remember thinking maybe it wasn't a dream.

In an instant I realized that what I had heard was the creaking of the floor boards in the hallway outside my bedroom. But the sounds had stopped. Then I realized I have a thick carpet in my bedroom.

I started to reach for the 9mm in my nightstand, but it was too late. I felt a body pushing me down, back into my bed. Not his hands. It was more like his whole body was falling onto me. He was big and heavy, and he smelled like booze. Under his crushing weight I heard the breath explode from my lungs, then the sound of rustling fabric. I felt a cool, thin cloth, like the nylon shell of a down vest or jacket, close over my nose and mouth.

I tried to push him off my face, but he was too heavy. The pillowy stuffing beneath the nylon fabric closed in over my face.

I knew it was only a few seconds before I would lose consciousness. I tried to jerk a knee up, hoping I could land it between his legs, but my own legs were pinned under the sheet and two blankets and the guy's suffocating weight.

I struggled to free my arms from under the blankets, but my right arm was pinned under his body. With my left I started to scratch at his face, then formed a fist. I landed a blow on his right ear and another on his face, but since my fist was hooking around from the side I wasn't able to generate much force. He groaned, low and slow, but he didn't react otherwise.

I felt along his right flank, but it was protected by his coat. I slid my hand down until it reached the bottom of the coat. Grabbing the fabric, I heard it rip as I pulled it up toward his shoulder to expose his flank. Forming my hand into a spear, I jabbed it into his flank between the bottom rib and the hip bone. He didn't respond.

I started to see spots. I could tell I was losing consciousness. Even though I had been without air for only fifteen or twenty seconds, I was exerting too much effort trying to push him off me. I knew I had only a few more moments. I tried again to spear his flank, this time twisting my fingers back and forth after they landed.

He cried out in pain. I repeated the spear and twisted again, harder. Then again and again. He made some groggy sounds, the way drunks do when they start to come to, and began to roll off of me. I gasped for air as his jacket pulled away from my face, but the weight of his trunk as it rolled toward the side of the bed crushed my ribs on the right side.

I knew if I could get him to roll off the bed I might have a chance. For an instant his movement stopped, and I feared he would fall back onto me. I took a deep gulp of air in anticipation.

But he kept rolling, and finally his enormous weight lifted from my ribs. I heard a thunk, then he cried out as his head hit the corner of my end table. The table where I keep my 9. I reached into the drawer and pulled it out. I keep it loaded—I live alone—but I wasn't planning to shoot him. At least not yet.

It was too dark for me to see him clearly, but I could make out the outlines of his head and body well enough. I lifted the pistol high and swung it down, toward his head. I felt it land, almost silently, on his scalp. This time he didn't make a sound, didn't move. I stayed there a few moments, the pistol trained on him. He was out.

I swung my legs out of the bed and turned on the light on the end table. That's when I saw who it was.

Chapter 9

"Oh, Jesus," I screamed. "Oh, God, no." I was out of the bed, on the floor next to his body. I put my ear next to his mouth. He was breathing, but it was very faint. The blood on the right side of his scalp matted his brown hair. I slapped his face. "Come on," I cried. "Come on." But he didn't seem to hear me.

I started to shake, out of control. I picked up my phone, opened it, and tried to dial 9-1-1, but my fingers couldn't hit the right numbers. My stomach started churning real bad. The acid swept up into my mouth. I put the phone down on the end table and vomited all over the wall and the carpet. I began to choke. I held onto the window frame, gasping for breath. After a few seconds I was able to cough the crap out of my windpipe and start to breathe again. I was on my knees, puke all over my tee-shirt and my thighs, trying to get my breathing under control. I dug my fingernails into my thighs, trying to get my hands to stop shaking. It took another ten or fifteen seconds.

I looked down at Mac. He was on his back, his bloody head twisted to the side. His eyes were closed. I picked up my phone and dialed 9-1-1.

"9-1-1. What's your emergency?"

"I need an ambulance."

She asked me for my address, with the cross-street. Then, my full name and phone. I gave her all the information.

"All right, ma'am. I'm dispatching an ambulance. Please stay on the line. Tell me what happened," the voice said.

"This man fell, hit his head on a table."

"Are you with the man now?"

"He's right here."

"How old is he?"

"Not sure. Maybe fifty."

"All right, ma'am. Is he conscious?"

"No, he's not."

"Is he breathing?"

"Yes, he is. I think he is. He was a minute ago."

"Is he bleeding, ma'am?"

"Yeah, a little. On his head."

"Okay, try to stop the bleeding if you can. Get a cloth, apply a little pressure. Just sit tight, okay? The ambulance will be there in about six minutes."

I grabbed a sweatshirt and stopped the bleeding on Mac's scalp. There wasn't that much blood, but the scalp felt soft and squishy. I started to cry, panicking as I thought maybe I'd fractured his skull. I took a pillow off the bed and put it under his head. I didn't know why.

As I waited for the ambulance, I kept checking to make sure he was still breathing. I looked down at his head. There was another red bruise, near his left eye. That would be from when he hit the night table.

He looked like shit. His tousled hair had an oily sheen. I'd put his beard at three to five days. The hangdog bags under his eyes were greyer than usual. His dark blue down coat was encrusted with dirt, grease, and solid stuff I didn't want to identify. His gym-grey sweatpants had piss stains near the crotch. He wasn't wearing socks. The black sneakers were untied. He smelled like Scotch and shit.

I'd met Mac at AA about a year ago. It was some time after my drinking had cost me what was left of my self-respect, long after it had cost me my family and my job. Our bond, based on intense self-loathing earned over years of lying, deceiving, and betraying the people in our separate lives, made us quite comfortable with each other. When you feel you don't deserve anything good in your life, you don't waste a lot of time trying to look your best.

Mac left me about six months ago, when his wife got a really bad diagnosis. It was the right decision for him. We didn't stay in touch.

I didn't know whether he was back on the booze full-time or whether he was simply spring-breaking it. It wasn't news to me that Mac was weak, of course, but I assumed he was gone from my life. Those were the terms, and I'd lived up to them. I'd never called him, not once.

Now I checked him one more time. He was unconscious but still alive. The bleeding had stopped. I went into the bathroom and washed the puke off my face and my thighs. Brushed my teeth and put on a bra and a clean tee-shirt and a pair of jeans.

I heard the doorbell and went out to let the paramedics in. Then I realized how Mac had gotten in. A big chunk of the door frame was splintered, and a sliver of trim dangled from the chain. I must have been out pretty deep.

"This way," I said to the two young paramedics, one beefy middle-aged guy and a skinny young one behind him. They half-lifted, half-dragged the gurney up my concrete steps. As I turned to lead them into the bedroom, I noticed the middle-aged guy running his finger down the busted doorframe.

"Over there." I pointed to Mac's legs, which were visible between the bed and the wall.

The older paramedic stopped when he saw my pistol on the night table. He turned to his partner and pointed to it. "Call the police."

"I'm the police," I said. I hadn't realized my pistol was still out in plain view.

"Excuse me?" he said.

"My name is Seagate. I'm a detective, Rawlings Police Department. I'll take care of it."

He was shaking his head. "Is that your gun?"

"Yeah, that's mine."

"And you busted down your own front door?"

"No." I didn't know what to say. "Yeah, this guy broke in. But I know him. It's complicated. I'll take care of the breaking and entering."

The young guy looked up from his phone, his gaze shifting from me to his partner. He didn't know whether to call it in, like his partner said.

"Listen, Detective," the older guy said. He turned to the young guy. "Call it in, Ronnie." Then, he turned back to me. "My protocol is clear. If I see evidence of a crime, I call the police. I don't know what the hell happened here. Me and my partner are going to get this guy's vitals and do what we need to do to keep him alive while we wait for the police, but we're not getting in that ambulance without a cop sitting right next to us. You understand me?"

I nodded. The young paramedic called it in.

While the paramedics took Mac's vitals, put him on the gurney, and set up an IV, I stood there, not knowing exactly what to do.

Mac had always been real good about my job. He gave me plenty of space, never tried to interfere. He knew he was toxic. Standing there, watching the paramedics work on him, wondering whether I'd just fucked him up bad, I began to think about how this was going to fuck me up, too.

The paramedics were right to call for the police, to insist on having a cop in the bus with them. It's in their protocol for a good reason. Not that Mac would ever get violent with them. Not when he was sober, anyway.

Couple minutes later, I heard the knock on my door. The paramedic must have told them not to use the lights and siren.

It was two uniforms: Garcia and Abernathy. I recognized them.

"You okay, Detective?" Abernathy said. He was the senior one, about forty, couple years younger than me, a big, strong guy who liked to do community work. No interest in becoming a detective. He looked concerned.

"Yeah, thanks." I shook my head and looked down at my feet, which was my way of acknowledging that bad shit had happened here tonight while signaling I didn't want to talk about it.

"You're gonna have to come in and make a statement."

"I know that." I paused. I pointed to the hall closet and the two officers stepped out of the way so I could get my coat.

Abernathy turned to his partner. "You go in the bus with the paramedics, okay?"

Garcia nodded and walked back toward the bedroom to check in with them.

Abernathy shifted his weight. "You ready, Detective?"

"Let me just get my bag." I went back into my bedroom and grabbed it out of my closet. I took a quick look at Mac, who looked pale and fragile and pathetic.

Abernathy escorted me out to the patrol car and opened the door for me, which I took to be his way of saying he was sorry for having to bring me in. We didn't talk on the drive to headquarters.

Abernathy carded us in and walked me into the detectives' bullpen. There must be a couple of things more embarrassing than hearing a uniform tell the detective on duty that there was an incident at your home and you need to make a statement, but none that came to mind at that moment.

Pelton was the night detective. He was about fifty-eight or sixty, a little bit on the short and stocky side, but a good cop. He had two more years, I think.

"Let's go into an interview room, Karen," he said. I appreciated that he was trying to do this as quiet as possible.

We got settled. "Do you have to do that?" I said as Pelton turned on the recording unit from its controls on the wall.

He hit a button to pause it. "Way I see it, Karen, you want to get out in front of this. Be absolutely straight with us. If this guy broke into your house, that's what you say happened. If it turns out he's hurt bad and you had something to do with that ..." He paused. "If his lawyer comes after you—or his family's lawyer does—what you say over the next few minutes is gonna make the difference in whether you're on the force. Or in prison." He still had his hand on the button.

I nodded.

He hit the button again to start up the system. He came over and announced the time and who was in the room.

"Detective Seagate, do you want to have counsel present or do you want to make a statement now?"

"I'll make a statement now." I realized Pelton was right. This was important. I realized, too, that I was clean, and that not asking for a union rep or a lawyer would help make that point. This was all on Mac.

Pelton walked me through what had happened. I told him the truth: I was awakened by the sound of someone outside my bedroom. He fell on me, I couldn't breathe.

"At this point, were you afraid for your safety?" Pelton was lobbing the slow pitch over the plate for me.

I told the truth. "Yes, I was. I didn't know who the person was, but I was suffocating under his weight. I didn't know what he was going to do." I knew I had to say the next sentence. "I thought he was trying to kill me. Or rape me."

And with that on the record, I knew I had just put Mac in a very bad place.

But as I was telling Pelton what had happened, telling it straight, I realized that it was Mac had put himself in that place. And that I didn't have any other option. It would be up to Mac and his attorney to deal with what he'd done.

"Did you try to defend yourself?"

I tried to keep my voice steady and clear as I described how I pushed him off of me, how he hit his head as he fell off the bed, and how I hit him with the barrel of my pistol.

"Why did you hit him with the pistol?"

Again, Pelton helping me out. "I was afraid he might keep coming at me."

"Detective Seagate, did you tell the paramedics that you had hit Mr. McNamara with your pistol?"

"No, I didn't. I wasn't thinking clearly. I was upset. I was hoping this whole thing didn't have to get written up."

"Why is that, Detective?"

"I didn't want to get Mr. McNamara in more trouble than necessary."

"If your account of the incident is true, shouldn't Mr. McNamara have to take responsibility for his actions?"

I was silent for a moment. "Mr. McNamara and I were in a relationship. It ended some months ago."

"But you didn't know it was Mr. McNamara who had broken into your house, is that correct?"

"That's correct."

"And regardless of whether you knew it was Mr. McNamara who had broken into your house, as the incident was occurring, you were trying to defend yourself. It was only after you had defended yourself against the attacker that you learned the identity of the attacker. Is that the case?"

"Yes, that's the case." I wiped at my nose. Suddenly I was dead tired, struggling to keep my eyes open. I saw Pelton lean in, looking hard into my eyes. He announced the time and ended the interview, then got up and walked over to the controls and shut down the system.

I heard myself crying as I put my head on the battered, scratched-up steel table. I was out for a few seconds. I felt Pelton's hand on my shoulder. He was half lifting me out of the seat. Next thing I knew I was in the storage closet where we had a couple of cots for cops who were in the building when they should've been home. My head hit the pillow, and I was out.

Chapter 10

"Karen?"

I felt a hand on my shoulder. I tried to rouse myself. All I could see was a silhouette of a man framed by a rectangle of light coming in from an open door. I had no idea where I was.

"It's Ryan," the voice said. I heard him walk toward the open door, then the fluorescent tubes in the ceiling started buzzing and lit up. I covered my eyes with my hands. My eyes stung and I had a screaming headache. It took me a few seconds to orient myself, and then I remembered the episode with Mac. I started to cry but tried to cover it up so Ryan wouldn't see me falling apart. I wiped at my nose.

"What time is it?"

"Eight-twenty."

"Shit." I sat up quickly, which my head really didn't like. "We were supposed to interview that professor at eight-fifteen."

"It's okay. I called her. Told her something came up. We'd be there at nine."

I sighed. "Great, thanks." I tried to pull myself together. "I'm really sorry about this."

He raised his eyebrows. "About a guy breaking into your place and attacking you?"

He'd been briefed by Pelton, or the chief, or someone. "I don't know what the hell happened." I shook my head.

"A guy pushed your door open hard enough to pop the chain, break the door frame. He's in your bedroom. You had to assume he was going to attack you."

"Yeah." I looked at my clothes: a tee shirt, sweatpants. "Do you think we could swing by my place so I can get some clothes?"

"You ready to go now?"

I looked around for my coat. Ryan retrieved it from a utility desk in the corner of the room and held it for me to get into. "Thanks."

He led me out to the Charger. "I'll drive, okay?" He gave me a gentle smile.

The sun was an indistinct glow above the horizon as we headed over to my place. "Who filled you in?" I said.

"Pelton," Ryan said. "He told the chief, too."

"Shit."

"Don't jump to conclusions."

"Yeah, I know. But I was kind of hoping I could go a whole year without bringing any personal shit into headquarters."

Ryan pulled into my driveway and shut down the Charger. "It was that guy did it. You didn't have any other options."

I looked at my watch. It was 8:35. "You think I have a moment to call the hospital?"

"I called over at eight. They're still working on him."

"That doesn't sound good." I was crying again.

"Don't get ahead of yourself. It doesn't necessarily mean anything." Ryan paused. "It's that man you were with? Earlier this year?"

I nodded.

"I'm sorry, Karen."

"Let me put some clothes on." I got out the cruiser and tried to run into my house but I slowed it to a walk when I felt some acid flowing north into my throat. It took me just a minute to throw on my Cop Casual outfit: a pair of wool slacks, a blouse, a sport coat, and pair of flats with thick soles in case I had to spend any time outside. I also grabbed a couple of Tylenol and swallowed them.

Getting dressed for work helped me focus. I really wanted to get back to thinking about the case, not about this mess with Mac. And I wanted Ryan to think of me as the senior detective, not as his fucked-up older sister who his mother told him he had to take care of.

I tried to lock my front door, but the frame was too busted up and the door wouldn't even stay shut. I went back inside, grabbed a magazine rack and pushed it up against the door so it at least closed and looked normal. I left the house by the back door and made it to the driver's side of the cruiser. Ryan lowered the window. "Let me drive," I said.

"You sure?"

I opened the door and he got out. "All right," I said when we got in the Charger. I looked at my watch: 8:42. "Thanks for letting me stop."

"We'll get to campus on time."

On the way to the university, we went over our strategy for the interview. My usual approach is to display my stupidity and ignorance, the theory being that if the suspect is innocent, no harm done, but if he's guilty, he'll lie to us or at least mislead us, which might make it a little easier to catch him out.

Ryan was arranging some things in his leather briefcase. "I take it you want to stay away from her writing?"

"I'm not going there since I can't figure out most of what she's saying. But I'm fine with you doing whatever you want."

We pulled into the lot at the Sciences Building on the Central Montana State University campus. There were only a handful of grumpy-looking students in sight. I was hot from all the heat the big engine in the cruiser pumped out, but the frigid air cut through my cloth coat when we walked the forty yards to the building.

We took the elevator to the third floor and found room 319.

I pointed to a shiny silver sign over the door. Rossman Mining Environmental Laboratory, it said. "Look at that," I said.

"We should ask Dr. Wilcox about that," he said.

The door was closed, but the light from inside was visible through the drawn blinds on the glass wall. I knocked.

Lauren Wilcox opened the door fast. She was about fifty, with too-long, frizzy salt-and-pepper hair parted down the middle. Her eyes, green with gold flecks, were bright. She looked at me, and then at Ryan, and broke into a big smile, showing long crow's feet. "You the detectives?"

"Karen Seagate." I gave her my official smile. "My partner, Detective Ryan Miner."

She was wearing a thick plaid wool shirt, reds and tans, which I could tell was officially women's only because the buttons were on the left. The brown corduroy pants and engineer's boots could have gone either way. No jewelry, no rings, no makeup.

"This is our new home," she said with a broad smile.

It was as big as the detectives' bullpen back at headquarters, maybe twice the size of a standard classroom. Off to one side were some round tables for students. Along one wall were eight or ten different pieces of equipment, most of them with places in front where you would load in some kind of soil samples or liquids for testing. All of them had computer screens of various sizes, and a few of them were hooked up to wide printers.

But the star of the show was this enormous fish tank, maybe three feet wide and twenty feet long, with all kinds of plumbing running along the floor to feed it.

"This is our new flume," Lauren Wilcox said, pointing to it like a proud mother. "Come take a look." She walked me and Ryan over to it. "It's a stream—but a stream we can control. We put the water in it." She gestured to the wall where the tank was attached. There were knobs and controls and a big computer screen built into the wall. "But we put in exactly as much as we want, from any number of locations. And we put whatever we want on the stream bed."

Ryan was wearing a big grin. "This is so cool," he said. "You use this for showing fluid behavior?"

She cocked her head, surprised. "Yes, in the intro courses. Laminar and turbulent flow, sediment entrainment, transport, depositional processes. That kind of thing."

"And in the advanced courses?" Ryan said.

"We're working on modeling how the pollutants from flowback water get into the rivers and then the purification plants."

"We put the dirty water right into the streams?" I said.

"No," she said. "By which I mean it's illegal to do that. But that's where a lot of it ends up. Five years ago they used to put it directly on the roads to keep the dust down. And since it's full of salt, they used it for de-icing. Now it gets into the streams from runoff, pipe leaks, spills. And leaks in the containment ponds." She shook her head. "So we use the flume to test different models of what happens to it when it hits the sediment. You know, whether it gets bound up in it."

Ryan said, "What doesn't get trapped gets into the water supply?"

Lauren Wilcox smiled. "You study some engineering?"

"Just enough to be confused." He turned on his big smile. He was officially in Flirt Mode now. She nodded and held his gaze for a few moments.

I pointed to a shiny aluminum contraption straddling the glass walls of the flume. It looked like a high-tech range hood. "What's that thing?" I said.

"That's the data-acquisition cart. It rides along the top of the flume, taking laser and sonar readings of the sediment surface as it moves. So we can map the flume in real time as water moves through it. It lets us extrapolate what's going on in different rivers and streams with different bed conditions and organic materials."

"This is amazing," Ryan said.

Lauren Wilcox looked at him and smiled. In that instant, I saw what she looked like thirty years ago—and what kind of guy she would've gone after.

I turned to face her. "I noticed this lab is named for Lee Rossman."

She nodded, her expression serious. She'd heard about Rossman's death. "He endowed this whole thing."

"Help us understand that," I said. "Aren't you two on opposite sides?"

"Yes, we were. But there was one project we were working on that caught his attention."

"Which was?"

"We're working on a fracking-fluid tracer, a substance you put into the fracking fluid when you inject it into the shale. The tracer acts like a fingerprint. If that tracer ends up in someone's well water or municipal water, that tells you where it came from."

"Why would Lee Rossman want to help you do that?"

"From his perspective, it makes him look transparent. He says the chemicals don't pollute. It's a way to prove he's right."

"You don't see it that way?"

"I'm not going to speculate about his motives. But I look at it differently. If he looks transparent, that buys him time before the public demands that the industry disclose the chemicals they pump into the ground. Right now, the actual mix of chemicals is legally a trade secret. Companies don't have to disclose it. But the public is waking up to the obvious problem. Rossman—and everyone else in the industry—was betting the public would be satisfied if there are tracers."

"That's a pretty big bet, though, isn't it?" Ryan said. "What if the tracer shows up? They're opening themselves up to millions of dollars in damages, aren't they?"

Lauren Wilcox turned to him. "The industry is betting that the tracers won't actually work. Right now, they only last a few weeks before they degrade. They can be destroyed by UV light, by interactions with other chemicals. All that the oil companies will need to do in court is introduce reasonable doubt. If the tracers don't work perfectly—every time, in every circumstance—we'll be back to where we are now: We can't prove you're drinking Rossman Mining's chemicals."

She gestured to a small, round conference table and sat down in one of the four plastic stacking chairs. "What do you need?" she said, leaning toward me.

"We assume you've heard about the death of Lee Rossman," I said.

She nodded. "Caught it last night on the news."

"We believe it was murder."

"They said that."

I paused. "Do you know of anyone who would have wanted to hurt him?"

"'Hurt him'? If by 'hurt him' you mean injure him or kill him, no. Make him get out of the oil business? Renounce everything he has ever done to rape the planet? Donate his many millions of dollars to repair an infinitesimal portion of the damage he has caused over the decades? Go away and never come back? Yes, absolutely. Almost everyone I know would welcome any or all of those things. And put me at the top of that list."

"Could you tell us a little about the student group you oversee?"

"I founded Students for a Green Montana right after I got here, four years ago." She nodded. "I wanted to educate students about environmental science—sure—but really I wanted to help them understand how to engage in public life, how to work constructively with various stakeholders. The only way the environmental movement is going to become a potent force, especially in a conservative state like Montana—where the zeitgeist favors extractive industries, and the ethos of radical freedom and government non-interference is well-entrenched—the only way is to become enmeshed in the business and political environment."

"Tell us about the students in the group."

"Most of these kids are twenty years old." She gave me an "it's all about the kids" smile. "They're full of enthusiasm, and they don't understand how people who come from the land, who've worked this land sometimes for four and five generations, can poison it—for a few bucks. To be honest, I don't, either." She shook her head in sadness. "And when some of my kids write inflammatory things in the paper, it's my job to rein them in. But for me the question is simple: Would you rather have a generation of kids lined up, eager to join the polluters, or a bunch of kids who sometimes go a little overboard in criticizing their predatory business forces?" She tilted her head. "I know what my answer would be."

"I hear what you're saying." I nodded. "Anyone in your group you think might be capable of violence?"

She closed her eyes and exhaled, like she understood I had to ask it but I was way off base. "No," she said. "Not in a million years. They're just not fully housebroken yet."

"Tell us about Nathan Kress of Rivers United."

"I work with Nathan. He's always very generous about letting my kids work with him: you know, internships and volunteer activities with him."

I waited for her to continue, but apparently that was all she wanted to say. "You don't think Rivers United does valuable work?"

"Nathan and I have a very good professional relationship, and I believe he's a good person. A very good person. But I believe—and I'm not telling you anything I haven't told him to his face many times—he lets himself be used by the political-industrial complex."

"How's that?"

"He's happy to play the role of the official environmental guy in town. He's the one who sits on all the panels and commissions, right alongside the mining guy and the Chamber of Commerce guy, and they sort of balance each other out. Then the county planning board, the public-utility commission, and the governor all nod their heads solemnly and say they've listened to all the voices, this has been very valuable, we're going to have to give this serious thought, *et cetera*."

"Isn't that what you want?" I say.

"Then they go ahead and waive the corporate taxes, suspend the oversight, and grant the permits. The game is rigged. We always lose. No, that's not at all what we want."

"What is it you want?"

"We need to replace the current paradigm." She looked at me, then at Ryan, to make sure we were paying attention. I remembered some of my professors doing it. "Today, we think of the environment as an interest that needs to be balanced against other interests, such as energy needs and employment. If the mine produces pollution, that's a negative. If it creates jobs, that's a positive. That's the model. What we need is a paradigm that sees the environment not as an interest but as the ecosystem in which we all live. When we're talking about an industry—especially an extractive industry such as mining, and this kind of mining, which is so damaging to the land, the water, the air—the first question needs to be this: Should we even consider it in the first place?"

She paused to give us a moment to take in what she was saying. "We have to get to the point where an initiative is off the table as soon as its *potential* environmental damage is determined. I say *potential* because you can't predict what the damage will be, but common sense tells you that if the industry won't even divulge what's in the carcinogen cocktail they blast into the shale, there will be significant damage. Once you get into a debate where one side says an industry is poisoning the earth—to some extent, and one day we'll be able to prove it—and the other side says it provides cheap energy or it creates this many jobs or whatever—today—well, it's game over.

"Nothing demonstrates this better than global warming. Every year, the tipping point—the date when the earth will no longer be able to support human life if we don't eliminate global warming—is re-calculated, and it always gets closer. Yet half the population thinks there's no such thing as global warming. It's insane. It must stop." She paused and shook her head, like she couldn't believe there are people out there so stupid. "It is our responsibility to stop it." Lauren Wilcox sat back in her chair and took a breath.

"Professor Wilcox," Ryan said. She turned to him. "Can you tell us where you were Sunday night, after, say, nine o'clock?"

She flinched, then gave him a confused look. "You're kidding me, right?"

I put on a sad expression. "Unfortunately, no," I said. "It's just a routine question we have to ask all of the victim's associates."

"I was by no means an associate of Lee Rossman," she said, a flash of anger in her eyes, "which I have just explained in considerable detail."

"I apologize for saying that." I put up my palms in a show of contrition. "But can you tell us where you were Sunday night, after, say, nine o'clock?"

She sat up straight in her chair. "I'm sorry." She lowered her eyes, then raised them again and gave me a smile. "What I just said was rude." She turned to Ryan. "I apologize, Detective."

Ryan shook his head to dismiss it.

"When I start to talk about fracking …" She paused, then

exhaled a long breath. "I mean, what we are doing is just so tragic. And so unnecessary. When the detective asked me where I was Sunday night … I understand you're investigating a murder. It just caught me by surprise." She turned to Ryan and bowed her head. "Again, I'm sorry."

"Don't mention it," Ryan said, smiling. Then the smile disappeared. "So, can you tell us where you were Sunday night, after, say, nine o'clock?"

"I teach two classes Monday. Sunday night I was at home, preparing."

"Can anyone corroborate that?" Ryan said.

"Unfortunately, no. I live alone." She smiled.

I stood up and pulled a card from my big leather bag. "All right, Professor, thank you for that information. Would you get in touch if you can think of anything that can help us in this investigation?"

"Of course," she said. "I'm sorry I couldn't be more helpful." She turned to Ryan. "Detective."

"Not at all," I said. "You've been very helpful." Ryan and I turned and left her office.

When a suspect calls the victim a rapist—of a woman, a kid, or even of a planet—yes, that could be very helpful, indeed.

Chapter 11

"We wanted to catch you up." We were sitting in the chief's office, having just gotten back from campus. He nodded, telling me to go on. "We finished up our first round of interviews here in town, and we want to go out to the rigs."

"No forensics yet?"

"Harold said later today," Ryan said.

"Who've you interviewed?"

"We already told you about Florence Rossman."

"Yeah," the chief said, shifting in his chair. He saw me squinting a little. The light was coming in from the window behind his head. He turned and adjusted the blinds.

"Thanks," I said. "We interviewed a bunch of people at the bar where Rossman's body was found."

"And?"

"And zilch. Guy who owns it is a scumbag, and some of the girls might be hooking, but nothing about what Rossman was doing in the alley."

The chief let out a long, slow breath. He was looking down at his desk, his brow furrowed, like he was thinking about how to phrase something. He looked up at me. "Maybe Harold can put someone's DNA on Rossman."

I shrugged. "We could get lucky. Maybe he was doing one of the employees. But we'd still need probable cause to be able to make that link. Same night, there might've been a hundred girls—amateurs—willing to suck him for a quick hundred."

The chief looked at me, his face a blank. "Next?" he said.

"We interviewed Cheryl Garrity, his director of operations. She's a little strange."

The chief turned to Ryan, signaling for him to comment.

"I couldn't get a clear read on her." Ryan raised his palms. "Maybe she was traumatized—I think we got there right after they heard. She was kind of robotic. Maybe it was how she handles stress."

The chief turned to me. "Do you like her?"

"She and Lee Rossman go back more than twenty years," I said. "She's the right age to have been in a relationship with him back in the day."

"But now with Florence on the scene?"

"Yeah, Cheryl could be pissed about that," I said.

"One thing she did mention," Ryan said, "was how Florence is the co-owner of the business. If Cheryl's the woman scorned, that would be my vote for motive."

"Good to know." The chief nodded. "She have an alibi?"

I shook my head. "She lives alone."

"Who else have you talked to?"

"Cheryl Garrity put us onto two environmentalists in town." I forgot the guy's name, so I looked at Ryan.

"Nathan Kress," Ryan said. "Rivers United."

"I know who you mean," the chief said.

"He has an alibi," I said, "plus he owed Rossman."

"For what?"

"Rossman paid the medical bills when Kress' son got really sick," I said. "Kress wouldn't hurt a fly. No way he'd ever hurt Rossman. He's the kind of guy wants us all to get along."

The chief turned to Ryan. "You see him that way, too?"

"I do," Ryan said.

"And the second environmentalist?"

"We just talked to her," I said. "Lauren Wilcox. A professor in town."

"Like her?"

"I haven't had a chance to talk with Ryan, but, yeah, I do. First off, Cheryl Garrity calls her an eco-terrorist—"

The chief tilted his head. "She used that term?"

"Sure did."

"She explain what it means?"

I shook my head. "No such luck. But she spelled out the name to be sure we'd look her up."

The chief turned to Ryan. "And when you looked her up?"

"We found a professor who's well-published," Ryan said. "A little more radical than Nathan Kress—I mean, about environmentalism. She runs this student group at the university that gets the kids involved in the politics."

"She point you to a kid?"

"No," I said. "She called them puppies. Just not housebroken."

"One thing Karen thought of," Ryan said. "We put in a call to the FBI to see if they've got her in some sort of database."

The chief looked wistful. "That would be nice, wouldn't it?"

I said, "She does have a temper. When we asked her if she had an alibi—which, by the way, she doesn't—she gave us some lip."

"She's sitting there in a brand-new lab," Ryan said. "It must have cost a million bucks. Guess who paid for it?"

"Lee Rossman?"

"Exactly."

"So she owes Rossman, too, like Nathan Kress?"

"No," I said, "she's got a real set of balls on her. She said she wouldn't hurt him—what's she gonna say?—but she was up-front about how she wanted to put him out of business permanently."

"But not with a knife," the chief said.

"She was clear about that."

"You stay in touch with the FBI."

"Absolutely."

"So who you want to talk to out at the rigs?"

"We want to start with Bill Rossman, Lee's son," I said. "You know him?"

"Heard of him. Never met him." The chief frowned. "What's he doing out at the rigs?"

"Florence told us he works on the rigs sometimes and lives here in town sometimes. When he's here he's going to college."

"His father's just been killed. Why isn't he here in town with Florence?"

"We haven't quite figured out that relationship," Ryan said. "His step-mom said it's a work-in-progress."

"Is he in our system?"

Ryan looked down at his notebook. "Some misdemeanors. Criminal mischief. Underage drinking. Possession."

"Was he selling?"

"No." Ryan shook his head. "Just a couple of joints. These go back six or seven years. The only recent arrest was last year. Simple assault. He got into it with another student. They beat each other up. They'd been drinking. Neither one pressed charges."

"That's all we know about that incident?"

"The other student," Ryan said, reading from his notebook, "is Kirk Hendrickson. Don't know what they were fighting about. You want us to track him down, or the arresting officer?"

The chief sighed. "Not yet. Let's see where it goes. I'm more interested in why Bill's still out at the rigs."

"And whether he was out there when his father got killed," I said.

"Maybe Harold can help us with that." The chief paused. "Anyone else you want to talk to out at the rigs?"

"There's a rancher named Mark Middleton who's had some

confrontations with Rossman Mining," Ryan said.

"What kind of confrontations?" the chief said.

"Middleton is unhappy because he thinks Rossman wasn't honest with him when they leased his property for drilling. So he organized some other unhappy landowners, bought some billboards, made some obnoxious YouTube videos. Then he started denying the company access to his property—"

"Which violates his contract."

"Yes. Then Rossman equipment on his property started taking some small-arms fire."

"During the day?"

"No, just at night," Ryan said. "Middleton denies he had anything to do with it. But whoever was doing the shooting knew how to hit the expensive parts on the equipment."

"Any arrests?"

"No. The local police have talked to him a couple of times, since it's all happened on his property, but they didn't have enough to charge him."

"So Middleton is trying to intimidate the company?"

"That's the way I'd read it. He figures the workers are going to start worrying about whether he'll fire when they're on his property. If they refuse to work the three rigs on his ranch, maybe the company will decide it's not worth the trouble and just shut them down."

"But Middleton hasn't made any specific threats against Lee Rossman?"

"He stops just short. Calls Rossman a ghost, says he has him dead to rights. That kind of thing."

"Well," the chief said, "I think you two ought to try to talk with him. Maybe he just crossed that line."

"So, we're good, Chief?" I said.

"Yeah," he said.

Ryan and I stood up and turned to leave.

"Ryan, could you give me and Karen a minute?"

"I'll see you back in the bullpen." Ryan left the chief's office.

"Sit." The chief pointed to a chair. I sat. "I wanted to see how you're doing."

It took me a moment to figure out what he was referring to. "I'm good. A little tired." I shook my head. "I'm fine."

He looked at me, didn't say anything.

"You mean the incident at my place, last night, right?" I said.

He scratched at an earlobe. "If you want me to assign someone else—it's a long drive out to the Bakken."

"No, chief, I'm fine. I'll sleep in the cruiser. I mean, if I get tired."

"Karen, we've been through some stuff together—"

"Which is why I'm telling you I'm fine."

"This man—McNamara—that was the man you were involved with a few months ago."

I stood up. "Listen, Chief, I appreciate what you're doing, but it's not your problem. I'm telling you I'm okay, so I'd appreciate it if you could just …" I showed him my palms.

"All right, Detective, I hear what you're saying." He stood up and buttoned his suit jacket. "Do you intend to tell Booking whether you plan to press charges?"

I had forgotten that the hospital would release Mac to the Department, and he'd show up here. We'd need to decide what to do with him. "I'm sorry, Chief, I haven't had a chance to think about that."

"Would you like my advice?"

"I don't want you to have to get involved."

He pulled his head back. "I'm the chief of police for the city of Rawlings. I have to either release this man or charge him. Now, do you want my advice?"

"I understand what you're saying, Chief." I felt my legs go a little wobbly, the fatigue catching up to me. "But I want you to think of me as just another cop."

"Charge him with B&E. That's a felony. We hold him. When you've had a chance to get some sleep and decide what you want to do, you can add assault. Whatever you decide."

I nodded and stood up to leave.

He stepped out from beside his desk and walked over to me. "Karen, trusting people doesn't make you weak."

I started to weaken. "I trusted Mac."

"I'm not Mac."

"No, Chief, you're not," I said. "I know you're not." I knew if I said anything more, I'd fall apart. I pointed over my shoulder. "Ryan and I need to get going."

He nodded and I left his office. I made my way out past Margaret, his gatekeeper, down the hall, and out to the detectives' bullpen.

Ryan was sitting at his desk, looking at his computer. He looked up. "Everything okay?"

I nodded. "You ready to go?"

"Sure," he said. "You want to try to make it there and back today?"

"What is it? Two hours' drive?"

"About."

"There probably isn't anyplace to stay out there, is there?"

"I hadn't thought of that," he said.

"Let's see if we can do it all today."

We headed out to the Charger, gassed it up, and started out on State Road 12, a two-lane, east toward Marshall, Montana, a little town on the Yellowstone River, a few miles shy of the North Dakota line.

"I'm driving," I said as Ryan headed toward the driver's side. He stopped and gave me a hesitant look, but I wasn't asking. "You can drive us back," I said.

Two miles out of town, the car dealers and RV places gave

way to pastureland, dotted by the occasional farmhouse, with barns, sheds, and grain silos. The sky was turning a nasty grey. I hoped we wouldn't get caught in a storm. Roads out here are fast—unless they get slick.

"Were you able to get an address on Bill Rossman?" I said.

Ryan was looking out the windshield. He didn't turn to face me. "He's in a Rossman man camp couple miles east of Marshall."

"Were you able to contact him?"

"He didn't pick up. I left a message."

The wind had picked up, charging across the empty prairie, pushing the Charger back and forth across the median line. An eighteen-wheeler carrying a load of steel pipe covered in canvas tarp approached us. As I steered the Charger onto the rumble strips to give us a little margin of error, the wind ripped a grommet off the tarp, snapping the heavy canvas like a whip. "Holy shit," I said.

I could tell we were getting closer to the oil fields when we started spotting the truck turnouts, wide paved strips a few hundred yards long for the guys to sleep. Even though the turnouts were full of brightly painted garbage cans, the black pavement was littered with trucker bombs, the two-liter plastic bottles full of frozen urine. When it gets down to twenty below, with thirty-mile winds, keeping Montana tidy just doesn't seem worth the effort of getting out of the cab.

Ryan used the GPS to lead me to the Rossman man camp. It looked like a one-story warehouse, painted cinder block with small windows every few feet. Off to the side was a paved driveway that led around to the back, where the guys parked their pickups and rigs. We took one of the handful of spots out front and went into the lobby. It looked like a low-end hotel chain, with a simple reception area. A few chairs lined the wall, and a plain cloth couch sat in the middle, flanked by two end tables.

I walked up to the reception desk and introduced me and Ryan, said we were hoping to speak to Bill Rossman.

The forty-year old woman wearing a Rossman sweatshirt looked at her computer screen. "He's working now," she said with an official smile.

"You can tell he's not in his room?"

"Everyone here works for Rossman Mining. We know who's on shift, who isn't," she said.

Ryan walked up to the desk and gave the woman a big smile. "Can you tell us if Bill Rossman is in a single or a double?"

She looked down at the screen. "Double."

"Is the roommate in?"

She glanced down. "Andy Bellows. Room 156. Down the hall, first right."

"Thanks very much," I said as we turned to head toward the glass door with the card reader next to it on the wall.

"Put these on, please." The receptionist handed us a couple of visitor badges. We heard a buzz and the door unlocked. We clipped on the badges and walked through the door. In a big room on the left, some bleary-eyed guys were playing pool under fluorescent lights. On the right was a smaller room with a dozen computers on desks lining the wall. Next to the desks, a small storefront sold candy, cigarettes, chewing tobacco, little boxes of detergent, and plastic razors. Past the laundry room with ten washers and dryers, we turned right into a hallway with individual rooms. Except for the fire extinguishers mounted on the beige walls, it looked like a standard motel.

I knocked on the door of room 156. A slightly nauseating chemical smell hung in the hall. Ryan pointed down at the industrial carpet, colored a mud-friendly brown with pale yellow stripes. It looked new and quite clean. We waited.

"He might be playing pool or something."

Ryan stepped up to the door and rapped on it with a little

more authority. "Or maybe he's just sleeping."

We heard some movement from inside and a muffled "Shit."

"Andy Bellows?" I said when a big guy in a tee-shirt and boxer shorts opened the door. He was rubbing his eyes. I introduced us and apologized for waking him up.

"Where the hell you say you from?" I picked up a Southern twang.

"Rawlings. Couple hours west of here."

He shook his head, like he didn't know there was anyplace couple hours west of here. "What you want with me?"

"We're investigating the murder of Bill's father, back in Rawlings. Just wanted to ask you some questions. Five minutes, tops."

"Who's Bill?"

I looked at him. "Your roommate." I pointed to the other bed in the eight-by-twelve room. "Bill Rossman."

"That's his name?"

"Yeah, that's him. You know, you work for Rossman Mining? Your roommate's dad was the boss."

He rubbed at his eyes. "Didn't know that."

"You heard Lee Rossman died couple days ago?"

"I do twelve-hour shifts, fourteen of them in a row. I haven't heard much of anything."

"Okay, Andy, just let us come in and ask you a couple questions. I promise we'll be out of here fast."

He stepped back and gestured for us come in. I took the plastic chair that went with the tiny desk bolted to the wall. Ryan sat on Bill Rossman's rumpled bed.

"Thanks, Andy. So you didn't know Bill's the boss' son?"

"Never put that together. We just sleep in the same room. We're not on the same crew. He don't talk much. Not to me, anyways."

"The murder happened Sunday night, late. Or early Monday."

"Here in Marshall?"

"We're not sure. Do you know whether Bill was here in his room Sunday night?"

"This is Tuesday?"

"Yeah."

"No, I don't think he was. I was here, though."

"Is it common for him to be out all night?"

"I been here less than two weeks, so I can't say what his patterns are. And he don't tell me shit. But judging by the way he smells when I do run into him, I'd say he's out a lot of the time."

Ryan said, "What does he smell like?"

"Beer." He paused a second. "And pussy." He looked at me and shrugged his shoulders, like it was my partner who asked. What was he supposed to do: not answer the question?

Chapter 12

"Beer and pussy," I said as we walked back out toward the main lobby of the man camp. "I wonder what he was trying to say."

"It's a real head-scratcher," Ryan said. "We get back to Rawlings, I'll run it by some of the older guys. See if they know."

The receptionist gave us directions to the drilling rig Bill Rossman was working. I thanked her and handed her the two visitor badges.

"Ah, shit," I said as we got outside. "Look at this." It had started to sleet, and the black Charger was covered in ice. The doors crackled as we opened them. Ryan got a scraper out of the trunk. I turned the defroster on high as he hacked away at the windshield.

We crunched our way slowly the three miles out to the rig, which was perched on a bluff. The steel derrick, painted red, a good hundred feet tall, looked like what the guy who did the Eiffel Tower would have designed if they'd told him to make it ugly and sturdy enough so you could screw an eight-inch diameter pipe a couple miles down through rock.

The derrick sat in the middle of what must have been three or four football fields' worth of bulldozers, pallet movers, construction trailers, water trucks, and a few dozen racks holding hundreds of thirty-foot lengths of black steel pipe. I recognized generators and tanks, squat like propane tanks but bigger than pickup trucks. Off to the side was a pond as big as a municipal swimming pool filled with a thick, clay-red liquid that was cascading out of a wide white PVC pipe leading back to the rig.

I stopped the Charger on the edge of the drilling pad, almost fifty yards away from the derrick. We got out of the cruiser, our feet crunching on the clay surface that was dimpling up with ice, and walked toward the construction trailer with the most lights on.

The noise from the diesel generators was deafening. Ryan shouted to me, "They're bringing the guys in. Because of the rain." A guy on a steel platform sticking out from the derrick, forty feet up, guided a length of pipe into position so a couple of men at the base could lower it into the well. The guy unhooked his harness and started climbing down the ladder. He hooked his boot heel on the icy rung and slowly lowered himself to the next rung.

A half-dozen roughnecks started walking toward the construction trailer where we were heading. Ryan walked up one of them, a burly guy whose full beard was encrusted with ice. "Can you point me to the foreman?"

He pointed to the trailer. "Jim Doering. In there."

I thanked him and we walked up the wooden steps to the trailer. I knocked.

"Come," we heard from inside. We walked in, wiped our feet on the rubber mat just inside the doorway, and I introduced us. "Can we have a few minutes with Bill Rossman?"

"As long as you need. We could be down for an hour, maybe more."

"Could you point him out to us?" I said.

Doering stood and walked over to the window. He pointed. "The young guy over there. With the goatee."

Ryan said, "Bill didn't ask for any time off? You know, about his father?"

Doering shook his head and walked back to his desk. "That's something, isn't it?"

"Why do you think that is?" I said.

"If he was any other guy on my crew, I'd say he doesn't want to lose the pay. But Bill? No idea."

"So he doesn't talk to you," Ryan said.

"Far as I can tell, doesn't talk to anyone."

I thanked him and we went back out into the sleet. The wind was picking up, the sleet coming in sideways and stinging my face. We caught up with Bill. I told him who we were. "Is there somewhere we can talk for a couple minutes? Out of the weather?"

He nodded and started to walk toward the derrick. He led us into the base of the unit, a little enclosure, open at the sides but with a steel roof and floor. The space was packed with control panels for all the electronics. Another guy came in and flipped some switches to shut down the generator powering the main drill rig. Except for the clanging of chains and the whooshing of some orange water still flowing into the pit twenty yards away, it was finally quiet enough for us to hear the sleet drumming on the steel roof.

The guy who had shut down the generator made some notes on a clipboard. He looked at Ryan in his suit and black wool overcoat, then he glanced at me. He gave us an official nod, as if we were from corporate, or maybe the government.

"First, Bill," I said, after the other roughneck left the little room, "we want to say we're very sorry for your loss. We're the lead detectives on the case. Our chief knew your dad, and he's promised us every resource we need to solve it."

Bill Rossman nodded again. He still hadn't said a word. His dark brown eyes, almost black, looked at me intently, like he was trying to figure out what we really wanted. Then he turned to Ryan and looked at him for a long moment, too. Apparently, he wasn't automatically buying the idea we wanted to catch whoever killed his father. Or maybe he wasn't confident we'd succeed.

"Tell us about why you work out here." My arm swept across the room. "Are you learning the business to take over for your father?"

"I have no idea what my father's plans for me were. He wasn't real hands-on. I work here because I like it." Bill was a little over six feet, with his father's broad shoulders but no fat on him.

"What do you like about it?"

"It's physical. No games, no lies. Spin the bit fast enough, it's going to crack the shale."

"Unless the bit breaks," I said.

He rewarded me with a hint of a smile. "That can happen." Then he started to take off his heavy, rubber-coated gloves. His hands were cracked and red. He clenched and unclenched his fists slowly, as if he was trying to get the blood flowing back into his fingers.

"Can you tell us why you aren't back in Rawlings with Florence?"

He tilted his head, like that was an odd question. "I don't think she needs me there." He paused. "She'll be fine. She has friends."

"What do you mean? You're family."

"Not really. Not blood." He slid his gloves into the big pockets of his muddy orange overalls, then looked up at me. "She has plenty of money, she looks good. She'll be fine."

"Are you coming back to Rawlings, I mean, for your father's service?"

"I've talked with Aunt Cheryl. She'll keep me informed of that."

"That's Cheryl Garrity?"

This time Bill just stared at me, like it was a dumb question. Like, of course, everyone knows that when Bill Rossman says "Aunt Cheryl," he's referring to Cheryl Garrity, the director of operations for his dad's company. Because it's impossible that there could be two women named Cheryl in Montana. And therefore I should assume that Aunt Cheryl is Cheryl Garrity so as not to waste his time. And if it turns out we assume there's only one Cheryl but there's really two and therefore we don't figure out who killed this guy's damn father, well, that's okay, we'll just suspend the lead detective, the moron named Karen Seagate, who's standing here with slush soaking through her shoes and one foot's already numb and the other one's tingling. I turned to my partner.

Ryan said, "Tell us about that arrest last year. You know, that fight you got into?"

"I'd been drinking. I really have no memory of that."

"You don't even remember what the fight was about?" Ryan stepped a little closer to Bill Rossman.

Rossman didn't move. "I don't remember what it was about. Or who it was with."

"His name was Kirk Hendrickson," Ryan said. He and Bill Rossman were standing about a foot apart.

"If you say so." The tone wasn't obnoxious. Just matter-of-fact.

"Can you tell us where you were Sunday night?"

"I was in town here somewhere. Not exactly sure."

"What do you mean?"

"I was with a girl, at her place."

"Can you give us her name?"

"Don't know her name."

"Address?"

He just smiled.

"Well, Mr. Rossman," I said. "Again, we're sorry for your loss." I handed him my card. "You get in touch with me—anytime—with information. Anything at all."

He took the card, turned, and left the small metal room

underneath the derrick.

I put up my collar and followed Ryan out to the Charger. I got in and turned it over as he started working on the windshield again.

"Did you pull that kind of shit when you were single?" I said when Ryan got in the cruiser.

He was brushing the sleet off the sleeves of his overcoat. He stopped, furrowed his brow, and turned to me. "Exactly what kind of shit are you referring to, Karen?"

"The manly man working with his hands because it's real?"

He laughed. "No, that doesn't work for Mormons."

"How's that?"

He put on a seductive voice. "'I want to serve the Lord and the Church and my family.' Is that turning you on?"

"I see." I put my hands over the vent, which was pumping out the hot air. "So is Billy Boy completely full of crap, or just mostly?"

"I think his roommate figured him out pretty well."

"Him being all about beer and pussy?"

"I believe him about being out with some girl Sunday night—and not even knowing her name." Ryan adjusted the vent on his side of the dash. "I mean, it's plausible. There's no shortage of bars here in Marshall, and no shortage of girls looking for guys with a lot of time on their hands and money in their jeans."

"Now that you mention it," I said, "it's a pretty good line of bullshit he was peddling. If the girl sees herself as deep, then he's her soulmate and he gets laid. If she isn't into that shit, she knows he's got three hundred bucks and he gets laid anyway."

"Works either way," Ryan said.

"But we still don't know where he was Sunday night."

"Very true. He might have taken a drive to Rawlings to stab his father."

"The father who wasn't very hands-on," I said.

"You notice his step-mother isn't family—"

"But Aunt Cheryl apparently is?" I shook my head. "Yes, I did notice that."

"You believe him that he doesn't remember getting arrested?"

"No, I don't," I said. "After twenty or thirty collars, you start to forget some of the early ones. But a potential felony? Earlier this year? You remember that one."

"Even if you were drunk?" Ryan said.

"Sitting on a wooden bench in Holding for eight or ten hours clears your head."

Ryan was writing in his notebook. "We're going to want to learn a little more about Kirk Hendrickson."

"Yeah, but if it turns out Bill was telling the truth—that the fight was just about beer and pussy—we don't know one fucking thing more about Bill Rossman than we did this morning."

"We just keep spinning the bit, breaking the shale."

"Yeah, that's exactly what I want to do." I leaned against the door and lifted my right leg up and rested my wet shoe on the vent. "Can we go home?"

"You want to get some sensible shoes and come back again?"

"Yes," I said. "Because it's so lovely here."

"We should interview Mark Middleton."

"Ah, shit." I'd forgotten. "The guy who denies shooting up the Rossman equipment?"

"Yes, that Mark Middleton."

"You know where he lives?"

Ryan pointed to the laptop. "I know where everybody lives."

Chapter 13

We got back on 12, took it two miles east, then turned off onto
Dry Creek Road, a one lane, unpaved, two ruts with grass growing
between them, which led us almost a mile north to Mark
Middleton's spread. A metal sign, swaying in the sleet and wind,
said it was the Double M Ranch.

At the end of a hundred-yard drive sat a modest one-story
brick house with black shutters, probably from the fifties or
sixties. Off to the side were a big unpainted barn and a couple of
small outbuildings and tarp-covered hay-storage units.

White plastic fencing made to look like wooden post-and-rail
rimmed the buildings. I stopped at the gate. Ryan got out and
opened it, then we drove in toward the house. Off to the left we
could see into the barn. I spotted a flatbed pickup for hauling hay,
a couple of livestock trailers, a baler, and an ATV, all of them
shiny and new, all of them white.

"Look at that." Ryan pointed off into the distance, west of
the house.

"I can't see anything." All of a sudden a flare of burning gas
lit up a drilling rig. I heard the hissing sound coming in over the
tapping of the sleet. Nearby were a couple of horse-head jacks,
twenty- or thirty-feet tall, the horse heads bobbing up and down
slow and steady.

The roof on the Middleton house extended out over a
concrete patio that ran the width of the house. On the patio was a
set of wrought-iron chairs and a table, all protected by plastic

covers cinched tight at the bottom.

I knocked on the door. A thin curtain covering the window in the door slid aside for a moment, revealing a lined and leathery face of an older man. The door opened.

"Mark Middleton?" I said.

He was about sixty, wearing overalls and a blue work shirt. His baseball hat said Kawasaki. In his right hand, pointed at me, was a .45.

"Who are you?" His mouth was twisted into a scowl as he looked first at me and then at my partner. Scanning Ryan from top to bottom—the black topcoat, white button-down, and blue silk tie with a subtle paisley pattern—Middleton shook his head in disgust.

As I reached into my bag to pull out my shield, Middleton stepped back, wary, and raised his pistol. "My name is Karen Seagate. This is my partner, Ryan Miner. We're police detectives from Rawlings."

He looked puzzled. "Rawlings?"

"That's right, Mr. Middleton."

"What do you want?"

"Mr. Middleton," I said, holding up my palms, "do you think you could put the pistol down? We're hoping you can help us with a case we're working on."

"Let them in, Mark." It was a woman's voice from inside the house. "Where are your manners?"

Middleton didn't say anything as he stepped aside. Ryan and I brushed some of the sleet off our shoulders and sleeves and walked inside the kitchen. I smelled tomato soup and something baking.

"My wife, Doris," Middleton said, still scowling.

Doris Middleton remained seated at a worn wooden country table. There were four battered wood chairs with navy cloth cushions tied to the seats and the backs. Identical food at the two

places: a bowl of tomato soup, a sandwich, and a cup of coffee.
Along the wall behind the table were stainless-steel appliances. I
couldn't read a name on them, but they looked really nice, really
new.

"We're sorry to interrupt your lunch, Mr. Middleton." I
turned to her. "Mrs. Middleton. We're just out here for a little bit
and wanted to talk with you for a couple of minutes."

"Of course," Doris Middleton said. "Please sit down."

"Thank you." We left our coats on and took the two other
chairs at the dining table.

"You'll have to excuse my husband." Doris Middleton took a
sip of her coffee. "He thought you were from the oil company."

"Rossman Mining?"

"Yes," she said. "We're in the middle of a conflict with
them."

"We read a little about that."

"But if you've driven all the way from Rawlings, I imagine
you're not here to talk about vandalism."

"You're right, Mrs. Middleton." I nodded. "We're here
because of the murder of Lee Rossman."

Doris Middleton took a sip of her soup. "Excuse me. I'm
going to heat this up." She stood and walked over to a big
microwave above the matching stove. She put the soup inside, hit
a few buttons, and gave me a gentle smile as the machine
hummed softly. A slim woman of sixty with perfect posture, she
wore tailored corduroy slacks and a cashmere sweater over a
simple button-front blouse. Her coiffed hair, a well-dyed auburn,
was cut short. "Yes, we read about that." The microwave dinged,
and she retrieved her soup. She concentrated on carrying the bowl
back to the table, and then sat down and took another sip. "Oh,
that's much better." She looked up at me. "How can we help?"

"We're interviewing a few people from Rossman Mining, and
we were hoping, with your ties to the ranching community, you

might be able to help us identify others we should interview."

Mark Middleton cleared his throat loudly, as if to comment on what I'd just said. "How'd he die?"

I turned to him. "He was stabbed."

"I'm surprised."

"Why is that?" I said.

"Surprised anyone would be willing to get that close to him."

"Had you ever met Mr. Rossman, Mr. Middleton?"

He shook his head. "The son of a bitch never took the time to come out here to talk to any of us. Not once."

"You invited him?"

"Of course I did." He barked it out, like I ought to have known it. "Many times."

"He never got back to you?"

"Oh, he got back to us. He sent out the salesman. The same bastard who talked us into signing those leases." He cleared his throat. "It was like he was rubbing our noses in it. First we're going to take advantage of you. Then, when you finally realize what just happened and you want to know what we're going to do about it, we'll send the salesman back. The same damn salesman. That's what we think of you."

"Did the company go back on its contract?"

"I'll show you what the company did." He stood up slowly and walked over to the sink. He turned on the tap and looked at me. "Are you paying attention?" He picked up a butane lighter sitting next to the faucet, held it next to the running water, and flicked it. There was a popping sound as a foot-long flame shot up next to the stream of water. He pulled the lighter away, and the flame disappeared.

"That's what the company did," Mark Middleton said. "Then they send that damn salesman out here to tell us there was no proof the water wasn't full of methane before they drilled. He points to something on page 18 of the leasing contract says the company won't be responsible for pre-existing 'methane migrations.' He actually said that to my face. Used that phrase. Like half the ranchers in the whole county already had poisoned water before his company came to town. Now half the ranchers in the county can't drink their own well water. Can't take a shower in their own water. Can't even water their livestock. You ever heard of a working ranch without water?"

He came back to the table and sat down. His Kawasaki hat slid back on his head as his hands came up and covered his face. He was crying.

Ryan said softly, "That's a terrible thing happened, Mr. Middleton."

Mark Middleton wiped at his eyes and turned to Ryan. "Now where do you get the nerve saying something like that to me? You, sitting there in your fancy suit and tie, what do you know about what happened?"

Ryan put his hands on the table and laced his fingers. He looked right into Mark Middleton's eyes. "My father was a farmer. Outside Salt Lake City, in Utah. The farm had been in our family for four generations. It wasn't much. Forty-five acres. Year-to-year, we never could pay off any of the loans. Not the bank for the machinery. Not the supply house for the seed, the fertilizers, the chemicals. It was a hard life, but it was an honorable living, and it meant everything to my father." Ryan paused and gazed out over Mark Middleton's shoulder.

"It was seven years ago, next month, on the nineteenth of December. My father had lost a long legal battle. It had gone on almost three years. It was about access to water. I wasn't home, but afterwards I found the sheets of paper on the kitchen table. He had done the calculations. What he realized that day was that he was worth more to our family dead than alive. He left the papers on the kitchen table. He didn't need to leave a note. He walked out to the barn and raised his pistol to his temple and pulled the trigger."

Ryan's head sagged and he started to weep. "It was a .45, almost the same one you have right there." He pointed to the pistol sitting near the salt and pepper shakers in the middle of the table.

Mark Middleton got up from his chair and walked over to Ryan. He hesitated, then put his hand on Ryan's shoulder. "I'm sorry about what I said, son," he said to my partner. "I'm real sorry I said that."

Ryan nodded and put his hand on Mark Middleton's. Middleton squeezed Ryan's shoulder and then walked back to his place at the table and sat down.

"Listen," Mark Middleton said. He wiped at his eyes and his nose. "I don't know how we got onto this, but you two have a long drive ahead of you, and it doesn't look like the weather's going to cooperate. Here's what I have to say about Rossman. He was a crook, and till the day I die I will regret letting his salesman set foot on my property. But it's one thing shooting up Rossman's equipment. It's quite another to kill the man himself. You have to know that I am a Christian. Not a perfect Christian, by any means. But I am a Christian. I would never hurt anyone. That's not me." He was shaking his head. "That's just not me."

"We know that, Mr. Middleton," I said, my gaze fixed on his red-rimmed eyes. "Do you know anyone you think might have been mad enough at Mr. Rossman? Anyone at all?"

He shook his head. "We're good people out here. We got a beef with the company, but nobody out here would kill. Nobody would." He covered his face with his hands.

"Mr. Middleton, Mrs. Middleton," I said as Ryan and I stood up. "We want to thank you for taking the time to talk with us."

Doris Middleton stood. "It was our pleasure," she said. She paused a second, like she wanted to say something. "What my husband said just now—about shooting up Mr. Rossman's equipment? If he gave you the impression that he was suggesting that he ever did that, that was a misstatement. He did no such thing. And on the question of the murder of Mr. Rossman, we both categorically deny that either of us had anything to do with that. I am willing to testify that my husband and I were together all night long—right here—and that neither of us left the house.

"Mr. Rossman's remains were discovered in Rawlings," she said, gesturing to me and Ryan. "Which would suggest that either we were in Rawlings, where we killed him, or that we killed him here, transported his body to Rawlings, then returned here. If you'd like, you could check with our daughter, Emily—I'd be happy to give you her contact information. Emily, her husband, Richard, and our grandson, Alan, stayed overnight with us Sunday; it was Alan's eighth birthday, and he loves to come out to the ranch. They left Monday morning, after breakfast. They live about three hours east." She paused. "Would you like Emily's contact information? It wouldn't be a problem."

I nodded to Ryan, who slid his notebook and a pen across the table to Doris Middleton, who started writing.

"One other thing, if you could give us just another few seconds. The name of that salesman? From Rossman Mining?" I said.

She nodded and wrote a little more in Ryan's notebook. When she was done, she looked up and smiled. "Could I wrap up some cobbler for the trip back? I just made it this morning."

"That's a very kind gesture." I wanted to say yes. It did smell good. "But no, thank you. Again, we appreciate you talking to us."

Mark Middleton held the door open for me and Ryan.

The cold and damp hit me as the door closed firmly behind us. I buttoned up my coat. The sleet was mixing with snow, which threatened to make the trip back a little more interesting than I had counted on.

I held my collar up against my neck as we started walking toward the Charger. "You want to drive, or are you too grief-stricken?"

"I'll pull myself together." He smiled as I handed him the keys.

"Where'd you learn how to do that?"

"Cry?"

"Yeah."

"I had a bunch of older sisters," he said. "When I wanted to blame stuff on them, it worked better if I could squeeze out a tear or two. I practiced biting the inside of my cheek and thinking about really sad things." Ryan scraped and brushed the windshield and then got into the cruiser.

"Like what a disappointment you must be to Jesus?" I said.

He closed his eyes and lowered his head. I could see him working his cheek.

"Can't do it?"

He shook his head. "I'm not a machine. I have to be in the moment." He gave me his big smile.

"You're full of shit," I said.

"That's just the jealousy talking, Karen."

"Okay, so we're agreed Mark Middleton didn't kill Lee Rossman?" I said.

Ryan turned over the big engine in the Charger. "No," he said. "I don't *think* he killed Lee Rossman."

"That was an act?"

"I hadn't thought of that," he said. "He might've had older sisters, too."

"Then what?" I said.

"I assume he really was broken up about his polluted well."

"But that doesn't mean he didn't get into it with Rossman Sunday night and stab him?"

"Very true." He nodded.

"You think Middleton drove to Rawlings and stabbed him there?"

"No, I don't think that happened."

"You think he stabbed him here, threw him in the pickup bed, and drove all the way to Rawlings to dump him?"

"No," Ryan said, "I don't think that happened, either."

"His wife? All hundred-and-ten pounds of her?"

"No, I'd be very surprised if that happened."

"Okay, Sherlock, I give up. Why don't you *think* Middleton killed him?"

"Because I don't know who *did* kill him. So I'm not ready to say Mark Middleton didn't."

I let out a big sigh. "Well, obviously, you little shit," I said, "if we know Lee Rossman was murdered but we don't know who murdered him, we can't say for sure Mark Middleton *didn't* kill him."

"Isn't that what I just said?"

"Why do you do this to me?"

"Use rigorous logic?"

"No, asshole. Why do you break my balls? If you say you don't *think* Middleton killed Lee Rossman, that means you have a reason to suspect that maybe he did. That's what I was hoping you were gonna explain to me."

"Interesting," he said. "The things you hope for."

"How about you just drive us back to Rawlings? I'll be sitting here with wet feet, getting pneumonia, okay? Then I hope I die—and they blame it on you and it really fucks up your career."

"The point I was trying to make is that, since we haven't ruled anyone out, don't you think we ought to interview the salesman who pressured Mark Middleton into signing that lease?" He pulled the notebook out of his suit jacket pocket and opened it. "Mr. Ron Eberly. I mean, as long as we're out here? He might have an interesting perspective on Mark Middleton."

"Pneumonia will take too long. Just drive me into a utility pole. Say you slid off the road. I don't give a shit anymore."

"I'll phone Rossman Mining, get Mr. Eberly's phone number. See if we can track him down. Wouldn't you feel foolish if he's here, and we go back to Rawlings and then have to come back to interview him?"

I waved my hand at him dismissively and closed my eyes.

Chapter 14

Mac and I were in a dark, empty space, all concrete and steel, like an underground garage or a warehouse. Even though there were no lights, somehow I could see him walking away, slowly, his body hunched over as if he was in pain. He was wearing a soiled down jacket and sweatpants, shoes with no socks. I raised my arms and got into a firing stance. I pulled the trigger, a puff of smoke shot out of the barrel, and I heard the explosion, the sound stretched out and followed by three long echoes. It seemed quite normal that the round flew through the air slowly enough that I could see it, even watch it spin. When he heard the shot, Mac turned his head around to see who had fired, but he kept walking. After the longest while, the round hit him, squarely in the back, but he didn't flinch. The smoke from the barrel of my pistol traced the path of the round, and then enveloped him. He kept walking, but his shape started to fade into smoke. He turned to grey, then a dirty white, and then he disappeared in a wisp.

"Karen, wake up." I felt Ryan's hand on my shoulder. "You were screaming, Karen."

It took me a few seconds to come out of the dream. I didn't know where we were. I looked around. We were parked outside a big grey stone building. A silver-white mix of snow and sleet covered the pickups and SUVs parked on either side of the four-lane street.

"The county commission building." Ryan's concern showed in his eyes. "In Marshall. Ron Eberly's inside. The salesman for

Rossman Mining?"

"I was screaming?"

"Yeah," Ryan said. "You want to take a minute?"

I closed my eyes for a few seconds, to try to call up the dream so I could dismiss it. "No." I opened my eyes. "Think I'll be okay. Sorry."

"Forget it." He shut down the cruiser. "By the way, Eberly's called a landman. Not a salesman."

"Got it." I unbuckled my seatbelt and grabbed my bag from the seat behind me. "All right, let's go."

We both gripped the handrail as we climbed the icy courthouse steps. The stone building, a squat two stories, simple and solid, looked like it dated from when coal was the fuel that was supposed to make everyone rich. A brass plaque next to the wide glass doors said it was built in 1934 under a grant from the Works Progress Administration.

We wiped our feet on the huge rubber mat under the portico and walked through the revolving glass doors. The central hallway, thirty feet wide and a hundred feet long, was a drafty shell with dark brown floor tiles. Mahogany benches with scrolled arms were built into the walls. Gold lettering on the dark wood doors identified the offices of the various county departments. Fluorescent tubes hanging from the double-height ceiling cast a yellow glow on the hallway. Between the office doors, the tan plaster walls were filled with primitive murals of muscular and straight-backed farmers, ranchers, and coal miners going about their work, their gleaming muscles rippling against their rolled-up shirtsleeves, determined smiles on their faces.

A small group of men sat at heavy, old wooden tables clustered around one of the doors. Some were wearing business suits; others had on western sport coats and jeans. All of them were poring over large, leather-bound deed books and taking notes on legal pads.

"Do you know which one is Eberly?"

"Will in a second," Ryan said. We walked over the landmen. He called out, "Ron Eberly?"

One of the men looked up.

"Mr. Eberly," Ryan said as we walked over and he introduced the two of us. "Could we go over there and talk with you?" He pointed down the hallway to an empty spot. "It'll just take a couple of minutes." Ron Eberly stood and followed Ryan and me, our damp shoes squeaking on the tile floors. We huddled outside the door to the Highway Maintenance Department.

Ryan and I have been together long enough for him to know when to lead the interviews. Since I looked and felt like crap, he took over.

"We're investigating the murder of Lee Rossman," he said. "Let me start by saying we're very sorry. You and Mr. Rossman were close for a long time."

"That's right." Eberly shook his head. "Almost thirty years." He looked like he used to be an athlete, a little under six feet but broadly built. He put his hands on his hips and shifted his weight, the way some guys do to display the testosterone. I used to think they did it only to make women go all damp, but I've seen it often enough when macho guys talk to Ryan that I think they want to signal it to other athletic men, too.

"We just talked with Mark Middleton and his wife, Doris," Ryan said.

Ron Eberly nodded slightly to tell us he knew who the Middletons were. Although he must have realized they told us he was a total shit, he was experienced enough not to show us anything. He was going to listen to us respectfully and say as little as possible.

"Tell us about the conflict they're having with Rossman Mining."

"Nothing really unusual about it," Ron Eberly said.

"Everyone in mining sees it all the time. Landowners bring a set of unrealistic expectations about drilling, and the reality can catch them off guard."

"The Middletons showed us the methane in their water."

Eberly nodded his head. "I'm aware of the migration."

"They say the drilling caused that."

He shook his head, just a little bit, like he was weary of having to refute an obvious mistake. "There's really no evidence of that."

"You mean the Middletons never tested their water for methane before the drilling, right?"

"That's right, legally. They'd need to be able to document their claim that the drilling caused the methane migration—or at least that the water was methane-free before the drilling. But in terms of geology, there's methane in all the shale. That's what natural gas is." He put out his hand, palm up, as if to say that's why the company came to town, started giving people money. "It'd be hard to find water wells without some methane in them. Plus, we drill more than a mile below their well, with a thick solid-rock layer in between." He shifted his stance. "Did they get a chance to mention the water buffalo we put in?"

"No, they didn't."

"We bring them fresh water. It's a one-thousand gallon reservoir, stainless-steel lined. We fill it up once a week. And cases of bottled water for drinking. As much as they ask for. Did they mention that?"

"No, they didn't."

"Did they mention our offer to drill them a new water well?"

"No."

"I didn't think so." The index finger pointed at Ryan was the only sign of Eberly's anger and frustration. "All we asked for was his signature on a confidentiality agreement. We asked him to cease-and-desist on his videos and other publications, and we stated we were not admitting liability for his methane problem. In exchange, we offered to do the geological assessment, site the new well in the best place, drill it, and hook it up. Free of charge." Eberly paused to catch his breath. "He said no."

"How do you interpret that?"

"He's a proud man. I respect that. I do. But if he'd been willing to work with us, we would have solved that problem for him—even though we didn't cause it in the first place." Ron Eberly noticed his finger pointing at Ryan and pulled his arm back. "I think he'd rather make videos about flames coming out of his faucet than admit that maybe he was at fault."

"How do you see him being at fault?"

"He didn't read the contract. Didn't get a lawyer. Some of these owners aren't willing to do any homework. Aren't willing to learn the difference between net and gross. It's not that hard. Aren't willing to pencil out the difference between a big signing bonus and a big royalty percentage. Aren't willing to look up the word *easement*—then they get mad at us when we put in a road for the trucks. You know the question I get asked most often by landowners?"

"What's that?"

"'You got a pen?'"

"Mark Middleton called Mr. Rossman a crook," Ryan said. "He blamed the company for ruining his ranch. Some of the things he's written about Rossman and his company are pretty nasty. You think he could've wanted to hurt Lee?"

"Tell you the truth, I didn't get to know him. I spend half my time right here." Ron Eberly pointed to the tables at the other end of the hallway. "I'm researching four or five leases every week. I did maybe three trips out to his place. Total time with him and his wife: maybe a couple of hours. My job is to do the research, draw up the contract, present it to the landowner, get the signatures. Once that's done, I'm off to the next piece of dirt. Yeah, I know he's angry. Deep down, I think he's angry at himself. From my perspective, nothing bad has happened at his place, certainly nothing that isn't covered in the leasing contract. And Rossman Mining has lived up to the letter of the contract." He was silent a moment, gathering himself. "You know how I know that?"

"How's that?"

"They haven't taken any legal action against us."

Ryan spoke. "Mr. Middleton told us he tried contacting Mr. Rossman a number of times but that he never replied."

Ron Eberly shrugged. "If you buy a Ford and don't like it, do you expect the president of Ford to come out to your place?"

"Tell us a little about Cheryl Garrity."

Ron Eberly paused, like he wasn't expecting us to mention her. "What do you want to know?"

"A little bit about her history with Lee Rossman. I take it you and Cheryl were both working for Lee when he was married to his first wife."

"That's right."

"What was the first wife's name?"

"Helen."

"How did Cheryl get on with Helen?"

Ron Eberly's brow was furrowed. "I'm not sure what you mean."

The question seemed pretty clear to me.

"Cheryl and Lee spent a lot of time together on the business," Ryan said. "They must have traveled a lot together. You know, on business. Any problems there with Helen?"

Ron Eberly looked at Ryan for a moment, and I thought I could see a hint of a smile. "Lee's had a corporate jet for many years. He'd always invite Helen along."

"So she'd travel with him?"

"Not always. When Billy was little, she'd stay home most of the time. If there were any problems between Lee and Helen about Cheryl, I didn't see them."

"Cheryl Garrity is single, is that right?" Ryan said.

He nodded.

"Never married?"

Ron Eberly looked like he was trying to pull up a distant, trivial memory. "I think she was married for a little bit, maybe twenty years ago. Just for a year or two."

"To someone with the company?"

"No, I don't think so. An attorney or something like that. Maybe a businessman. But, no, he wasn't with Rossman Mining."

"Did she have a personal relationship with Lee?"

This time he let us see the smile. "She was his subordinate. He was her boss. As far as I know, that was the relationship."

"You get to see Bill Rossman much out here?"

"Not really." Ron Eberly frowned. "He keeps to himself these days."

A woman carrying a briefcase came out of the office a few feet away. She gave us a polite smile as she passed by us on her way toward the building entrance. We waited a few seconds.

"Why is that?" Ryan said.

"Can't say. Except maybe he's twenty-three."

"So you used to have more contact with him?"

"Oh, yeah, Billy was a great kid. Smart as a whip. Wanted to be an oil man, like his daddy." He paused. "He took his mom's death pretty hard. That was tough for him."

"You see him as taking a bigger role in the company now?"

"I could see that. He's working as a roughneck now. A lot of kids these days, they go to college, study engineering, geology—whatever—they've never touched a length of pipe. Hell, they never had a beer with a guy who worked a rig. But Billy's doing the right thing. If he decides to get into the business, the guys are going to respect him. They know he gets dirty."

"How did you get into the business?"

"It was Lee. He was a couple years older than me. I think he saw me as a little brother—a little brother who used to get into trouble after he picked up his pay packet." He smiled with that mix of pride, shame, and nostalgia that I've never seen on a woman. "But I was straight with him, and over the years I guess I grew up a little. He came to trust me. He paid for me to take a landman course, let me do the job wrong, then learn how to do it right. You know the thing I'm most proud of in my whole life? That I can honestly say I never let Lee down. Not once."

"You know of anyone who might have wanted to hurt Lee?"

"Like I said, there's a group of landowners who think they got a raw deal from the company."

"Like Mark Middleton."

"That's right. You ask around in town here, look at the flyers on some of the bulletin boards, you can get yourself a half-dozen names. I want to be clear: I'm not accusing the Middletons or anyone else of anything. But I am saying if you look at the videos, read the letters to the editor, check out their blog—some of them have said things that could be seen as threats."

"Threats to Lee Rossman personally?"

"I'm not a lawyer. But Lee and I have talked about it off and on, last few years."

"What did he say about it?"

"If you knew Lee like I did, you could predict it word-for-word. 'Oh, they're just running their mouth,' he'd say. 'They don't mean nothing by it.' There were a few landowners got riled up when they found out we paid their neighbors a bigger signing bonus. But everyone was going to make so much money on the royalties it would all blow over soon enough. With Lee, the glass was always three-quarters full."

"He didn't take any security measures? Bodyguards?"

Ron Eberly laughed. "Lee was a country boy. If he thought he needed security, he'd carry it in his waistband."

"But he didn't think he needed any security Sunday night," Ryan said.

Ron Eberly gazed out over Ryan's shoulder. "I didn't say Lee was always right." His eyes were shining a little bit.

"Mr. Eberly," Ryan said, "I have to ask you this next question. Can you tell us where you were Sunday night?"

"Mondays are always busy. Here at the deeds office. Meeting with landowners. I've got a room at the Marshall Residence Inn. I was working on leases."

"So, you were here, not in Rawlings?"

"You can talk to the manager. Guy's name is Tony. I use the Business Center at the Residence Inn a lot."

"Thanks very much." Ryan handed Ron Eberly a card. "Get in touch if you think of anything, would you?"

"You bet," he said, nodded to me, and walked back to the table where the other landmen were bent over the deed books.

"You got that?" I said to Ryan. "Tony at the Residence Inn." I glanced over at my partner, who was already writing in his notebook.

Chapter 15

Wrung out from the incident with Mac that kept me up about four hours in the middle of the night, I was glad to let Ryan drive us back to Rawlings. The snow was coming down heavy, but the tires from the big trucks carrying water, generators, tanks, chemicals, pipe, and the big steel rigs had cleared wide strips on the road out of Marshall. Still, it was hard driving because the constant truck traffic busted up some of the asphalt and grooved serious ruts and dips into the rest of it. Ryan and I sat for fifteen minutes a couple miles east of town when a truck hauling pipe spilled its load after getting in a wreck with a pickup. When tons of steel pipe hit the asphalt, they have to call in a bunch of equipment to corral it; we were lucky because there was a solid shoulder we could use to get out of there.

"Think we'll make it back before the chief leaves for the day?" I said.

Ryan looked at his watch. "Unless the weather turns bad or we hit another problem, yeah, I think so."

"Let's go over what we got today—before I fall asleep, I mean."

"Okay, Bill Rossman is following in his father's footsteps, working on the rigs sometimes, going to college sometimes."

"Yeah," I said. "Plus he's drinking and screwing girls he doesn't know their names. But he doesn't have much to do with any of the guys. What did he say was his reason for working the rigs?"

Ryan was really good at remembering the phrases people used when we interviewed them. "It's honest. No bullshit."

"Which of course was probably bullshit."

"I agree," Ryan said, "but that doesn't tell us who he is or what he's doing—or whether he's the kind of kid who'd hurt his own father."

"Well, we don't have enough information to say. We could say he's pissed at his dad for replacing his mom with Florence. Or for not replacing her with Aunt Cheryl."

"Or for being rich and driving a BMW. It could be anything. I think Ron Eberly might have nailed it: Bill is twenty-three."

"All right," I said. I felt my spirits nosedive as I watched the snow fly past us. I realized my son, Tommy, now a sullen seventeen, started being miserable at thirteen and gave every indication of staying miserable for many more years, maybe forever. "Methane Mark Middleton. You like him?"

"I like him for shooting up Rossman's trucks. The fact that he does it carefully—at night, so he won't hurt anyone or get caught—suggests that's he's got a healthy passive-aggressive side. Plus, he's probably a coward—physically, I mean. I don't see him stepping up to Lee Rossman and shanking him."

"You never know. He could be all weaselly, then, one day, he gets in his pickup and drives to Rawlings, pissed off because Lee Rossman won't return his calls or whatever. He confronts him. Rossman pushes him away. Out comes the blade and before either of them knows what happened, Rossman's on the pavement, bleeding."

Ryan said, "You think we ought to get in touch with their daughter? Check out their alibi?"

"Not yet. The way Doris Middleton offered it up, it seemed a little forced. The daughter might be in on it—or at least willing to say Daddy never left the house that night. Which would be what she believes—or wants to believe. Anyway, it's not that good an alibi to bother chasing down unless we see some other stuff that makes us like the Middletons more."

"One more: Ron Eberly." The silent snow was starting to ice up on the windshield on the outside edges where the wipers didn't sweep. Ryan turned up the defroster.

I pulled my coat tighter as the air coming out of the vents started to cool. "Yeah, Ron. I think he's clearly a liar."

Ryan smiled. "Because he's a salesman?"

"Hadn't thought of that, but yeah. That doesn't help."

"What did he lie about?"

"I think he was lying about the methane," I said. "I believed Mark Middleton that his well was clean before the drilling—and that all the other ranchers with methane had clean water, too. He wouldn't've been able to run his ranch with the water we saw coming out of his tap. The oil companies always say there's solid rock between the water wells and the drilling. But fracking doesn't make sense to me. The drill bit goes through the rock—the impermeable rock—then the guys set off explosives inside the pipe. No way you can guarantee there won't be methane going where you don't want it to go. Isn't that a law of physics or something: how shit doesn't stay where you put it? That it goes wherever it wants to go?"

"Not sure that's an official law of physics, but I get your point," Ryan said. "Any other lies? That one might be just a professional lie. You know, a salesman saying he believes in his product."

"The one I'm willing to bet my life on is when he said he never let Lee Rossman down."

"How do you know that's a lie?"

"I know that's a lie because I'm an adult. The two of them've worked together thirty years. No way he didn't let Lee down. Take me, for instance. The best relationship I've had since I'm an adult is with you, and I've let you down a couple dozen times in the two years we've been partners."

Ryan was concentrating, like he was checking the math. He started counting on the fingers on his right hand, then his left. Then he did the right hand again. "Couple dozen sounds about right."

"Exactly my point," I said.

"So how did Eberly let Lee Rossman down?"

I let out a long sigh. "Could be anything. Maybe Eberly nailed Rossman's first wife, and Bill is his kid. Maybe Eberly steals money from the company. Maybe Eberly's pissed that he's still writing up contracts and doesn't own a piece of the company, so Sunday night they go drinking at Johnny's Lounge and Eberly knifes him. Lot of ways Eberly could let him down."

"We could check with the guy at Eberly's motel to see if he can alibi him," Ryan said.

"Same as with the Middletons and their daughter. How much you think it would cost Eberly to get the motel guy to alibi him for Sunday night? One-hundred? Two-hundred, tops. No," I said, "we just don't have enough to work with on any of the good people in Marshall, Montana, to rule them in or out."

"It's only about thirty-six hours since Rossman was killed," Ryan said. "We'll figure it out."

"Or we won't," I said as I reclined my seatback and closed my eyes. "Let me know when we get to headquarters—or when you figure out who killed him." The rocking of the Charger put me out quick.

I didn't know how long I was asleep when I recognized Ryan's voice calling my name. "I think it's your cell."

I listened for a moment and recognized the buzzing coming from my leather bag on the seat behind me. I retrieved the phone and checked the screen. It was Allen Pfeiffer from the FBI. "Hey, Allen, thanks for getting back to me." I put my phone on Speaker.

We exchanged small talk for a few seconds. Then he said,

"I'm not seeing a Lauren Wilcox in any of our databases. But maybe we can find her through facial recognition. You got a picture?"

I looked at Ryan. He was nodding his head. "You bet. Just a second." I said to Ryan, "Can we email Allen a picture now?"

"Yeah, I think so. Get his email and I'll find it."

"Okay, Allen, sorry. My partner thinks he can get you a picture within a few minutes. Is your email secure?"

"Secure enough for what we're doing. Make the subject line 'Vacation pics.' That way, maybe the FBI won't open a file on me."

"All right," I said as he read me his email. "Thanks a lot, Allen. We'll get that off to you as soon as we can."

"Not a problem," he said, and we ended the call.

Ryan swiveled the computer toward me and pointed to the screen. "Start with the state DMV."

It took me a few seconds to get oriented, but I pulled up her photo.

"Right click, then Save Image As."

I did it.

"Why don't you go to the Web, try cmsu.edu, then go to the Biology Department."

I found the faculty section of the Biology Department, but she didn't have a photo up. "Nothing doing," I said.

"Try Googling her."

I did. "There's thousands of hits."

"Go to the top of the page and select Images."

There she was: dozens of pictures of the frizzy-haired ecology professor. I selected and downloaded a couple of them, then attached them to an email to Allen Pfeiffer. "Okay, done."

"Very good," Ryan said. "Maybe Allen will find something."

I was looking at my email. I had one from Harold Breen, the medical examiner. He still used email rather than messages. "The autopsy is done," I said to Ryan. "Says he'll be in until about six if we want to stop by."

Ryan looked down at his watch. "We'll be there by five."

His estimate was off by five minutes. I carded us in the back entrance. "Let's see if we can get him." We headed down the hall and took the stairs down to the basement, where Harold Breen's office and the autopsy room are. We hurried past the rifle range and past the office of Robin, our evidence tech.

I could smell the autopsy room before we got there, which was a bad sign. I pushed open the heavy swinging door. Even though the HVAC system was sucking out air as hard as it could, the place still stank of shit and mold.

Harold looked up from the table where he was cutting the scalp off a beat-up guy with a grizzled beard and long hair. "Hey, sweetheart," he said to me. Then he turned to my partner. "How are you doing, Ryan?"

"Listen, Harold, I don't want to be rude," I said. "But if I have to stand near this stiff for another minute, I'm gonna blow lunch."

Harold smiled. "Yes, Mr. John Doe does have a bit of a tang about him, doesn't he?"

"Can we at least move over there?" I pointed to the other side of the autopsy room and, pinching my nose shut, started walking over there.

Harold was wearing a lab coat with a plastic apron over it, some kind of plastic pants, argyle socks, and orange Crocs. He put his scalpel down on a white cloth on the steel tray next to the remains of the late Mr. Doe. He began to heave his considerable bulk in my direction.

"Do you need any of your papers?" I wanted to catch him before he started to get his big body rolling toward me. He would need a while to stop and change direction.

"No, I'm fine." His breathing was labored. He wiped at his

forehead, which was gleaming with sweat. "Don't need any paperwork on Mr. Rossman."

"Great," I said. "You gonna tell me who killed him?"

Harold made it over to me and Ryan and reached out to grab the edge of a desk to steady himself. "I do know who killed him, Karen. Before I tell you, though, would you mind peeling back that gentleman's scalp, sawing off his skull, scooping out his brain, and weighing it for me?"

I looked at him. "Is that your way of saying it's my job to figure out who killed Rossman?"

"That's a very good guess." He smiled.

"Okay, Harold, how did he die?"

"He bled out."

"That's it?"

"That's it. He got stabbed. The blade tore up some blood vessels—nothing major—then penetrated his pancreas, which is full of blood. It probably took a half-hour to bleed out."

"What can you tell me about the blade?"

"It was about an inch wide, double-edged. Probably a hunting knife or something like that. Nothing remarkable about it. Probably at least five inches long. The wound track was over six inches long. It's likely the victim doubled over after getting stabbed, compressing the tissue. There was some bruising around the entry wound, which suggests that the blade went in all the way to the handle. If you get me a knife, Robin and I can probably tell you if it was the one."

"Any shit on the wound that told you anything?"

"Robin said it was clean. Only thing in the wound were some fibers from the victim's undershirt and shirt."

"Tell me about the angle."

"The guy was holding it underhanded, which is unusual, so the blade went in on an upward trajectory. He pulled it out straight."

"The killer right handed?"

"Yeah, the wound is in the left upper quadrant, three inches off the midline. The wound track is oblique, angled toward the midline. So, yeah, right-handed."

"How tall?"

"The killer was between four feet tall and eight foot."

I just looked at him. "So we shouldn't be looking for someone works for a circus."

He smiled at me, his eyes almost disappearing in the folds of fat on his face. "Most likely between five feet and six feet."

"Why do you say that?"

"Because most people are between five feet and six feet."

"Are you enjoying this?"

"I always enjoy talking with you."

"Male or female?"

"Sorry, the killer didn't leave any DNA—at least Robin hasn't recovered any. He was probably wearing gloves. Robin tells me the knife blade was sharp enough that it went right through the two shirts quite cleanly. So an adult female of average strength could easily have done the damage."

"Any evidence that he was killed inside and dumped outside in the alley?"

Harold Breen shook his head. "Robin didn't find anything that would suggest he was picked up and moved. When we took his clothes off, his shirt was tucked in normally. No stains or anything on his clothing to suggest he was dragged. Our conclusion: He walked into that alley on his own steam. I put the report in the system."

"Okay, Harold, thanks." I looked at Ryan to see if he wanted to ask anything. He shook his head.

We left the foul-smelling autopsy room and headed down the hall toward the staircase. Robin's door was open. I knocked.

Robin was seated at one of her computers. She was wearing

bright red headphones and didn't hear me. I knocked again, harder, and she looked up.

"Hey, cops," she said brightly.

"Anything we should know from Lee Rossman or the disgusting alley?"

She shook her head. "Nothing yet that can help you. There's all kinds of DNA in the alley—mostly cigarettes and a couple of used condoms. Two needles. But nothing that can be tied to Rossman. There's a long hair, dyed brown, European origin, on his outer coat, but no way of knowing if he brought it into the alley with him or it just blew onto his coat and stuck there. The wool on the coat has good adhesion."

"His fly was down. Any sticky stuff on his dick?"

She shook her head. "He hadn't gotten laid since his last shower."

"Saliva? Lipstick?"

"Or blown."

"Shit." I was hoping for some vaginal fluid from a hooker in our database. "Anything on the rest of his clothing that tells us what he was up to?"

"He was wearing leather-soled shoes. No tread on them or anything to collect any soil. Didn't see anything other than traces of gasoline, which he could've picked up in any garage or street. There was another hair, also European, from a different person, dyed a different brunette, on his suit jacket. About nine inches long. He got a brunette wife or girlfriend?"

"A brunette wife. Don't know yet about a girlfriend."

"Do you want me to start typing the hair samples?"

"No, not yet. Maybe he hangs his coat up in some kind of closet at work. The hair could come from anyone in his office. I'll let you know." I tapped on the doorframe with my knuckle. "Shit, I was kind of hoping you'd have something for us."

"Well, when you and Ryan were out joyriding today, I did find something: a throwaway cell phone in the BMW. It was stashed away pretty good under his seat."

"Very good, Robin. Thank you." I looked at my watch and turned to Ryan. "Why don't you head home? I'm gonna run upstairs and do the form to get authorization to run the phone down."

"I already brought it to the chief," Robin said. "He authorized the search. The report's on your desk."

I turned to Ryan. "That was excellent police work, wasn't it?"

"Beyond excellent." He nodded.

"Robin, you have outdone yourself." I don't know what crazy shit happened to Robin when she was a kid, but sincere expressions of affection or gratitude made her really uncomfortable. Therefore, I looked for opportunities to praise her. "Are you blushing, Robin?"

She put her hands up to cover her pale, freckled cheeks, which only made it worse. Her neck was the color of a rosé, well on its way to a red. I walked over and kissed her gently on the top of her head. She had some new pale blue streaks.

She let out a yelp and shuddered. "Get away from me, you hideous hag."

I laughed, and Ryan and I headed upstairs to take a quick look at Lee Rossman's phone records. When we got to our desks in the detectives' bullpen, we discovered two copies of a printout of the call log and text messages for the disposable phone.

"This doesn't look like the reports we usually get," I said. It had the same data—numbers, duration of calls, names of account owners—but it looked homemade, like we had printed it ourselves. "What's going on?"

"It's a throwaway phone. There's no record that associates it with a particular person."

"So we go to the phone company."

"They're not required to store that information," Ryan said.

"The phone is just like a notebook or a diary we found in the car. We can crack it open and see what's in it."

I held up the paper. "That's what this is? We cracked it open?"

"Jorge's got some software that can do a complete system dump on any phone—regular cell or disposable. I bet he just grabbed these logs for us."

"How 'bout that," I said, and we started scanning the printout. "Who's Warnock, Susan? I recognize that name."

Ryan grabbed his notebook from the inside pocket of his suit jacket. It took him a few seconds to locate the name. "She's one of the strippers at Johnny's Lounge."

Chapter 16

It was after eight when I pulled into the lot at the Rawlings Regional Medical Center. I could tell the temperature was going down fast because I had my heater all the way up but I could still feel the chill coming off my windshield. The thermometer on my dashboard read three degrees, which meant we'd hit minus ten, easy, by midnight. The snow and the winds had stopped, as if the weather god wanted to strut around, proud of how brutal he could make it in Montana even with one hand tied behind his back.

I got out of the car, the frozen air wrapping itself around me, tingling as I pulled it into my lungs. I gathered my coat tight and started crunching across the parking lot toward the main hospital entrance. Right next to the main entrance, sharing the paved semi-circular driveway, was the emergency entrance, with a big, bright red neon sign in all caps. I realized I should have been glad I wasn't arriving in the back of an ambulance. The feeling of gratitude lasted a good two or three seconds. Spiritually, I'm quite retarded.

I assumed that Mac would be in the ICU, which was on the third floor. There was nobody in the elevator when I got in. Ordinarily, when I'm trapped in a big metal can with strangers, I'm relieved to not have to smile and discuss whether we all agree it's awfully cold out there, but now the isolation seemed to push in on me from all four sides and I started to cry.

In a moment, the elevator beeped, the doors opened, and I

was looking directly into the eyes of the woman on duty at the main nurses' station. She saw me wiping at my eyes. I must have looked as scared and bedraggled as most people getting off on the third floor, and I probably was. "Excuse me—" she said, ready to inform me that I had missed visiting hours.

I pulled my shield out of my bag and held it up for her to see. "A patient named McNamara. ICU?"

She looked confused, as if she wasn't expecting anyone who looked like they'd gave a damn about a drunk son of a bitch who attacked a woman. She rallied, offering a polite smile, and pointed me down the hall. I didn't need directions; there was only one room had a young cop sitting on a chair out in the hall, reading a magazine.

I didn't recognize the uniform, who was so new he wore his black polyester tie even though the department didn't require it. Apparently, he recognized me and jumped to attention, sending his magazine and his eight-point service cap flying, as if he thought I'd come to inspect him. As a matter of policy, we don't often send detectives out, off-shift, to make sure uniforms are doing a satisfactory job preventing unconscious drunks from making a getaway. I was never as young as this guy.

He picked his things up off the floor and stood out of the way as I shielded my eyes to look in the big window. In the dim light I could just make out six beds arranged in a semi-circle. With the eerie green and amber glow from the readouts on the equipment, I needed a moment to recognize Mac. Like all the other patients, he was lying flat. Near the foot of his bed sat a woman in a wooden chair. Her back was to me, her coat draped over the chair.

I walked into the room, not right up to his bed but close enough to confirm that it was Mac. He had an IV in his arm and an oxygen tube in his nose, and his head was bandaged. A tube stuck out of the bandage. His eyes were closed, and except for the shallow rise and fall of his chest, he looked pretty much dead.

With the humming and beeping from all the machines, the woman at Mac's bed hadn't heard me. Her hair was brown, cut medium-length. She was wearing a sweatshirt and jeans. I still hadn't seen her face, so I couldn't tell her age. She could have been his wife or a girlfriend.

One of the machines hooked up to the patient at the end of the semi-circle started flashing a red light and beeping, a nasty, high-pitched screech engineered to get your attention from fifty feet away. I stepped aside as a couple of nurses rushed in. One of them started fiddling with the machine while the other trotted back out, presumably to get more help. The guy in the bed hadn't moved and showed no sign of whatever hell he was experiencing on the inside.

When the commotion started, the woman at Mac's bedside turned around. She stood and pulled the chair away, although the medical people didn't seem to know or care she was in the room. She looked concerned for the guy attached to the squawking machine. Then she noticed me, holding her gaze to determine whether I'd come to see the guy in trouble.

She was in her late twenties, medium height. Even in the bad light, I recognized Mac's full face and long nose. In one of our conversations about the many people we'd fucked over, Mac had talked a little about his daughter. Her name was Maureen. We'd never met; Mac and I weren't meet-the-family types.

Two doctors came in, trailed by two nurses, and walked briskly over to the crashing guy. They looked at the green lighted numbers and wavy lines, hit a couple of buttons, and the beeping stopped. They checked his chart and talked quietly among themselves for half a minute. I couldn't hear them, but the doctors' body language suggested the bed would likely be available by daybreak. The two nurses looked grim as the doctors left to get back to whatever they had been doing.

Maureen walked over to me. "You here to visit someone?"

I wasn't thinking fast enough to come up with a plausible lie. "Mac."

She seemed glad someone had come, and she forced a smile. But the bags under her eyes and her hangdog expression said she was completely wrung out. She didn't look scared that her father might die—right here, right now. She just looked incredibly weary and defeated. I didn't know what had been going on for the last six months, since Mac left to take care of his wife, but whatever it was, it was real bad, and his daughter wasn't just getting the occasional phone call. She looked like she was smack in the middle of it.

"I'm Maureen," she said.

I tried to smile. "What happened? I mean, to Mac."

She closed her eyes and looked down, then she started to cry. "The policeman said Mac attacked some woman. She defended herself, hit him with something. On the head."

"I'm so sorry." Which was true.

"Apparently the woman has to decide if she's going to press charges." Maureen's voice was slow and almost expressionless, as if this was just the latest bad thing she didn't see coming, couldn't have stopped if she had, and didn't know how to fix.

"Is Mac hurt bad?"

"The idea that Mac could attack someone is … it's just crazy. Most days I have to help him get dressed. Half the time he has no idea where he is. Sometimes, doesn't even know who he is." She shook her head. "'Attacked someone.' That's ridiculous."

We stood there for a minute, silently.

"How bad is he?" I said.

Now she was crying pretty hard. "They said it's a depressed skull fracture. Means the skull is broken and the broken pieces were, like, pushing down on the brain. He's in and out of consciousness. They're afraid he might have seizures or he might need more surgery. You know, if there's some damage to his brain that they didn't see from all the tests."

"They had to do some surgery?"

"He had some kind of blood clot, you know, under the skull? So they're worried about pressure on the brain. Something like that. Tell you the truth, I didn't understand half the things the doctors told me. They talk like you went to medical school." She wiped at her eyes with a tissue. "It's not their fault. They try to explain everything. I'm just so tired."

I could see she was starting to get wobbly. "Why don't we go sit down?" I helped her get back to her chair. "Just a second." I walked over to the other side of the room and got another chair and brought it back.

"How do you know Mac?" Maureen said as I sat down next to her.

"I was in AA with him, a few years ago." She gripped the wooden chair arm to try to control the trembling. I grasped her hand. "He reached out to me. He helped me a lot."

"What's your name? Maybe he's mentioned you."

"I'm Eleanor," I said. That's my mother's name.

She shook her head. "Mac's helped so many people … it's too bad he can't help himself."

I squeezed her hand. "He's drinking again?"

"The last month has been … horrible. When my mom died … he was just so exhausted. I don't know if you've ever watched someone die like that. Cancer."

"I have."

"I really don't blame him. He started drinking. He said he just needed it for a little while, but I think he knew he'd never get free of it if he started again. Probably didn't want to keep going."

"He'd been sober for a while?"

"When he moved back in with my mother, after her diagnosis, I could see him struggling with it. But he really tried, did everything right. He leaned on some of the people from AA."

He hadn't leaned on me. It hurt me deeply at the time, but I had come to see it as his generosity.

Maureen squeezed at her eyes. "I thought … I thought he'd be okay when she … you know. Because she was in so much pain. I thought he'd be okay. But he was laid off—I don't know if you knew that—hasn't worked for the longest time. They lost the house. He was living with me, and he started drinking. Which, I told him, I can't have that. I have a little girl, and I couldn't take care of the two of them."

She covered her face in her hands and began to sob. "Three days ago I told him I couldn't have him drinking in front of my little girl and he'd have to leave. Which he did. He didn't give me any trouble about it. But he didn't tell me where he was going. That was three days ago. I still have no idea where he was all that time. Then I get this call from the police that he's attacked some woman and she hurt him."

"Who's going to take care of him? I mean, when he's released."

"If this woman presses charges—" She raised her palms in confusion. "I don't know, the county or state or whoever takes him. I guess they have some kind of program for medical care until he's well enough to be tried."

"What if she doesn't press charges?" I said. "What happens?"

"Then I don't know what we're going to do." She was silent for a moment. "I mean, I don't know what *he's* going to do. Maybe the VA can do something for him. I can't." She paused. "I wish I could, but I can't."

"Maybe there's someone who can help him," I said. "He has to want to help himself, get better. This incident … I don't know what I'm saying, I don't know what he went through … maybe what happened with the woman will help him. Once he gets out of here, he might see things different. It could give him the motivation he needs."

"I almost think he'd be better off if this woman goes ahead and, you know, tells the police to charge him. At least that way he'd be put into some kind of program."

"I think there are those programs."

"He was involved with a police woman, a detective, I think she was. They were together for a while." She paused to see if I knew who she meant.

I looked at her and shook my head.

"Do you think she could help him?"

"How do you mean?"

"I … I really have no idea," Maureen said. "It's just, when he comes out of this, he has no one." She looked at me. "Did he mention this woman? Do you know who I'm talking about?"

"I'm sorry," I said. "I don't know anyone who can help him." I felt myself starting to cry. "I wish I could help. I really do."

"I don't know what to do," she said between her sobs.

"Can I tell you something I've learned?" She nodded but didn't say anything. "Most of the shit that happens, you can't do anything about it. If you try to stop it, it'll kill you—and then it just happens, anyway. Only thing you can do is just let it happen."

Sobbing and out of control, she put her arms around my neck and pulled me in.

"It's going to be okay, Maureen," I said softly, stroking her hair. "It's going to work out okay."

Of course she was old enough to know this was untrue. Maybe even old enough to forgive a stranger who has nothing better to offer than empty clichés.

Chapter 17

I heard a ringing, like one of the machines Mac was hooked up to in the ICU, but it was faint enough and far enough away that I just let it go. I didn't think I'd be able to focus sufficiently to do anything about it, anyway. After a while—I don't know how long—it stopped, and I slipped back into sleep. Then, it started again. This time I realized it was my phone. I opened my eyes. The sun was coming in my big picture window in the living room.

Something was wrong. November, it's dark when I get up. I tried to focus my eyes. I wasn't in bed. I was on my couch, still dressed from yesterday. I sat up quickly, cracking my leg against the coffee table, knocking over the empty bottle of Jack Daniel's. Then it came back to me, what had happened.

My mouth was dry and foul tasting, and my head felt like someone with steel hands was pressing the front and back together with all his strength. As I struggled to get off my couch, I saw the time on the big grandfather's clock next to the fireplace: 8:10. Holy shit, I thought. Don't let it be the chief calling me.

I rushed into my bedroom and looked at the screen on my phone. It said "Miner, Ryan." I breathed a sigh of relief. It was Ryan, calling me on his own cell.

I picked it up. "Hey, Ryan."

"You okay, Karen?"

"Yeah, I'm fine. Just had a dead battery. Had to get my neighbor to give me a jump."

"Want me to swing by and pick you up?"

"No, no, that's okay." I tried to sound awake, but I could hear my voice, thick and full of crud. "I'll be there in twenty," I said.

"All right," Ryan said. "We need to get over to Susan Warnock's and interview her. I'll see if she's in the system and get her address and all." He paused. "You sure you're all right, Karen?"

"Yeah, absolutely." I tried to clear my throat without him hearing me. "I should've called you when I realized I was gonna be late. I'm sorry."

He was silent a moment. "See you soon." He hung up.

I ran into the bathroom and took a shower so quick the water never got hot. Ryan knows I live about eight minutes from work. If it took me twenty minutes to get to headquarters, he'd know I was lying about a dead battery. Dead battery, for God's sake. You'd think a person who lies as much as I do would be better at it.

The ride in took eight minutes. I'd concluded that Ryan had figured out I was lying—and why—so there was no sense in sticking to my story. I carded myself into the building and ran down the hall toward the detectives' bullpen. The clock on the wall said 8:29.

Ryan's expression was concerned as he glanced at my wet hair. I knew my face was more of a mess than usual. My eyes were red-rimmed, the grey bags under my eyes greyer than usual, my skin pale and puffy.

"I went to see Mac last night." I didn't intend to say it as an excuse, but before it was out of my mouth I knew that's how it would sound.

"How is he?"

"Skull fracture."

"I'm sorry."

"Me, too."

"You'll be okay?"

"Yeah," I said. "I'll be at the meeting tonight. Eight sharp."

"Good," he said. Not like a boss. Not even like a father who's telling you how disappointed he is. Like a friend who wants you to stay well. "Ready to head out?"

"My coat's already on." I tried to smile.

"All right, let's go."

He pulled his topcoat off the back of his chair and slipped into it. He grabbed his briefcase and started to walk when I came over to his side of the desks and touched his arm. "Ryan," I said. "I'm very glad I know you."

He looked embarrassed and turned away. "You want to drive?"

"You probably can get us there faster," I said.

We went out to the Charger and headed toward the Walnut Street Apartments, where Susan Warnock lived in apartment 214.

"We got a sheet on her?" I said.

"Couple of traffic citations. That's all."

It was a two-story stucco complex with maybe fifty units. Ryan parked us in one of the three visitor spots, next to the numbered parking spaces. The cars looked miserable, their glass covered in spider webs of frost, their hoods and trunks spotted with snow that had blown in under the steel roof.

"Just a second," Ryan said as we were heading toward the entrance to the complex. He walked back toward the cars, pulled his notebook from his inside suit jacket pocket, and opened it.

"What is it?"

He pointed to a silver sedan parked in spot 214. The nameplate on the trunk said Audi7. "I've had my eye on this car." He walked around it slowly, his eyes fixed on it, like a teenager looking at a Mustang at a used-car dealer's.

"So why don't you get one?"

"Because I don't have seventy-five thousand dollars?"

"For just one of them?" It looked nice, long and graceful. I glanced down the row of other cars. Lots of small pickups, Honda Accords like mine, Saturns, small Hyundais and Fords. "I think we might want to talk to Susan about her car."

We took the stairs up to the second floor. It was a decent enough complex, with bulbs in all the wall sconces, reasonably clean carpeting, and no garbage sitting outside the apartment doors. Definitely a step up from the student slums I used to visit on weekends when I was a uniform. I put my shield around my neck and knocked with a little force. Nothing.

Ryan said. "The car's here. Let's give it a second."

"I think one of the other strippers said she has a kid." I looked at my watch: 8:42. "She could be getting the kid to school."

We walked to the end of the hall, where a window with snow rounding the corners looked out at another apartment complex, some duplexes, and, in the distance, the Rawlings River and the Greenpath, hidden behind a ribbon of black, leafless trees.

Neither of us said anything. If I hadn't fucked up and gotten drunk last night, I'd have liked to talk with Ryan about Mac and his daughter. Ryan was really good to me when I crashed and burned, right after we became partners a couple years ago. I'd been quite shitty to everyone, including him, but he seemed to understand that I couldn't help it. He gave me the space I needed and never judged me.

Finally, we heard the elevator door open. It was Susan Warnock, bundled up in a down coat and a wool hat. She fished her keys out of her purse then stopped when she saw me and Ryan walking toward her. We met about twenty feet from her apartment door.

"You're here to talk to me?" she said.

"Yes, please."

I saw a hint of a frown as she nodded. "This way."

We followed her to 214. She opened it up and led us in, then hung her hat and coat in the little closet in the entryway. "I was bringing my son to his bus." She smoothed her hair back. "Can I take your coats?"

"No, Ms. Warnock, thank you. We need to talk with you a few minutes about Lee Rossman."

She gestured for us to sit on the couch. It was a medium blue, leather, with tan leather pillows in the corners. She sat in a tan high-backed chair.

"We talked Monday afternoon, a little after one," I said. "At Johnny's Lounge."

"I remember."

"I asked you if you went out with Lee Rossman. You said no."

She shook her head. "That's not exactly what happened … I'm sorry, I don't remember your name."

"I'm Detective Seagate. This is Detective Miner. What exactly did happen?"

"You asked me if I went out with Lee Rossman. I said that's not why I work at Johnny's. You asked me why I work there. I said it's for the money."

"You go to law school?"

She held her gaze.

"Why didn't you tell me the truth?" I said.

"This is why." She gestured to me and then Ryan.

"You do understand, don't you? I ask you if you go out with Lee Rossman, you lead me to believe you don't, then I find out he calls you from his burner couple times a week, talks to you for ten, twenty minutes at a time … you do understand that gets me interested in you, don't you?"

"Yes, I do, Detective. I was hoping you'd find out who did kill him and my name would never come up." Like it was my fault for not having caught the real killer—after all, it's been forty-eight hours. "Do you understand that?"

"Tell me about your relationship with Lee Rossman."

"Lee used to come to Johnny's Lounge."

"How often?"

"I'd say every few weeks. He'd be there with other guys. Some were dressed nice, like he was. Others were roughnecks. He tried to pass me a note, but you know the drill: We're not allowed to date any of the customers."

"But the note eventually made its way to you?"

"Yes, it did. I assume he paid someone. I don't know who."

"So you started going out with him?"

"I wouldn't call it 'going out.' We never went out in public. He made that clear at the start."

"Because he was married?"

"Yeah, because he was married. So we wouldn't be seen together in public."

"And that didn't bother you?"

"I've never been married," she said, "so I have no firsthand knowledge of how wonderful it is." I saw her looking to see if Ryan or I were wearing wedding bands. "The only guy I ever went out with the last fifteen years who wasn't married is Tyler's father, and for some reason he didn't seem to want to get married. I'll accept reasonably honest."

"What did you get out of the relationship?"

"Besides the uncomplicated sex?"

"Yeah, besides that."

"Money."

"Tell me more."

"He helped me with some expenses. Tyler needs some tutoring. Tyler, my son."

"And the Audi under the carport?"

"Actually, I do pretty well at Johnny's Lounge. I could have afforded that myself, but yes, that was a gift from Lee."

"And what did Mr. Rossman get out of the relationship, I

mean, besides the uncomplicated sex?"

"I think he liked me." She raised her jaw a little bit.

"Well, yes, I can see you're quite likeable, but could you be a little more specific?"

"We'd talk."

"What about?"

"Things."

I paused. "Ms. Warnock."

"Art, for instance." She gestured to the prints and posters all over the walls.

"What kind of art is that?" It was all bright colors and swirly shapes. One of the prints looked like it might have been a nude woman. If you kind of titled your head, squinted, and used your imagination.

"Most of it is abstract expressionism."

"You studied art."

"Yes, I did. I have most of an MFA."

"Most of?"

"Did I mention my son, Tyler?"

"And you and Mr. Rossman would talk about art like these pictures?"

"That's what I said. He knew nothing about art, and he was completely comfortable with that. Very unself-conscious. I've found that successful people don't try to hide their limitations. But he would ask me questions. He had a good eye. In another world, I mean, if he'd gone to college, he could have become a very good student of art. He was very respectful, and very grateful. I think that was the aspect of our relationship that gave me the most satisfaction. A sixty-five year old oilman, sitting on this couch," she said, pointing to me and Ryan, "talking to me about art."

"You've been stripping how long?"

"Like I told you, two years. I was a grocery checker, until the oil started up. Then Johnny's Lounge took off. I went over there, got a job right away."

"When was the last time you saw Lee?"

She thought about it. "I think it was last Thursday."

"Where was that?"

"At a hotel, the Cumberland, downtown. He used the name Dallas. James Dallas, if you want to track it down. He always paid in cash."

"Did you two have some kind of fight?"

"Not at all. We never fought."

"You never fought?"

"That's what I said." She took a breath. "In my experience, people only fight—couples, I mean—if they want different things. Lee and I didn't want different things. He appreciated my companionship and my willingness to sleep with him without asking for any commitments. I felt the same way—and was very satisfied with the relationship exactly as it was."

"You mean, the free Audi and the money for tutoring your son?"

She looked at me, then smiled slightly. "Is this where I'm supposed to become offended that you're implying I'm a prostitute? Then I lose my temper and break down in tears and tell you I killed Lee because he wouldn't divorce his wife and marry me and make a beautiful home for me and Tyler to live in, happily ever after?" She leaned forward a little. "Let me explain something about my life. I've made it on my own since I left home at fifteen. I've raised Tyler on my own. When I go to work, five nights a week, drunken assholes call me *whore* and *bitch*. That's just to break the ice. Little later in the evening, they tell me how they're going to fuck me in my cunt and up my ass and in my mouth—and how I'm going to love every moment of it. You understand what I'm saying? That's what I do for a living. So if you want to sit here and suggest I'm a whore because I had sex with Lee and he gave me money, you go right ahead and suggest it. Because I don't give a damn what you think about me and the way I live my life. If you have any evidence that I killed him, you get in touch, okay?" She stood up and turned to walk away.

"Please sit down, Ms. Warnock. Just a few more questions." She sat, her expression blank. But I could see her ribcage rising and falling beneath her cotton sweater. She had a very nice figure. I'd put the waist at twenty-six. "Where were you Sunday night? Were you working?"

"No, I was here."

"Can anyone alibi you?"

"My son and I were doing a bunch of things. I do my grocery shopping with him, usually after dinner Sundays. Then, I clean the apartment for an hour or two. He's in his room, in bed, by nine. When did you say Lee was killed?"

"So, nobody to vouch for you after nine?"

She shrugged her shoulders.

"Can you tell us about anyone who might have wanted to hurt Lee?"

"Since we didn't spend any time with any of his associates, I really can't."

"No other gentleman callers except Lee Rossman?"

She sighed. "None that I'd call gentlemen."

"But you do understand my question."

"I sometimes see other men, but not Sunday."

"Did Lee mention any problems he was having with other people at work? Anybody who didn't like what he did for a living?"

"No, nothing like that. He never talked about people who didn't like what he did for a living."

"What do you think about what he did?"

"Not a fan," she said. "But I think there's someone who might have disliked him for a more personal reason."

"Oh, who was that?"

"I don't know his name."

"What do you know about him?"

"Nothing, except that he's screwing Lee's wife."

"Did Lee know who it was?"

"I couldn't tell, and I didn't push it."

"How did Mr. Rossman feel about his wife's affair?"

"Lee was fairly traditional in that way."

"As in, he could have a lover but his wife couldn't?"

"That's what I mean by *traditional*."

"Did he say what he was gonna do about it?"

"Not in so many words. But from his body language, I assumed there would be a confrontation. A physical confrontation. I mean, if he found out."

"Is there anything else you'd like to tell us, Ms. Warnock?"

"I'm very sorry he's gone. I liked Lee very much. Our times together were always positive. He was a good friend. I knew that our relationship could never have become anything more than it was, and I didn't want it to be. And I knew that eventually he would have moved on. But still, it was a wonderful experience."

"Ms. Warnock, did you kill Lee Rossman?" I said. "And please answer the question directly."

"No, Detective. I did not kill Lee, and I do not know who did."

Ryan and I stood and I handed her my card. "Let me know if you think of anything that can help us figure out who did."

Chapter 18

"You want to look at her Audi again before we leave?"

"Well, now you're just being hurtful." Ryan smiled. "You want to drive?"

"Yeah, I'm fine. I'd rather you do the computer stuff." We got in the Charger and I started it up, cupping my hands over the air vents.

"Of course," Ryan said, "maybe Susan Warnock was just making that up."

"About Florence screwing someone?"

"Maybe she was just saying that so she doesn't look so skanky."

"No, I don't think she's interested in appearances," I said. "What she said about all the shit she gets as a stripper—I believed what she was saying."

"Maybe Lee told her he thought his wife was fooling around so *he* doesn't look all that skanky."

"You mean, her fooling around justified him fooling around? Nope, sorry. He didn't need an excuse for it. Like Susan said, he was a traditionalist: As long as he provided for his wife and screwed around discreetly, he wouldn't see anything wrong with his behavior."

Ryan turned to me. "Okay, you don't like any of my theories, what do you think is going on?"

"Just what Susan said: Lee was nailing her because he's a rich guy—"

"A rich guy who likes to discuss abstract expressionism."

"Yeah, that's it. He'd look at the fingerpainting on her walls and get all hard. And Florence Rossman was fucking someone because—shit, I don't know, there could be a dozen reasons. Because she'd seen her husband nude, or he wasn't willing to use up all his blue pills on her, or she knew about Susan and it's payback, or they fought all the time, or she was a skank. You don't want to start naming reasons husbands and wives cheat. You'll be there a while."

"So what's our next move: go to Cheryl Garrity? She'd know whether there's a guy from the company involved with Florence."

"Yeah," I said, "I think she would. But I want to hold off on her. I want to be able to tell her she was holding out on us about both affairs—if it comes to that."

"Why's that?" Ryan said.

"Because she's our best link to the company. I want her to know we can find this shit out on our own. That way, we can put more pressure on her. Remember, she could be a former lover, too, who didn't like Lee taking up with Florence or the stripper."

"So you want to come at Florence? Two days after her husband is killed?"

"I don't give a damn about that. Our job is to find out who killed Lee Rossman. Odds are, it's family. Here's this rich woman with ten more years before her tits collapse. She kills her husband, she has twice as much money as the day before. Compared to Florence, what's Susan Warnock got to gain by killing him? She's already got the Audi. She's not gonna get another one now."

"Okay," Ryan said, "how do you want to come at Florence? Do we know about his affair with the stripper?"

"Let's go to her house." I navigated us out toward the river and toward the big house overlooking the reservoir. "Yeah, I think we do. If we tell her we already know about the stripper, she might be less embarrassed about telling us about her boyfriend."

"How aggressive do you want to be?"

"Aggressive enough to get the truth out of her."

"You could call her a whore, like you did Susan." He smiled.

"If that's what it takes to make her uncomfortable, that's what I'm gonna do."

With the recent snow, it was hard to recognize the landscape as we snaked up the hill. The car bottomed out as the pavement turned to gravel, hidden beneath the blanket of snow. We parked near the entrance to the big house hanging over the cliff. Next to us was a small black Nissan.

I rang the doorbell. When the door opened, I recognized the housekeeper but didn't remember her name. "Policemen," she said to us.

Ryan said, "Ms. Hidalgo, Detectives Seagate and Miner. Is Ms. Rossman home?"

"She with the reverend now," the housekeeper said, pointing to the black car parked next to the Charger.

"Can we wait?" Ryan said.

"Yes, you wait." She waved us in. "This way," she said, leading us down the hall with the glass walls overlooking the river and the reservoir. The reservoir was a mean-looking grey, with a white collar of snow. "I tell her."

We were in the library, bigger than my living room. It had two matching high-back chairs, in burgundy leather, and a black love seat. Each chair had a side table with a tall brass reading light. The shelves were oak, stretching to the ten-foot ceiling. A couple of ladders in matching oak were attached to tracks at the top so you could get the books above your head.

I walked over to one of the sets of leather-bound books. "Complete Works of Twain, it says."

Ryan came over and took one of the volumes off the shelf. He opened it and looked at the first page.

"What are you looking for?"

"To see if it's real."

"What?"

"Some people—people rich enough to have rooms for their books—buy books by the foot to fill up the shelves. The books are fake. The pages are blank, or old newspapers." He riffled the pages. "These are real."

"Can you tell if anyone read them?"

"A hundred years ago, the pages were uncut when you bought them. Those, you could tell if they hadn't been read."

I walked over to a large painting above one of the leather chairs. "Look at this," I said. "It's like the refrigerator art in Susan Warnock's place."

Ryan came over and looked at it for a moment. Then he leaned in, focusing on the southwest corner, near where some blue stripes turned into some red ones. He pointed and turned to me.

I pulled my reading glasses out of my big leather bag. "Son of a bitch."

"Detectives," a voice said. I turned around. It was Florence Rossman. She was past the crying and sobbing, but she had put on a thicker layer of makeup, probably to hide the puffiness beneath her eyes. She wore a high-necked black sheath dress with a scalloped hem and chiffon sleeves, which showed off her well-toned arms. The only jewelry was a string of real pearls. "I'm sorry for keeping you waiting. I was with Reverend Chalmers. We were discussing Lee's service."

"Not a problem," I said.

"Won't you take a seat?" she said.

"You look well." Which is what you say to a woman who doesn't. I've heard it a lot.

"It's been a tough few days." She folded her hands in her lap and crossed her legs. The sheer black stockings showed off her slim ankles. "I've found that staying busy is the best way to deal with unpleasant circumstances." She paused. "I learned this from my parents."

I assumed she wanted me to follow up on that. "Your parents?"

"They were killed in a boating accident when I was fifteen. I was raised by my auntie, my father's sister, a single woman who ran a company. She interpreted her job as to help me make the transition from a well-off but spoiled girl to an independent woman who didn't need to rely on a man for her economic security."

Just once, I'd like to meet a woman with money who says she's never made a dime on her own, she has absolutely no skills or brains or ambition, and she wouldn't know what she would do if the guy stopped supporting her. There's got to be a rich woman like that.

"And you made that transition," I said.

"I did. I was put on a small allowance. I began working immediately, worked my way through college. I created four or five different companies before I was twenty, and I made considerable profit from each of them. I started a van-rental business for college students. I imported Italian suede goods. Set up a local food co-op and managed to get the university dining halls to contract with them."

"That's very impressive," I said, my bullshit-detector beeping in my ears like the machine in the ICU hooked up to that poor bastard. My experience has been that people with remarkable accomplishments don't talk about themselves—because everyone already knows. Me? I talk about myself almost every day. My name is Karen, and I'm an alcoholic.

"How can I help you today?" Florence Rossman said, her head tilted a little to show I had her full attention and she would do what she could.

I stood and walked over to the painting. "Do you know the

person who painted this?"

Florence Rossman looked confused. "I'm sorry?"

"I said, 'Do you know the person who painted this?'"

"That was something Lee bought." She smiled and rolled her eyes. "Last year, he started to show some interest in art. He began to collect some pieces from a gallery downtown."

"Did that surprise you?"

"As a matter of fact, it did. I'd never known that side of Lee. I suggested that he might consider getting in touch with some of the larger galleries—I mean, in Los Angeles, Chicago, New York. I thought some of their work might turn out to be better investments."

"How did Mr. Rossman respond to that?"

"He said he wasn't ready for that. He just liked this painting." She smiled sadly and put up her hands in a what-are-you-going-to-do gesture.

I walked back to the chair and sat down. "The artist is Susan Warnock."

Florence shook her head to say she didn't recognize the name. "Is she a local artist?"

"More of a stripper. At Johnny's Lounge, downtown. Where Mr. Rossman's body was found Monday morning. Your husband had a throwaway phone, which he used to call her."

She pulled back. "You've spoken with … what did you say her name is? Susan Warnock. You've talked with her?"

"Yes, we did. A half-hour ago. She said she and Mr. Rossman were having an affair, that it's been going on for some months."

Florence Rossman paused for a moment, and her gaze drifted over my shoulder. She swallowed hard, smoothed her black dress, and re-crossed her legs. "No," she said, "I don't know anything about that. I had not heard of her."

"Do you think she could be telling the truth, Ms. Rossman? I mean, that Mr. Rossman was having an affair?"

She blinked a couple of times, rapidly. "Yes," she said, her voice a little shaky. "She could be telling the truth."

"Could you tell us a little more about that?"

"When I met Lee, he was in his fifties. I was in my thirties. I had no illusions about the sort of life he had led, the kind of relationships he had maintained."

"Meaning?"

"Lee was a very ambitious man, very competitive. In his culture—"

"What culture was that, Ms. Rossman?"

"The oil industry. He was a wildcat oilman. He never finished college—I was quite surprised to learn that he even attempted college at all. He started out working on the rigs. He earned good money—in cash, in an envelope—and if it there was any left at the end of the week, that surprised him. He liked American pickup trucks, American whiskey, and American women. I was aware that, when he was married the first time, there were rumors of affairs."

"And after the death of his first wife?"

She smiled briefly and wet her lips. "Yes, there were numerous affairs."

"Did he ever have any affairs with women in the company?"

She looked at me. "You know, Detective, I really can't say."

"But you're not particularly surprised to learn of a relationship with the stripper?"

"Well, I am somewhat surprised—only in that I did not know he was involved with Ms. Warnock."

"But that she was a stripper?"

"No." She spoke slowly, as if she was thinking it through as she spoke. "That does not particularly surprise me. As I indicated, he liked women, and I do not believe that … that socioeconomic background was a factor."

"One other thing we need to ask about. Susan Warnock said

that you were involved in a relationship, as well."

She was looking at her dress, smoothing it along a pleat. Her head jerked up. "Does that surprise you, Detective?"

"That you'd be involved in a relationship?"

She took a moment. "That she would say I am."

"I've been in this business for some years, Ms. Rossman. Really aren't that many things surprise me. So let me just ask you outright: Were you in an extra-marital relationship?"

She smiled. "I'd feel most comfortable if I knew the police were working diligently to determine who would want to hurt my husband, rather than asking me about my personal life."

"That didn't really answer my question, now, did it, Ms. Rossman?"

"Do you need a more direct answer?"

"You understand how a cop thinks about these things," I said. "If you were having an affair, that would suggest maybe you were having some problems in the marriage. Maybe you were making other plans. You know, with this other guy? Or that the guy had fallen for you hard and wasn't your husband's biggest fan. And one other thing I need to say. If you tell us you weren't having an affair, but we find out you were—and it would probably take a couple hours, a day at the outside—it would make us look at you different."

"I see." Her eyes were focused on a row of books over my shoulder. She was calculating her next move, thinking it through. "An adulterer and a liar, you're saying. Not a person of a very high moral character, am I correct?"

"I realize how that perspective is kind of obvious, but yes, I'd have to say that realizing you're an adulterer and a liar makes us look at you harder. The adultery presents all sorts of motives. And the lying? Well, if you didn't kill your husband—and your boyfriend didn't kill him—I have to wonder why you didn't simply tell us the truth. I can assure you, whether you were faithful to your husband or not—that kind of thing just doesn't interest me apart from this investigation. And we don't leak stuff like that to the media. You give us the name of your boyfriend, we track him down, find out you were with him that night and one of you can prove it. Simple as that: You're not a suspect, he's not a suspect."

"Yes, I can understand that logic." Florence Rossman nodded. "At the risk of incurring those consequences, however, I'm going to say the following: I was not having an extramarital affair."

Chapter 19

"Who was she doing?" I turned the engine over in the Charger. Usually the thing puts out a big, throaty roar, but all the snow was dampening the sound.

"Don't you want to start with whether she was telling the truth?" Ryan said.

I eased out of the parking area in front of Lee and Florence Rossman's big house and headed back toward town, the wide tires crunching the snow.

I turned to him. "If you believed her that she wasn't screwing someone, just give me your weapon and shield right now. You're too stupid to be a cop—and that's saying something."

Ryan laughed. "I just wanted to go step-by-step. All right, she was lying about having a lover. Do you know who the lover is?"

"No, I have no idea. Do you?"

"I think I do. Yes."

"Want me to stop the car so you can tell me?"

"No, keep driving. It was Ron Eberly."

"The landman? How do you get that?"

"They just fit."

"What the hell does that mean?"

"They look like they go together. I mean, physically. He's the college football player—"

"I don't think he went to college."

"He's the high-school football player. Good looking, athletic. More her age. Plus, he's a little bit mysterious, maybe even dangerous. She's the homecoming queen, very attractive. She'd go for the athlete."

"But she went for Lee Rossman."

"No," Ryan said. "She *married* Lee. That doesn't mean he's her type. It could have been a decision—a business decision."

"You know, when she started talking about her parents dying in a boating accident, I got the impression that was a little story for our benefit."

"We scratch the surface a little, we're going to find out Florence Rossman isn't exactly who she says she is."

"Well, you scratch anybody's surface … Still," I said, "a woman put together as good as Florence, with a lot of money—and the potential to come into a lot more—she could attract a lot of fifty-year-old professional guys, you know, doctors, lawyers. No reason she has to settle for someone like Ron Eberly, who's basically a door-to-door salesman."

"Sure, she could attract a lot of more presentable guys than Eberly. All I'm saying is I've got a hunch it's him. Think about it. If Eberly and Lee Rossman go back a few decades, Eberly would be over at Lee's house: dinners, parties. She'd know Eberly for four years, or however long she's known Lee. The timing would be right for her to start looking for someone more her style. And Eberly's got the shoulders," Ryan said. "It's all in the shoulders."

I thought about Ryan's very impressive shoulders. I wasn't sure I agreed with him that it was all in the shoulders. But he's such a pussy about language, that would be his way of saying what it was all about. "If I grant you that point—"

"If?" He showed me his wide grin.

"If I grant you that point, what are we going to do with it?"

"I can tell you what I would do with it. I'd visit Cheryl Garrity, tell her we know Lee Rossman was seeing Susan Warnock, and Florence Rossman was seeing Ron Eberly—"

"And if she says how do you know any of this?"

"We say phone records."

"What phone records tied Florence to Ron Eberly?" I said.

"Florence's phone records."

"We don't have Florence's phone records."

"Cheryl Garrity doesn't know that," Ryan said. "If she asks, we say it's routine in a homicide. We check the victim's phones and financials."

"So that gives us an opportunity to pump her on Ron Eberly," I said.

"That's right. We put Cheryl on the defensive because she wasn't forthcoming about Lee and Florence. She'll tell us what we need to know about Eberly, and we'll either like him more or rule him out."

"And if you're wrong about Florence doing Ron Eberly?"

"We'll see it on her face. One thing for sure: If Lee was killed by one of his own people, Cheryl Garrity either knows who did it or can help us figure it out."

"Let's stop by Rossman Mining and see if Ms. Garrity is available." I drove us down the winding road back toward town. As we got closer, the roads got cleaner and easier to navigate. By the time we made it downtown, the streets were pocked with little patches of snow and ice but basically dry. I parked in the underground garage and we took the elevator to fourteen.

Last time we were here was right after Lee's murder made the news. Two days later, things looked like they'd returned to normal, at least on the surface. The receptionist looked up and greeted me and Ryan with a company-approved smile. I told her we wanted to see Cheryl Garrity. She got on the phone.

A minute later Cheryl Garrity emerged from the hallway to the left of the reception area and led us back to her office. We all sat.

"Thanks for taking the time to speak with us," I said.

Cheryl Garrity took the chair at her desk to let us know she wanted to get back to her work. "Do you have some news to tell me about your investigation?"

"Not exactly," I said. "These things generally take a little longer than people expect. But we were hoping you could help us with something."

She nodded.

"It's about Ron Eberly," I said. "We need to know a little bit more about him."

"Why are you interested in Ron?"

"Here's what we've learned since we spoke to you two days ago. Lee was having an affair with a woman named Susan Warnock, and Florence was having an affair with Ron Eberly." I didn't put any attitude on it. I've learned there's no point trying to make people feel guilty that they waste our time. They basically don't give a shit.

She didn't flinch, didn't move, didn't seem to react in any way. "Who is Susan Warnock?"

"Ms. Warnock is a stripper at Johnny's Lounge."

"Near where Lee's body was found."

"That's right," I said. "In the alley next to it."

"She's not associated with Rossman Mining in any way, is that correct?"

"Other than having an affair with its president, that's correct," I said. "What can you tell us about her?"

"Absolutely nothing. I had never heard the name before you said it."

"You and Lee weren't that close personally? I mean, he wouldn't talk with you about his extra-marital relationships?"

"I've worked with Lee for close to twenty years, both here and at other locations. You and your partner here—you haven't worked together nearly that long. Maybe you don't know how work relationships evolve over time. There were times when we used to talk more, I mean, about our personal lives. Especially after the death of his first wife. I think he relied on me more then. But the last few years, with his marriage to Florence, it's only natural that she has taken over much more of that role."

"Are you saying he told Florence about his girlfriends?"

"I really have no idea whether he did or not. He didn't talk to me about his relationship with Florence—"

"You mean, when she was his mistress?"

"Either before they were married, or after," Cheryl Garrity said. "I mean that once she was in his life, I became what my job title suggests: director of operations. In addition, when you've been with a colleague twenty years, you get to know them so well—what they're looking for in life, their values, how they spend their time—some of the details kind of fall away."

"How do you mean?"

"That he was having an extra-marital affair?" She waved her hand in the air dismissively. "I saw that enough times that it didn't register with me. I didn't really care who it was. This woman you mentioned—the dancer or whatever she was to him—I'm sure he was very kind to her, very attentive and sweet when they were together. He probably gave her little gifts. But it would have lasted until it ended. Then he would have moved on."

"Well, he's done moving on. This Susan Warnock, the last girlfriend—you're saying you don't know whether she has a boyfriend or some guy? You know, some guy who might be unhappy that she's screwing this sixty-five year old rich guy?"

"I wouldn't know her from Eve."

"All right, what do we need to know about Ron Eberly? Not just what's in his personnel file."

"Lee and Ron go back many years—years before I came on board. They worked rigs together. Texas, Oklahoma, all over. Lee founded his own company, and Ron was his first hire. Ron doesn't have the drive that Lee had. Didn't want to make something. Ron just wants to keep working. When his body couldn't take it anymore—being a roughneck, I mean—Lee fronted him the money to learn to be a landman. Ron didn't finish the course and get credentialed, of course; Ron doesn't finish things. But Lee didn't care. He rode along with Ron on his first few calls, to see if he was doing it well enough."

"Apparently he was."

"That's right," Cheryl Garrity said. "At the start, Lee had to rein him in a little. Ron would promise the landowners a little more than the company could deliver. Lee told him how he wanted him to represent the company, and I think Ron has complied. One other thing: Lee made sure Ron was on salary, no commission. I think Lee understood Ron well enough that he wanted to remove any incentive for Ron to try to work the landowners—more than necessary, that is."

"So you don't have any more problems with the contracts Ron has written than you do with your other landmen?"

"That's correct. Ron does the job."

"Does he have a family?"

"An ex-wife. Lives in Houston with their two children."

"Did Lee know Florence was having an affair?"

"Yes."

"Did Lee know it was with Ron?"

"Yes."

"Did he tell you that?"

"Actually, I told him about the affair."

"Explain."

"I learned about it some months ago—"

"How'd you learn about it?"

"I was following up on some missed communications. I thought Ron was here in Rawlings. He told me he was out in Marshall. But I saw him here. I swung by his place that night. His lights were on. Florence's car was in his driveway. I confronted him about it. He admitted it and asked me not to tell Lee."

"He didn't want to get fired?"

"I think it was he didn't want to face the fact that he had betrayed his best friend."

"So what did you do?"

"I thought it would be best for Lee if Ron were fired. There are enough irregularities—minor violations of policy and such—in Ron's record to warrant termination."

"So why is he still working?"

"Lee found out about it and called me in. He asked me what was going on. I laid out the case for termination. He didn't buy it. He asked me what's was really going on. I told him Ron was engaged in an inappropriate sexual relationship with someone in the company."

"What did Lee say?"

"He smiled. He didn't believe I was firing Ron for that. The culture in this company: We're not sticklers on that issue. He asked me who it was Ron was involved with. I told him I couldn't tell him. He said, then you can't fire Ron. He wouldn't let it drop. Finally, I told Lee it was Florence."

"Why didn't you just refuse to tell him?"

"Because I realized I had a responsibility to the company. I'm the director of operations at Rossman Mining. My job is to protect the company. And the first order of business is always to protect Lee."

"What did he do when you told him it was Eberly?"

"He told me he'd take care of it. And that he appreciated that I told him."

"When was this?"

"About ten days ago."

"Between that time and Lee's murder, did you get any information about a confrontation between Ron Eberly and Lee?"

"No, I did not."

"Do you think Ron Eberly killed Lee Rossman?"

"No, I do not."

"Seems to me entirely plausible."

"Not if you know Ron Eberly."

"Everything you've told me says he had a number of reasons to do it, starting with the fact that he didn't want to get fired—or shot by Lee. Plus, maybe he thought he might have an opportunity to marry some of Florence's money."

"Ron Eberly loved Lee. It was the only real relationship Ron ever had with another person. Ron would kill himself before he hurt Lee."

"But he's okay with screwing Lee's wife."

"Self-control is not Ron's strength. In many ways, he is a very weak and needy man. But I stand by my statement that he loved Lee. I know that he did not kill Lee Rossman."

Chapter 20

"What have we got on Mr. Eberly?" I said. We were back at headquarters, having re-interviewed Cheryl Garrity, who confirmed what Ryan had suspected: Florence Rossman's lover was Ron Eberly. I'd given Ryan a half-hour to find out everything we needed to know about Eberly. With a phone and the Internet, Ryan needs only twenty minutes, but since he had figured out it was Eberly that Florence was banging, I thought he deserved a ten-minute break.

"Mr. Eberly is not good with money," Ryan said.

"For example?"

"For example, he has two personal bankruptcies and two business ones. And this is his house in Houston." He pointed to his screen. It looked like my place—a crappy three-bedroom ranch with scraggly shrubs, dead grass, and a few missing shutters—except his had a sign in the front yard that said BANK OWNED.

"This guy's pulling down—what, a hundred thousand?—and he can't make payments on this litterbox?"

"Child support?" Ryan said.

"Only if he had the world's worst divorce lawyer. No, there's something else going on."

"Drugs?"

"That, or gambling."

"There's three or four casinos out near the wells," Ryan said.

"Shit, long as he's got a computer he could lose all his money from the comfort of his home."

"Let me give him a call."

I nodded and Ryan leafed through his notebook to get Eberly's cell number. I don't pray, but I heard myself asking Someone to let Eberly be in Rawlings, not in Marshall.

Ryan got through, told Eberly we need to talk to him. "Order yourself another cup of coffee. We'll be there in five." Ryan ended the call and turned to me. "What are you so happy about?"

"It's just a beautiful day," I said. "Where're we going?"

"To Elmer's."

It took us four minutes to get to the diner. It was a little after ten. There were only five old timers in the place. Ryan and I slid into the booth across the table from Ron Eberly. He was halfway through a big plate of eggs, sausage links, toast, and a couple small pancakes on the side.

Not having eaten anything in close to twenty-four hours, I started salivating. "Mr. Eberly," I said, "did you know Lee Rossman was having an affair?"

He gave it a little thought. "Would you like a cup of coffee?"

I looked at him. "That would be lovely."

He waved the waitress down. She was a weary sixty-year old wearing her dyed-black hair in a spike. She walked gingerly, like her shift started when the diner opened at six. Eberly looked at Ryan, who said, "Decaf."

Ron Eberly ordered the two drinks, thanking the waitress by name.

"So, Mr. Eberly," I said again, "did you know Lee Rossman was having an affair?"

He placed his coffee cup down on the table carefully. "Where did you get that information?"

"We're detectives. We've been detecting."

Rod raised an eyebrow, just a little. "Lee has been known to have affairs."

"Do you know the current woman he was having an affair with now?"

"This particular woman?"

"Yes, this particular woman. This particular now."

The waitress came over and put the coffee and the decaf down at our places. She got three thank-you's, as well as a warm smile from Eberly.

"No, I don't know her."

"She's a dancer downtown. A stripper. Name's Susan Warnock."

Rod nodded and smiled, like Lee still had it. Then he shook his head. "Sorry." He reached for the cream in a little pitcher. "Never met her."

"So you can't help us with whether she had another boyfriend might've got angry she was seeing Lee."

He shook his head again and took a bite of toast. He wasn't going to interrupt his breakfast just because he had to talk with a couple detectives.

"You and Lee go way back. He never said anything to you about anyone threatening him? Blackmail, anything like that?"

He just shook his head and took a sip of his coffee.

"Something else Cheryl Garrity told us."

Ron was chewing a mouthful of pancakes. He looked up. "What's that?"

"Florence Rossman was having an affair, too."

His eyes darted off to the side for just a moment before he looked back at me.

"Any thoughts on that?" I said.

"What kind of thoughts?" He chewed some more.

"Do you think Cheryl was telling the truth?"

Rod put his knife and fork down, took a sip of his coffee. "Really can't say."

I was starting to get a little pissed at how content Eberly

seemed as he ate his breakfast. I decided to put off telling him we knew it was him nailing Florence; maybe I could give him a little heartburn as he wondered whether we knew. "You go back pretty far with Cheryl, right?"

"Twenty years, I guess. Long as she's been with Lee."

"Would she have any reason to lie about that? About Florence having an affair?"

"Lee met Cheryl Garrity back in Houston in the nineties. Both of them were married then. She was working for another oil company. They began an affair. Cheryl moved over to Lee's company. But it didn't work out, her being his mistress and working for him, too."

"Who ended the relationship?"

"Lee did. He told me it was a lot harder to find a good manager than a good lay."

"He tell her that?"

Eberly smiled. "Just me. But I think Cheryl would have agreed. She seemed okay with ending the affair."

"She was over him."

He had a pained expression on his face. "I'm not sure about that. Cheryl is a realist. Her own marriage broke up. She saw how Lee was giving her more and more responsibility within the company. She liked the salary—and the ego strokes."

"And liked being around Lee?"

"I think that was a big factor."

"So Lee hooks up with other women. His first wife gets sick, dies. Tell me about Lee marrying Florence."

"It was fast. He'd met her at some business conference three, four years ago."

"Did it surprise you? I mean, Lee deciding to get married. Why not just keep screwing all the women he wants? Let Cheryl Garrity keep running the office? That would keep things simple, right?" I heard my phone ringing in my big leather bag. I let it go to voicemail.

"I don't know. Maybe he fell in love with Florence." Rod smiled. "It happens."

"Florence *is* a very attractive woman." I couldn't resist. "How did Cheryl take it when Lee married Florence?"

"In public? Fine."

"In private, she go batshit?" I said.

"The way I'd put it," Eberly said, "Cheryl understood how Lee needed her to run the company. And even how Lee wasn't into fidelity. But then he marries a younger woman. Cheryl really didn't like that." He was most of the way through his eggs. I was eyeing a piece of toast.

"Getting back to Cheryl saying Florence was having an affair. You think maybe Cheryl was making that up? Like she wanted to show how Lee couldn't really have a successful marriage. How he had to fool around like he always did? You know, to make Cheryl feel better about herself?"

He shrugged. "I'm not Dr. Phil. I'm just an oilman."

"Interesting," I said. I looked over at Ryan, who was sitting there with a mildly amused expression on his face. One of the really good things about Ryan, he's willing to just sit back if I'm doing an interview. He doesn't feel he has to participate if things are going smooth with me and the guy.

I said, "You know who Cheryl said Florence is having an affair with?"

He cut a sausage link in half with his fork. He shook his head. "No, I don't." He started chewing.

I counted to five. "You."

He finished chewing the sausage and lowered the fork to the plate.

"Would you like to comment?"

"It's not true."

"I thought we had an understanding, Mr. Eberly. We keep

you up-to-date on the investigation. All you have to do is tell us the truth." I looked at him. He looked at me. "That's it? Nothing you want to say?"

"That's it. It's not true." He held my gaze. He was an awfully good liar. Better than me.

"Couple reasons I know it's true. First, she has a lot of money. You, on the other hand, don't. Bankruptcies, foreclosures."

He just looked at me, his face a mask. At least he had stopped eating.

I leaned toward him. "Where does all the money go, Ron?"

He leaned in toward me. We were maybe a foot apart. "Unless you can explain how this relates to Lee's murder, it's not really any of your concern."

"Well, like I say, it might go to motive."

He was wearing a dismissive smile, like I was going to have to do a lot better than motive. "You said there was another reason?"

"Well, yeah," I said. "Florence says she's having an affair with you."

"I don't believe you." His voice was low, but the tone was confident.

I raised my eyebrows. On the table, next to his Ford key ring with a dozen keys on it, sat his cell phone. I pushed it over toward him. "Call her."

The waitress came over and re-filled Ryan's cup from the carafe with the orange spout. "Thank you, ma'am," he said with a pleasant smile. Then she re-filled Eberly's coffee from the other carafe.

Ron Eberly sighed, pushed the plate away, rested his elbows on the table, and tented his fingers. This was him telling me he wasn't going to phone Florence to check up on my story. But I couldn't quite tell if it meant he was done talking with me, or done denying he was doing Florence.

"Were you with Florence Sunday night?" I said.

He nodded.

"What time?"

"Around eight."

"Till?"

"Six, six-thirty Monday morning."

"At her house?"

He shook his head. "My apartment, here in town."

"Can anyone else confirm that? I mean, besides Florence?" I took a sip from my coffee. "We'll have to check with Florence, of course."

He thought it over a few seconds. "It was the two of us."

I leaned back in the booth. "See how easy that was, Mr. Eberly? Telling the truth, I mean. If Ms. Rossman says she was with you—eight PM till six, six-thirty Monday morning—and we can corroborate that, then you're off the hook. You are, and she is. You can both go about your lives without a care in the world. You'll have plenty of money. Hundreds of millions, if the newspaper articles are right. You'll be able to buy your house back from the bank. The house in Houston, I mean. The one where your ex-wife and two daughters live. That one." I looked at him and smiled. "Lee Rossman dying like this, you and his wife having nothing to do with it—it's gonna work out real good for the two of you."

He was looking down at his plate. When he looked at me, for the first time I saw fear in his eyes. "I told you Florence and I were alone. How are you going to corroborate our story?"

I put on a pained expression. "You know, Mr. Eberly, that's always a tough one. Usually, you know, we get two people admit they were humping away, we believe them. But here? Here, it's a little tricky. Seeing as each of you had a motive to take Lee out, and each of you could've persuaded Lee to come meet you outside the tittie bar, and each of you had the physical strength to slide a knife into him—I'm just saying, the police chief's gonna ask us how we know it wasn't one of you two, with the other one covering with a lie about how you were together. Or how it wasn't both of you working together, so you can grab the old man's money and get back to fucking each other. I'm just saying."

"What do you want me to do?"

"You say you didn't do it, right?" I shrugged my shoulders. "If you're telling the truth, you got nothing to worry about. Because here's the thing: We're a little different from you. If our investigation shows you didn't kill your best friend, we're not gonna frame you. You're home free."

"I didn't kill him."

"Then you're fine. Actually, I shouldn't use the word *fine*. Just so you understand the difference between you and Lee, know this. When Cheryl Garrity found out about the affair, she wanted to fire you—get you out of the company, to protect Lee? But apparently Lee wouldn't have it. He didn't want to handle it like that. He wanted to resolve it, one-on-one. Like a man. You're still working because of Lee. In fact, all your life, you've been working because of Lee. And you're fucking his wife?" He didn't look up. "Out in Marshall the other day, at the deeds office, you told me and my partner the one thing you're proudest of is that you never let Lee down. Now Lee's dead, and you and his wife—you're both gonna be okay. Plus, rich."

"Is there anything else you want to say?" Eberly's complexion was a little pale.

Ryan and I slid out of the booth. Ryan folded a five-dollar bill and slipped it under Eberly's phone.

"You gonna eat that piece of toast?" I said.

Chapter 21

Back in the Charger, I pulled out my phone to retrieve the message. It was from headquarters. I put it on Speaker. "Bill Rossman is being medevaced to Rawlings. ETA ten forty-five. No word on his condition or what happened to him."

Ryan looked at his watch. "It's ten forty-five now."

I headed out of the lot at the diner. It was five minutes to the Rawlings Regional Medical Center. Both Ryan and I were scanning the sky, looking for the helicopter, but no sign of it.

As we got closer, Ryan spotted the tip of a blade on the helipad on top of the hospital. "I think the chopper's already arrived."

I pulled into the horseshoe at the Emergency Room and put down the visor with the Official Police Business sign. There were two squad cars parked in front of the big glass doors, and an officer standing there.

We got out of the car and rushed up to the uniform, Officer Hicks. I had my shield around my neck. "What's going on?"

"Not sure, Detective." He was a big black man with a gentle manner. "Something about a chemical contamination."

"The patient they just medevaced in?"

"That's my understanding," Hicks said. "They've got a decon unit in the hospital they use when it's only one or two patients. That's all I know. I'm supposed to keep civilians out. We're setting up an operations center in the main entrance." He pointed to the other set of doors.

"Thanks, Hicks." Ryan and I hurried to the main entrance, where another officer, Ellen Reynolds, greeted us. "You can get to the ER down this hall, first right. There's personnel there to brief you."

We made it to the side entrance to the ER and up to the desk.

"What's going on?" I said to the nurse on duty. "Where's the patient? Bill Rossman."

"He was deconned, then sent into the ER. They stabilized him and sent him to surgery."

"Is he in surgery now?"

"I don't know," she said. "Go to Post-Op, on the third floor. There's two paramedics there, from the medevac. The police department asked them to stay so you could talk to them. That's all I know."

We got on the elevator and rode to three. "What the hell is going on?" I said to Ryan.

He shook his head and exhaled.

We followed the signs to Post-Op, a large room with a reception desk and a bunch of soft upholstered chairs and couches. The two EMTs, young guys in uniforms, looked alert when they saw us, as if they wanted to tell us whatever they had to say, then head back in the chopper. On the other side of the room, on a dark blue loveseat with oak arms, sat Florence Rossman. She was crying, her head in her hands.

"Ryan, go over and interview the EMTs. I'll talk to Florence." He nodded and walked over to the two guys.

I went over to the couch and sat next to Florence. She didn't look up to see who I was, but she sensed someone there and slid a few inches over to her own side of the loveseat to make room. She was way out of control, sobbing, her shoulders hunched and rocking. I waited a few minutes, watching Ryan take notes as he talked with the two EMTs. They had an easy camaraderie, three strong young men doing their jobs.

I got up and walked over to the reception desk. "Do you have any idea what happened to the patient?"

"I know we did a decon on him before the ER sent him up here. That's all I know." She looked at her screen. "I have the surgeon coming out soon to tell you the patient's status."

"Was it some kind of accident?"

"I'm sorry." She shook her head. "You'll just have to wait."

I walked back over to the loveseat. This time, Florence Rossman looked up and, after a moment, recognized me. "You're the detective." She was still crying.

"Karen Seagate." I nodded. "I'm very sorry to hear your stepson's been hurt."

With that she started crying more, covering her face. After a minute, she spoke. "What are you doing here?"

"We got word that Bill was hurt. We don't know if it was, you know, some kind of accident at the rigs … Did they tell you anything?"

"Nothing."

"My partner and I, we're here …"

"You think he was attacked?"

"We don't know if it was anything like that. But if there was a crime—out in Marshall, I mean, we need to determine if it was related …"

She looked up at me, dabbing at her eyes with a handkerchief. "What is happening? First, Lee." Her hands started to shake. "I don't know if I can take this. I need Lee now." Her breathing was shallow and rapid. I had trouble making out what she was saying.

I took Florence's hand. It was hot and clammy, wet. But the shaking started to subside. "We'll just have to wait for a doctor to tell us what's going on."

We sat there. The two EMTs left, and a few minutes later I heard the muffled thwack-thwack sound of the chopper lifting off and felt the vibrations coming through the seat cushions.

Fifteen minutes passed. Twenty minutes. I held Florence's hands. We were sitting next to each other on the loveseat. At times, she pressed against me. We were silent.

Ryan stayed off to the other side of the room, as if he thought Florence Rossman might start talking to me, and he didn't want to distract her. But she didn't talk. Occasionally, she stared into the distance. Other times she closed her eyes, locked in her own private hell.

In the silent, sad room, the fatigue started to catch up to me, and I think I nodded off once or twice. I awoke when I heard a door open and a doctor walked in.

It was the surgeon. She was about forty, medium height, wearing blue scrubs and a little hat that held her hair back. The front of her scrubs was stained with blood and other fluids I couldn't identify. "Ms. Rossman?" the surgeon said, not knowing which one of us it was.

Florence Rossman stood up, gathered herself, and walked over to the surgeon. "I'm Florence Rossman."

"Would you come with me, please?" The surgeon started walking toward a little alcove off to the side of the room, the place where the doctor tells you what's going on.

I followed them, a few feet behind. As Florence disappeared into the little room, the surgeon looked at me. I touched my shield, and the surgeon nodded.

When Florence was seated, the surgeon said to her, "Do you mind if the police officer listens in?"

Florence Rossman shook her head. "I don't care."

"Let me tell you where we are," the surgeon said. "My name is Dr. Winwood, and I did the main surgery on Bill."

Florence looked petrified. "The main surgery?"

"Ms. Rossman, let me talk to you. Bill is going to be okay. He's a strong young man. But we needed to do several procedures today."

"What happened to him?"

"The EMTs reported to us that he had been attacked. He sustained many bruises, a few broken ribs. A broken leg and pelvis. All of those things we've got under control."

As the surgeon listed each of the injuries, Florence Rossman let out a little cry. I came over to her side, knelt next to her, and put my hand on her shoulder.

"Bill also sustained a ruptured spleen, and we had to remove it. But that will be okay, too."

"Doctor," I said. Florence Rossman seemed unable to talk. "Why did they have to decon him?"

The doctor's expression was serious. "When the patient was brought in, the EMTs told us he'd been found near a wastewater pit at a drilling rig. His clothes were wet and smelled of diesel and other industrial agents. The EMTs reported that he vomited several times during the flight here. He vomited, too, here in the hospital. It was orange, oily. We assumed it might be the wastewater. Our protocol is to decontaminate him. We got him into the decon room, got him out of his clothes, washed him up. We pumped his stomach, sent the contents to the lab immediately, and contacted the CDC."

"And?"

"The CDC is sending people over now."

"Do you have lab results?"

"The full analysis will take some time, but the preliminary findings are that the fluid from his stomach contained some chemicals that we're concerned about. The EMTs brought with them the MSDS from the—"

"The what?"

"Material Safety Data Sheet. It's the list of all the chemicals on the site. In this case, it's all the stuff in the fracking fluid."

"So, can't you match that with what you found in his stomach?"

"Yes. To some extent, yes. We've identified some heavy metals, radioactive materials, volatile organic compounds. BTEX—benzene, toluene, ethyl benzene, and xylene. A lot of oil, salts, sand. Some hydrochloric acid. Plus they identified some radioactive tracer isotopes used in the mining."

Florence was staring off into space, as if she could no longer listen to the surgeon. I stood up and gestured for the surgeon to follow me out of the alcove. When Ryan saw us come out of the alcove, he drifted over to us but stayed in the background.

"What are you saying?" I said to the surgeon.

"Listen, I'm not a pathologist. I took out his spleen, and we're taking care of the other injuries. The breaks and bruises. But I'm just not qualified to talk about all the stuff in his stomach."

"So you can't say what's gonna happen to him?"

"No, I can't. It depends on exactly what it was, plus the concentration and the length of the exposure. We did the best we could to get it out of his system as soon as we determined that some of it was toxic."

"But at least you know what it is, correct?"

"Most of it is pretty easy to identify, chemically, I mean. Some of it isn't specified on the MSDS."

"What do you mean?"

"Well, some of it is naturally occurring, got washed up from underground in the drilling process. And some of it the company doesn't have to list."

"What?"

"The EMTs told us this. Don't know if it's true. But the company doesn't have to list all the stuff in the cocktail."

"You're shitting me."

She shrugged and just looked at me, like she wanted to get back to whatever she was doing.

"These chemicals could mess him up, is that right?"

"He's going to have to be monitored."

"How long?"

"The rest of his life."

"Can you tell how he got all this shit in his stomach?"

"I have no idea."

"But there's no way he would've drunk that shit voluntarily."

"It smells like a gas station. Nobody would ingest it."

"What do you think happened to him?"

"Listen, Officer, I don't feel comfortable speculating on what happened. It's your job to figure that out."

"Doctor, I understand what you're saying. And I'm not asking you to make any kind of formal statement. But you know who this guy is, right?"

"Yes, I do." Her mouth was set in a scowl. "His name is Bill Rossman."

"And you know who his father is?"

"Officer," she said, "I don't have time for this. I don't know who his father is, and frankly I don't care. My job was to take out his spleen—"

"His father was Lee Rossman, the oil man. The guy who was killed two days ago."

The doctor furrowed her brows and took a breath. "Oh, my goodness, I had no idea."

"So you understand what I'm trying to do? We got the father murdered here in Rawlings, then two days later his son gets choppered in from the oil rigs, with a gut full of fracking chemicals and the crap beat out of him. You understand what I'm asking you to help me with now, right?"

"Yes," she said, "yes, I understand."

"Okay, great," I said. "Now, just between you and me, what the hell you think happened to him?"

"From the injuries, I'd say three or four guys beat him up, poured the fluid down his throat."

"All right, thank you. Can you tell when he got beat up?"

"Within the last three or four hours, I'd say. From the bruising. He looks like hell. There isn't a square foot of flesh that isn't bruised up."

"They could've killed him, right?"

"I think they decided not to."

"Can we talk to him?"

"He's still unconscious."

"How long will he be out?"

"Can't say." The surgeon glanced up at a clock on the wall. "Talk to the nurse. She'll set it up so we notify you when he's conscious."

I heard a phone ringing in the little room where Florence was still sitting.

"Okay, Doctor, thank you very much."

The doctor nodded, then turned and disappeared through the door that led to the operating rooms.

Florence walked over to me, full of energy.

"Ms. Rossman," I said, "I've had a chance to talk—"

I didn't see her right hand come up and slap me, hard, on the left side of my jaw. I started to stumble, and I felt Ryan grab me on my forearms and keep me upright.

She pointed her finger in my face. "You're dead." She turned and walked away, her chin in the air.

I turned to Ryan. "That call she just got? I'm thinking maybe it was from Ron Eberly."

He nodded. "That would make sense." He leaned in and looked at my face. "You okay?"

I opened my jaw, moved it left and right to see if it still worked. "I'd be good without getting attacked any more today."

Chapter 22

The chief paced back and forth in the incident room. I'd never seen him as agitated as this. "What the hell is going on?"

Ryan was standing, hands in his pockets, looking at the floor. I was sitting on a table. We looked at each other. "We have no idea, Chief."

"Can you tell me where Lee Rossman was killed?"

"No," I said. "Just that his body was recovered here."

"And Bill Rossman? Where was he attacked?"

"I think he was attacked out there, at the rig. In Marshall."

"Because that's where the fracking liquid is?"

"Yeah, most of it, anyway," I said. "There could be some here in town. At the company, maybe at the university."

The chief stopped pacing for a minute and stared at the board. He rubbed at his forehead. "Can either of you link the two crimes? Ryan?"

On the whiteboard, the photo of Bill Rossman was beneath the photos of his father and his step-mother. When we had set it up, we were working just the one crime: the murder of his dad. Now we didn't know if the attack on Bill Rossman was part of the same crime, or even if it took place in our jurisdiction.

"Except for the last names of the two victims," Ryan said, "I'm not seeing anything. Lee Rossman knew his killer, trusted him. The killer was able to get close enough to him to stab him without a struggle. No defensive wounds. Bill Rossman—from what the surgeon told us—was stomped on, probably by a bunch of guys, then presumably they poured the fracking liquids down his throat. The MOs couldn't be more different."

"Karen?"

"Like Ryan said, I'm seeing two unrelated incidents. At the moment."

"What do you want to do?" the chief said.

"I've been in touch with the Marshall PD," I said. "Talked with the detective. He said if we wanted to come on out, he'd show us the crime scene, open the file for us, whatever we want."

"You want to take a drive?"

"I don't *want* to take a drive, but I think we should." I looked at Ryan. He looked resigned as he nodded.

"Catch me up on where you are with Lee Rossman," the chief said.

"Lee Rossman was having an affair with a stripper here in town. Name of Susan Warnock. They talked about art. He bought her a nice car. Meanwhile, Florence Rossman was doing a guy named Ron Eberly, who's a landman for the company. He and Lee go way back. Cheryl Garrity, the woman who runs the company day-to-day, used to be Lee's mistress and was not happy when Lee married Florence."

"Jesus." He closed his eyes slowly and kept them shut a moment. "You interviewed Bill Rossman before he got beat up?"

"That's right," Ryan said. "He keeps to himself. Hard to figure out where his head is, but he was alienated from his father and didn't think much of his step-mother. He likes his Aunt Cheryl, though. Mostly, he drinks beer and sleeps with girls he picks up in bars."

"When you were out there, did you see anything that would help with the attack on Bill?"

"No," I said. "We interviewed an unhappy rancher, guy named Mark Middleton. Thinks the company polluted his well water. He's the one who shoots at the company's vehicles at night. He resents that Lee didn't stop by his place when he complained. And he's pissed at Ron Eberly, who wrote the contract he signed."

"You don't like the rancher for beating up Bill."

"No, that's not at all his style. Besides, I'd be surprised if he knows Bill exists, or that he's working on a rig."

"And Eberly, the landman? He's fooling around with Florence. He had motive for killing Lee."

"Yeah," I said, "but not for attacking Bill." I turned to Ryan. "My impression is that Eberly saw himself as a kind of uncle to Bill. Did you get that, Ryan?"

Ryan nodded. "Called him Billy. Anything Eberly had against Lee, it didn't extend to Bill."

"So you don't see Eberly hiring a few guys to beat up Bill to throw us off the track?"

"I guess anything's possible, Chief." I shrugged. "But right now, I'd say no to that. If he brought in people to help, that would just increase his risk. The guys who beat up Bill wanted to send someone a message. We just don't know what the message is—and who it's intended for. No, there's something big we're not seeing yet."

"Remember you said how Cheryl Garrity called that professor a terrorist. Pouring the fracking fluid down his throat, that's a message." The chief was scowling. "What's her name?"

"Lauren Wilcox. We hadn't thought of that one, Chief. But we did send her photos to Allen Pfeiffer at the FBI. We're waiting on him to tell us if he's got her in a database."

"I don't like Lauren Wilcox at all for Bill," Ryan said. "It's too brute-force for her. She likes to work the system, exert political pressure. When the attack on Bill Rossman goes public, that's going to create all kinds of positive publicity for Rossman Mining, which is the opposite of what she wants."

"But only if the attack can be traced to Lauren Wilcox," the chief said. "If she's a terrorist, we shouldn't expect her to play by the rules. One way to look at it: two Rossmans down in three days."

"You thinking someone's gonna go after Florence next?" I said.

"Let me talk to Florence, see if she wants some protection."

"Just so you know, Chief, she and I just got into it, a half-hour ago. She's not my biggest fan right now."

"What happened?"

"Ryan and I tricked Ron Eberly into admitting the affair with her. When we were with her at the hospital, he phoned her and told her we knew about it. That's our guess."

"At least, that's what we think happened," Ryan said. "Right after she takes a call, she slapped Karen pretty hard, Chief. And threatened her."

"What?" The chief had his hands on his hips.

"She pointed her finger in Karen's face," Ryan said. "Then, 'You're dead.'"

"You heard that? Those words?"

"Those words."

The chief walked over to me and leaned in to look at my cheek, which was still a little sore. Plus there was a one-inch scratch, presumably from a ring. "She do that?"

I nodded. "No big deal."

He shook his head. "Want to charge her?"

"No. Just be aware, if she calls you, she might ask you to fire me or have me killed or something." I tried to smile.

"I'm going to discipline you because you found out she's having an affair?"

"Just giving you a heads-up," I said.

"Okay, so you're off to Marshall," the chief said. "Stay in touch."

Ryan and I started to leave when the chief called me back.

"Can you give me a second, Detective?"

Ryan left. I stood facing the chief.

"Talking about Florence Rossman reminded me. You need to decide what you want to do, I mean, about John McNamara."

"Oh, shit." I had forgotten about Mac.

"I'm willing to back you up one-hundred percent. Obviously, he'd have to cop to the B&E. You know, the broken door. I don't know about the assault. That might be your word against his. Did you go to the hospital or document it?"

I shook my head. "No, I didn't do any of that." I felt a pressure rising up inside my chest. "I'll decide by tonight. Can you give me till tonight?"

"Sure," he said. "Have you gotten in touch with your sponsor?"

"Yeah," I said. "I did. She was really helpful." She would have been. "Thanks for your concern, Chief."

I met up with Ryan in the detectives' bullpen and we got ready to head out to Marshall. The drive would take more than two hours—if the weather was good. So even if we needed only an hour out there, we wouldn't get back to Rawlings before seven or eight. Since it was real important for Ryan to eat dinner with his wife at six and play with his little kids before they went to bed, he was not at all happy as we walked out to the parking lot.

I asked him to drive. He said sure. He probably thought I asked because my face hurt or I was upset or something, but really I just wanted to give him something to do so he wouldn't sit there and brood. Driving to Marshall took some concentration, with one beat-up, rutted lane in each direction and gusts that threatened to push the Charger onto a soft shoulder, which could flip it and send you rolling a hundred feet into a pasture. And of course there was always the possibility that the guy steering the eighteen-wheeler bearing down on you at seventy-five miles an hour was taking a little nap.

The sky was light grey, with wispy clouds moving fast, but at least it wasn't snowing or icing up. With all the big truck tires chewing up the road between Rawlings and Marshall, the surface was clean, and we made good time. We stopped for a quick lunch at a burger place an hour out of Rawlings. It was full of truckers. I recognized a faint odor of diesel. Ryan ordered three salads because they didn't serve anything vegetarian.

A little after three-thirty, we pulled into the little police department in Marshall, Montana. It was brick, one story, a couple thousand square feet. There we met up with Detective Carpenter, the lead on the Bill Rossman case, and Officer Lloyd, the first officer on scene. We talked in a little conference room.

"Thanks for meeting with us," I said to Carpenter, a tall, thin guy of about fifty in insulated rubber boots, jeans, and a western shirt with snaps. His head was shaved, and a pair of reading glasses rested on his nose.

"I wish I could've saved you the drive. We don't have much to report."

"Any forensics at the scene?"

"A thousand sets of bootprints frozen into the mud. There was a glaze of ice all over everything when Officer Lloyd got there early this morning. We're working with your hospital to get the victim's clothing and effects back here for analysis, but I wouldn't hold out much hope we'll find anything on them."

"Either there or nearby." Lloyd was a beefy young guy with a jarhead cut.

"Are those the photos?" I pointed to a case folder.

He pushed the folder across the table to me. The photos showed Bill Rossman on his back. He was wearing his orange overalls, which were soaked and stained with all kinds of fluids. I remembered that his overalls were stained when we talked with him yesterday. He was wearing only one glove. One of his legs was obviously busted. His face was all pulped up.

"Did you recover his other glove?"

"No," Officer Lloyd spoke in little bursts. "Might be in the pit."

"Your guess is that Bill Rossman was beaten up right at the edge of the pit, where his body was discovered?"

Detective Carpenter said, "There's all kinds of nooks and crannies at a drill site where you could bring a guy and beat him up so as nobody would see you. If you got yourself a bucket of spent water beforehand, you could do the whole thing out of view, then dump him by the side of the pit. It wouldn't take but ten seconds to carry him out there."

"Detective," I said, "you get a chance to interview the guys who were on shift?"

"They didn't see or hear anything."

"You believe them?"

"None of them jumped out at me as lying."

"What do you mean?"

"If any of the guys knew what happened—or thought it was a good idea to beat up the guy and were in on it—they had their story all worked out and stuck to the script."

"Give me a scenario," I said.

Detective Carpenter waved a hand. "Could be a lot of things. Maybe Rossman found out they were violating operating procedures and was going to report them. Or he caught them smoking dope—or selling it. Anything that could happen at any workplace."

"No CCTV on the rig?" I said.

Detective Carpenter shook his head.

Ryan said, "His roommate at the man camp? Did you get a chance to interview him?"

Officer Lloyd spoke. "Went home for a couple weeks. No roommate at the time of the attack."

I put my hands up in a shit-out-of-luck gesture.

Detective Carpenter smiled weakly. "Welcome to Marshall."
He let out a breath. "Want to take a ride out to the scene?"

We bundled into our coats and piled into Detective
Carpenter's big Jeep, parked behind the building. In seven
minutes, we were out at the rig.

When we were here yesterday, the place was full of machine
noise, with generators, winches moving pipe around, metal chains
clanging on metal, and a loud background hiss of dirty water
flowing through a big pipe into the wastewater pit. Today, the
place was silent. "You shut it down?" I said to Detective
Carpenter as we started walking toward the wastewater pit.

"Our evidence tech is not quite done."

It was fifty yards to the wastewater pit. It stank of diesel, and
the surface was orange and slick. "It doesn't freeze?" I said to
Officer Lloyd.

"Lot of chemicals in that water."

"Show me where you found Bill Rossman."

Lloyd pointed about twenty yards away and started walking
over toward it. We followed him to where the surface sloped
down toward the pit. I didn't go any closer. With the sheet of ice
on the red clay, I could see myself sliding right in. I looked
around. They were right in saying the forensics at the scene
probably wouldn't help much.

"You've already interviewed the foreman?" I said.

"He's the first one we talked to," Detective Carpenter said.
"He called it in when one of his men discovered Rossman a half-
hour into the shift."

"And he doesn't know anything?"

"Only thing he knows is we're not letting him operate his
rig."

"Can we go talk to him?"

"Sure."

We walked over to the construction trailer where we had

talked with the guy briefly yesterday. Today he looked mighty unhappy. No formalities.

"When are you going to let me get back to work?" he said to me.

"It's Detective Carpenter's crime scene," I said. "Up to him."

"As soon as we can, Mr. Doering. Soon as we can," Carpenter said.

"You want to help Bill Rossman?" I said to Doering.

He gave me a nasty look, like I was getting off track.

"He's in the hospital in Rawlings," I said. "They're patching up all the injuries. Busted leg, busted pelvis. Took out his spleen. One thing you could help with. They're trying to figure out what was in the soup he drank out at the wastewater pit. The more they know, the better they can monitor him. Down the line, I mean. They've got the MSDS sheet, but it doesn't list all the chemicals in the fluid. You know what's in the fracking fluid you shove down the hole?"

"No, I don't." His expression was hostile, like I was a crazy woman who was going to ream him out about fucking up the planet. "That's corporate. The fluid is delivered in a truck. I put it in a holding tank, then I pump it down the bore hole and collect whatever comes back up."

"You got any ideas why someone would want to beat the living shit out of Bill Rossman?"

Doering shifted in his creaky old office chair. "I pump the fluid down the bore hole and collect whatever comes back up."

"Thanks for all the help, Mr. Doering," I said to the shithead.

The four of us left, got back in the Jeep, and made our way back to headquarters.

"Like I said," Detective Carpenter said when Ryan and I were walking over to the Charger, "I wish we could help you more."

"We appreciate it," I said as we exchanged cards. "Keep us in the loop, would you?"

"Sure thing," he said. We shook hands all around and headed off on the long drive back. With any luck, this would be the last time we had to visit beautiful Marshall, Montana. Ever.

I drove toward the sun, a hazy yellow glow behind the pale grey sky. The wind pushed the Charger back and forth. Ryan checked his watch and gazed out the window at the endless ranchlands and coulees. Every few minutes we saw an orange glow off in the distance, the methane being flared off a drilling rig.

"You want to stop and get something to eat?" I said an hour or so into the drive.

"Can if you want," he said. "Not on my account."

"I'm all right," I said. We'd been together enough to not have to talk about the case if there was nothing new to talk about. "Kali let you wake up the kids if you get in late?"

"For some reason, she'd rather let them sleep." He was wearing a sad smile.

We pulled into the lot at headquarters and went straight to our separate cars. I remembered I promised the chief I'd make up my mind about whether we were going to charge Mac for that attack the other night.

I drove over to the hospital and up to the ICU. The nurse at the desk told me he'd been discharged.

"Home?" I said.

"VA."

It was only four blocks away. I headed over. A woman at reception gave me the room number. The lights in the hall were low, even though it was only about eight-thirty. The doors to most of the rooms were open. The place was full of old guys, some of them asleep, a few watching small TV sets. One room had a couple guys playing cards. I walked past two young guys, one missing both legs, in a wheelchair, the other on crutches and missing only one leg. They looked at me with hollow eyes.

I made it to Mac's room. The police officer stationed in the hall looked at me without much curiosity. Through the window I could see two beds. Mac was in one, his head still bandaged. His daughter Maureen was in a chair up near the head of the bed. I stood there for a good three minutes. Mac didn't move. I think Maureen was asleep, too. She shifted her position, trying to get comfortable in the chair. She didn't open her eyes.

"My name is Seagate," I said, showing the officer my shield. "I'm the one he attacked."

The officer stood up.

I pulled out my phone and called headquarters. "Is Detective Pelton in?" The operator connected me. "Pelton, this is Seagate. I've decided not to file any charges on John McNamara. Yeah, I'm at the VA. Can you tell the sergeant? I'm gonna pull the uniform off his detail, okay?" He answered and we ended the call.

"Report to headquarters," I said to the uniform.

Chapter 23

Thursday morning, a couple minutes after eight, I got a call on my cell. It was Allen Pfeiffer at the FBI. "Not sure when you punch in, Karen. Didn't wake you, did I?"

"No, you nailed it," I said. "Eight sharp. Got anything?" I put my phone on Speaker. Ryan was already at this desk. He opened his notebook.

"Yes, I do." He sounded upbeat. "The facial-recognition software for domestic terrorists gave us a hit on your professor, Lauren Wilcox. She used to be Lauren Atherton when she was in Earth First!"

"Shit, what did she do?"

"We know she was a researcher. This was in the eighties. She'd track companies they didn't like—loggers, resort developers, that kind of thing—then publicize their activities on their newsletters, make it easier for protesters to mobilize against them.

"So she was nonviolent?"

"She did some monkeywrenching. You know, destroying equipment, chaining herself to trees. Setting off pipe bombs to start fires at building sites. We have outstanding federal warrants on her for destruction of private property at a resort near the Tahoe National Forest and another incident at the BLM Wild Horse and Burro Corral in Litchfield, California."

"She ever kill anyone?"

"Not that we know of. But she wrote this defense of a

terrorist op that killed a logger when his chain saw hit a spike."

"You don't know if she was involved in the op?"

"Correct."

"All right, Allen. What's she looking at?"

"She's going to go to jail, probably at least ten years. And there's a number of tort judgments against her and the group for monetary losses.

"Is that additional jail time?"

"No, that's a lot of companies lined up to take all her money."

"Can you hold off a little bit before picking her up?"

"How little?"

"We got this case, the oilman knifed in the alley three days ago. Then, yesterday, someone beat the shit out of his son, made him drink a bunch of poison drilling fluids."

"He dead, too?"

"No—at least not yet."

"And you like Lauren Atherton on those two?"

"We don't think it's the same person did both of them, but we're not yet ready to clear her on either of them."

"I can give you twenty-four hours."

"Forty-eight?"

"She's a flight risk." Allen Pfeiffer's tone was calm. He was just explaining what he was going to do—and why. All very reasonable. "If she gets a whiff you know who she is, she can get to Canada in two hours, anywhere in Europe before nightfall."

"She's a professor. In the middle of a semester. You really think she's gonna run?"

"I think it's quite likely. She's been underground for almost thirty years. She knows what she's looking at."

"Okay, twenty-four hours."

"Don't let her know, Karen." Now his tone was firm. "We really want to clear this case."

"I hear you. Thanks, Allen." I ended the call.

Ryan stood up and slipped into his suit jacket. "We need to tell the chief."

We walked out of the bullpen, down the hall.

"Is he in?" I said to Margaret. She picked up her phone and talked to him, then told us to go in. The chief looked up from his computer. "There's a federal warrant on our professor."

"What kind of warrant?"

"She was an eco-terrorist in the eighties."

"The FBI going to grab her now?"

"No, Allen Pfeiffer is giving us twenty-four hours. He told me to keep it from her, so she doesn't run."

The chief tapped a pencil on the edge of his desk.

"Chief, what if we just let the FBI bring her in? She's facing jail time for the terrorism, she might be more willing to talk to us about Lee Rossman and Bill Rossman."

The chief was silent as he thought about it. "Let me put in a call to the prosecutor's office, see what Larry Klein thinks."

"What're you worried about?" I said.

"I'm not exactly sure," the chief said. "With the two different jurisdictions—federal and county—I don't know, I'm just not confident I understand the implications. I don't want to jeopardize either of the cases on a technicality I didn't see. If Larry has any questions, he can call Allen Pfeiffer."

"Got it," I said.

"In the meantime," the chief said, looking at me, then Ryan, "do what Pfeiffer said: Her federal warrant doesn't leave this office."

"Chief," I said, "if she's got this terrorism stuff in her background, I'm liking her a little more on the Bill Rossman case. You see it that way?"

"First, I don't know if Bill Rossman is our case. Until you can put the crime in our county, it's Marshall PD's case—"

"Yeah, I get that," I said. "But if she has a history of getting her way by intimidation …"

"True, but she was in her twenties then. She's almost fifty. Maybe she grew up."

I didn't take it as a comment about me. "Just saying: It's a possibility."

"Agreed." The chief scratched at his cheek. "The way I'd handle it—if she can't alibi out of it—"

"How can anyone alibi out of hiring three or four guys to beat the kid up?"

Chief Murtaugh looked at me hard for a few seconds. "As I was saying, the way I'd handle it, if she can't alibi her way out of it, is to see if she has any history with Bill Rossman."

Ryan stepped in so I wouldn't piss off the chief again. "I think we can figure that out, Chief."

"Yeah, we can do that," I said. "And I'm sorry I interrupted. I just—"

"Just don't step on the FBI's case, all right?"

"Absolutely," I said. "Thanks."

Ryan and I made it back to the incident room. I was looking at the board, as if staring at a dozen photographs long enough was going to make the whole thing fall into place.

"I think the chief's right," Ryan said. "We need to figure out if Lauren Wilcox has an alibi for yesterday—and yes, I know she can't alibi out of hiring three or four guys to beat the kid up—"

"Very funny, twerp."

"Can't I make fun of you when you're rude to the boss?"

"Sure you can, but then you have to call over to the university to find out if Bill Rossman's ever taken a course from Lauren Wilcox."

"I'm happy to do it, Detective," Ryan said, with a smile, "because I always show the proper respect to my superiors—"

"Asshole."

"Even when they act like inferiors."

"Just do it." I waved him off.

He started whistling as he left, heading toward the detectives' bullpen. I hung around the incident room a few moments, staring at the board a little more. Then I realized we hadn't put in a request to look at Bill Rossman's phone records. I hurried down to the chief's office and asked Margaret to get that request in.

I got back to the bullpen when Ryan was just hanging up. "Bill Rossman took a junior-level course in water pollution from Professor Wilcox last Fall semester."

"How'd he do?"

"B+."

"You get a copy of the roster?"

He hit a key on his computer, then cupped his hand to his ear as the printer off in the corner of the bullpen started humming. He walked over to get it.

"Okay, good," I said. "Let's head over to campus and see if we can chat with the professor."

We drove over, bucking the morning traffic. The trip took six minutes instead of the usual four. I parked in the lot behind the Science Building, and we took the elevator to the Biology Department, on the fourth floor.

The receptionist was a student, maybe twenty years old, with long blond hair.

"I got it," Ryan said to me softly as we approached her. "Good morning," he said to her, flashing his toothy smile. I stayed out in the hall to let the youngsters do their thing.

A minute later, he came over to me, carrying a slip of paper and waggling his eyebrows.

I rolled my eyes. "Professor Wilcox have an alibi?"

"If teaching a course counts, yes, she does."

"But that doesn't mean she didn't hire a bunch of goons to beat up Bill."

"Let me go back and ask the girl at the desk about that." He smiled at me.

"Is she on campus now? Can we talk to her?"

"No and yes. She's out on the river, in Municipal Park, doing something with a class of kids and their teacher."

"You're kidding. It's ten degrees."

Ryan shrugged his shoulders. We headed back out to the Charger and drove the two miles to Municipal Park, which borders the Rawlings River.

"Did the girl say where in the park?"

"Near the picnic tables."

At least we could park nearby. There were three cars in the lot. The place looked desolate. A strip of patchy brown grass led to the picnic area, a dozen long picnic tables and some grills bolted to the concrete slab, all under a shingled shade roof supported by four thick timbers. Kids' backpacks were scattered on the tables. Thirty yards away, where the grass led down to a little sandy area at the edge of the river, were maybe fifteen kids, two young women, and Lauren Wilcox.

The kids were sitting on two benches in the sandy area. The two women were standing guard between the kids and the river. Lauren Wilcox, wearing a puffy down coat and waders, was in the river, gathering water in test tubes and jars.

Ryan and I stood there a moment, watching her. She looked like a natural teacher, smiling and animated as she emerged from the river, holding up the samples. She walked over to the kids, who gathered around her as she showed them what she had taken out of the river.

"This is our terrorist?" I said to Ryan.

"Maybe she did grow up."

"I'll see if I can grab her." I walked up to one of the women, introduced myself, and asked if I could speak with the professor a moment. She turned out to be a mom; she pointed me to the other woman. After I explained what I wanted, she walked over to Lauren Wilcox and whispered in her ear.

The professor knit her eyebrows and frowned, then handed the teacher the water samples and walked up the bank toward me, shaking the water off her pale, chapped hands. I led her back to where Ryan was standing on the grass.

"Sorry to interrupt," I said to her when the three of us were out of earshot. "Just need a minute." The wind was gentle, but I could feel, out here by the river, it was a couple degrees colder than it was downtown.

She looked at me, annoyed that I was taking her away from something she obviously enjoyed.

"Do you know a student named Bill Rossman?"

"Yeah, he was in a class with me—last year, I think. He's the son of Lee Rossman." Her expression became clouded. "Why?"

"He was attacked yesterday."

"I'm sorry to hear that," she said. "Is he okay?"

"Not really. Beat up pretty bad."

"That's terrible." She waved her arm toward the kids. "I didn't hear about it on the news. I was preparing to do this little class for the kids."

"It hasn't been on the news. We were wondering if you had any ideas about someone who'd want to hurt him."

She shook her head. "Don't know anything about him, really. He's not a major of mine. I haven't seen him in months."

"We think the attack occurred out in Marshall. He was working out there, at a rig."

"Like I said, I'm sorry to hear it. Must be very tough on his family. I mean, coming so soon after his father was killed."

"Yeah." I nodded. "Must be."

"Why did you come out here to tell me this? Bill Rossman's a pretty big guy." She put her hands together in mock fists and put on a boxer's scowl. "You think I beat him up?"

"Someone poured a bellyful of fracking fluids down his throat."

"What?"

"He was beat up, then he swallowed a quart of fracking wastewater."

"Who would do that to someone?"

"That's what we were hoping you could help us with."

"You're not thinking I had anything to do with it, are you?" She stepped away, like I was contagious.

"No," I said. "But you know everyone in the environmental community. If there's someone who would do it, we thought maybe you'd know that person."

"Detective." She leaned back in toward me. "I have spent my life trying to keep poisons out of the drinking water. I am trying—this morning—to educate ten-year-olds about water pollution, in the hope that maybe one of them will study science." She paused, shaking her head. "The idea that I would ever poison someone—it's just obscene. It's unbelievable. I would never do anything to hurt anyone, under any circumstances." She paused, then stuck her finger right up toward my face. "I'm beginning to think you might be mentally ill."

She turned and walked back toward the kids, fast.

Ryan spoke. "She said it. Not me."

"She didn't do it."

"And she didn't arrange to have a group of guys do it," he said.

"No, she didn't," I said. "Shit." I turned and we headed back to the Charger.

Chapter 24

"You're an intelligent young man," I said. "What the hell is going on?" I turned over the big engine in the Charger.

Ryan sighed. "I have absolutely no idea. I'm reasonably sure Lauren Wilcox had nothing to do with the attack on Bill Rossman."

"She didn't even know he got stomped on by a group of guys."

"That's right. And therefore I conclude she had nothing to do with pouring the fracking fluids down his throat," he said.

"She might've been an eco-terrorist a few decades ago," I said, "but I'm not seeing it now."

"Unless we get some new forensics, the only thing left to pursue now is Cheryl Garrity. You think it's a coincidence she called Lauren Wilcox an eco-terrorist—and she turns out to be correct?"

"What is the link between these two women?" I said. "Allen Pfeiffer didn't say anything about Lauren Wilcox attacking any of Rossman's operations, right?"

"No, he did not." Ryan was silent. "Why don't we ask Cheryl?"

I pulled out of the parking area at Municipal Park and headed downtown, to Montana Street. I parked in the garage under the big office building that housed Rossman Mining. We rode up to fourteen and walked into the offices.

The young receptionist recognized me and Ryan and gave us

a corporate smile. "Sorry," she said. "Ms. Garrity called in sick today. She said she's a little under the weather. If it's important, I can call her at home."

"No, that's not necessary," I said, "We'll catch up with her another time. Thanks very much."

The elevator hummed as it delivered us to the basement parking lot. Back in the cruiser, I said, "Get us her home address from DMV, would you?"

Ryan logged on and hit some keys. "She lives in the Madison Condominiums. Number 1503."

"That's one of the penthouses, right?" I said. "I've always wanted to see those places."

"Well, this is your lucky day."

I drove us the six blocks to the Madison Condominiums, which sit on the two top floors of Rawlings' best and biggest hotel. It's got convention space on the main level and hotel rooms up through twelve. There are only four units on fifteen, each one with a wrap-around balcony. It's where I plan to retire, after I marry an extremely rich guy and kill him with my sexuality.

We nosed into the garage, and I pulled a ticket from the machine. The gate rose, and I parked us in a reserved spot. We walked over to the elevators for the residences, but they required a special card. We had to go into the hotel and show our IDs to the kid at the desk, who really wanted to call Ms. Garrity to get her okay. I really didn't want him to, and I almost had to pull the plastic card out of his hand.

The elevator opened to a small area with the doors to the four units in the corners. For some reason, the space included some fancy upholstered benches, side chairs, and narrow tables up against the walls. I rang the doorbell at 1503.

In a minute, I heard the deadbolt click, and the door opened. "Detectives," Cheryl Garrity said.

"Good morning, Ms. Garrity," I said. "We need to speak with

you for a few minutes. Can we come in?"

She hesitated a moment. "Yes, of course." She stepped back.
"Please come in." We walked into the hallway, which was covered
in large marble tiles. "Can I take your coats?"

"No, thanks. We'll just be a minute."

She led us past the kitchen and dining area into the living
room. Off to the left was a big gas fireplace, with a widescreen on
the wall above it and a leather chair and sofa ringed around it. Off
to the right was a conversation area with a big couch and two
matching chairs, and a coffee table made of a thick cross-section
of a really old tree. Straight ahead was a wall of windows that
opened to the patio. Cheryl Garrity gestured for us to sit on the
big couch.

"I wasn't expecting you," she said.

They always say that. The reason they never expect us is that
we try very hard not to tell them we're coming. Otherwise, they
wouldn't be there when we arrived.

A buzzer rang four times from a hallway that led to the
bedrooms. "Would you excuse me a moment? I'm just doing a
load of laundry."

"Of course," I said.

She stood and walked down the hall.

"She's washing the fracking shit off her clothes now," I said
softly.

Ryan nodded his head gravely. "The only explanation I can
think of."

We walked over to the wall of windows. The foothills ringing
the town were covered in snow, the river a black strip slicing
downtown in half. If I lived in a place like this, I'd spend a lot of
time just watching the silent cars and trucks moving around town
like little toys. "This is some view, huh?"

"About one point six million dollars' worth."

"Really?"

"Really," he said.

I turned when I heard Cheryl Garrity's footsteps on the marble floor in the hallway. "I'm sorry," she said as we all took our seats again. "How can I help you?"

"We stopped by your office. They said you were a little under the weather." She looked fine.

"Yes, that's right," she said. "The events of the last few days ... very disturbing."

"I take it you've heard about the attack on Bill."

She put a hand to her temple. "Florence called me soon after she heard."

"We talked with her at the hospital. How is she doing?"

"Yes, she mentioned that she talked with you there." I couldn't tell whether Florence told her we mentioned her affair with Ron Eberly. "She's not doing at all well, as you can imagine."

"She has friends?"

"Yes, of course, she has many friends—and I count myself among them. But still, this week has been an absolute nightmare."

"And how are you doing?"

"At times like this, I find it best to stay busy. I'm working with the medical team at the hospital."

"How do you mean?"

"They wanted all the information about the ingredients in the fracking fluid. I authorized giving them that information. And I tasked one of my chemical engineers to be the liaison—I mean, if they have any questions about any of the materials we use."

"Ms. Garrity, we have interviewed Ron Eberly. Several times. He mentioned that you were a very important person in Bill's life, especially after the death of his mother. When we talked with Bill, a few days ago, he called you Aunt Cheryl ..."

Cheryl Garrity looked down at her lap, picking at a cuticle with her thumbnail. When she looked up, her eyes were glistening. "Detective, a long time ago, I was married for a brief period, but we had no children. Because of my role at Rossman Mining, I worked closely with Lee for many years. Those years coincided with Bill's childhood. Naturally, I spent some time with him. Lee and Helen were very good about making me feel like part of the family. Thanksgiving, Christmas, Easter—all the holidays. I think they felt a little sorry for me: you know, noplace to go. When Helen became ill—she was seriously ill for three years—I did spend more time with Bill." She wiped at her eye with a finger.

"Bill was like your son."

"I cannot speak for his feelings toward me. But I do love Bill as if he were my son." She struggled to maintain her composure. "To learn that he was attacked—in that way—is devastating." She paused. "I cannot express my sorrow—and my outrage."

"Can you help us understand why someone would do that to him? Who would do that to him?"

She shook her head. "If I knew ... I would tell you."

"Ms. Garrity, something else Ron Eberly told us."

She looked at me, tears running down her cheeks now. "What is that?"

"He said that you had a relationship with Lee Rossman but that Lee broke it off when he realized that you could not be both his business associate and his mistress. Is that true?"

She looked at me for a long moment. "Detective," she said, "I don't know anything about your life. Your personal life, that is. You have asked me questions about Bill Rossman, and I have answered you honestly. I understand that you have a right to ask questions. You are doing your job. But I don't see that any relationship I might have had with Lee Rossman, decades ago ... I just don't see how that is relevant either to his death or the attack on his son."

"And Ron Eberly said that you were able to deal with the end of your affair with Lee, but that when Lee married Florence, you responded very badly."

Her head jerked up. "That is preposterous." She paused a moment. "God gave me many blessings. I am reasonably intelligent. I am highly disciplined. And I am extremely loyal. But look at me, Detective. I am a very plain woman. I am aware of that. I do not pretend otherwise. A man like Lee Rossman … does it strike you as reasonable that a woman like myself could expect to keep a man like Lee Rossman? When there are women who look like Florence? So many, many women who look like Florence? Please give me some credit. I have long since come to peace with what I might expect to receive in this life."

"Ms. Garrity, about something else you mentioned the other day. It's about Lauren Wilcox, the professor."

Cheryl Garrity was breathing a little heavily. "What would you like to say?"

"You mentioned that she is an eco-terrorist. You spelled out her name. We wrote it down."

"Yes, I remember."

"We did considerable research and—I have to be honest with you—we didn't find any evidence at all that she is an eco-terrorist. Can you help us with that? Why did you use that word?"

"I used that word because that is exactly what she is. She attacked Rossman Mining."

"What do you mean?" I heard my phone ring from inside my leather bag. I reached in and turned it off.

"She hacked our data system. She breached our security."

"How do you know it was her?"

"The attack came from her account at Central Montana State University."

"Did she try to sabotage your system?"

"She did not try to post anything offensive on it, if that is what you mean. However, she did attempt to install programs—I don't remember what my IT people called them—that would enable her to monitor our activities. And she combed through our e-mail system."

"Do you know if she found what she was looking for?"

"I don't know what she was looking for. We have nothing to hide, of course. All our operations are completely aboveboard and legal."

"Have you eliminated the threat? Removed the software?"

"We believe we have—but that's a question that cannot be answered definitively. We might learn, sometime in the future, that we have not completely eliminated the threat."

"Are you going to take legal action against her?"

"We are considering it. I mean, we were until … until this week. Now I don't know what Florence will decide to do. I certainly know what I will recommend, should she ask me."

"What is that?"

"I would come at Lauren Wilcox with everything I have. If the world knew what kind of person she is, she would be totally discredited."

"Which would help the oil industry."

"It would help the United States, Detective." Her voice was clipped. "Have you read anything she has written?"

"Some."

"Did you read the essay she wrote about her hero?"

"I don't believe I did."

"Her hero is Ho Chi Minh." She wiped at her eyes with her thumb and forefinger. "Do you know who I'm referring to?"

I recognized the name but couldn't place it. I turned to Ryan.

"From the Vietnam War?" he said.

"That's right." She nodded to Ryan, then turned back to me. "He was the leader of North Vietnam. He was a brutal dictator, a mass murderer. He said you can kill ten of our men for every man of yours we kill, and in the end you will tire of it and we will win. Lauren Wilcox sees the struggle against the oil industry as a revolutionary struggle. The oil industry is the colonial power, with endless riches and influence. And the environmental community—her corner of the environmental community, at least—are the freedom fighters." She paused, and the tears started again. "Ho Chi Minh cut down tens of thousands of American men. One of them was my father. In 1968. And yet she views him as a hero. She's not only irrational, she's a traitor." The tears were flowing freely down her face now. "And that is what I know about Lauren Wilcox."

I looked at Ryan, who nodded slightly. We stood up. "Thank you very much for your time, Ms. Garrity. Hope you feel better."

She didn't not respond, and Ryan and I let ourselves out.

Chapter 25

We sat in the Charger in the garage beneath Cheryl Garrity's extremely nice condo. "You believe her?" I said to Ryan.

"Absolutely."

"That she loved Bill Rossman like a son?"

"Absolutely."

"So she didn't have anything to do with attacking him."

"Don't waste our time, Karen."

"That she was okay when Lee Rossman dropped her and married Florence?"

"Absolutely."

"Why?"

"Because her explanation was completely rational, and she is a rational person."

"You mean the bit about how she knows she's a plain woman who couldn't keep a man like Lee Rossman?"

"That's the explanation I'm referring to."

"Which makes Ron Eberly a liar when he said Cheryl Garrity went batshit."

"The guy who said the thing he was proudest of in his life was that he never let Lee down—while he's sleeping with Lee's wife?"

"What's Eberly's motivation for lying to us about Cheryl?" I said.

"Three possibilities. One, he wants to portray everyone as powerless to exert any control over the emotions of love—"

"Why would he do that?"

"So he could pretend that his affair with Florence is a grand passion and he's therefore exempt from the bourgeois rules of sexual fidelity."

"I heard some sounds coming out of your mouth. Did you just say something?"

"So it wasn't his fault for nailing Florence."

"And the second possibility?"

"To deflect attention away from himself."

And the third?"

"Some people are just liars. They don't need a motivation."

"Okay, you believe Cheryl about Lauren Wilcox hacking the company's computers?"

"Absolutely. It's just the sort of thing Lauren Wilcox would do."

"The Lauren Wilcox out at the river? Showing the kids the crap in the water?"

"The Lauren Wilcox with a federal warrant," Ryan said.

"It's illegal. You see her as risking everything to snoop around on the company's system?"

"If you've never gotten caught, you begin to think you won't get caught. Nobody's smart enough to catch you. Besides, she's not blowing anything up. Nobody's going to be injured."

"What did you think about the Ho Chi Minh quotation?"

"I'm familiar with the quotation, although I wasn't aware that Lauren Wilcox had used it in her writing. But yes, it's totally plausible that Lauren Wilcox would see herself as a guerilla fighter battling a colonial empire. It helps her feel justified in breaking laws."

"Because the laws are there to protect the colonial empire," I said.

"That's right."

"And her father dying in Vietnam?"

"Absolutely. I did the math. Totally plausible."

"I was a little surprised you didn't mention an older brother dying in Vietnam."

"I wanted to, but, like I said, I did the math."

"All right, then. Who attacked Bill Rossman?"

"Why do I have to do everything? I just explained to you why Cheryl Garrity was telling the truth. Why don't you figure out who attacked Bill Rossman?"

My phone rang. I pulled it out of my big leather bag. It was Larry Klein, our prosecutor. I put it on Speaker.

"Hey, Larry, what's up?"

"The chief ran your question past me. About whether we should let the FBI grab up Wilcox on the old federal warrants."

"Yeah, what do you think?"

"I wouldn't do it that way. I'd use whatever time the FBI has given you to work on her for the Bill Rossman case. That one might be attempted murder, whereas the federal warrants are mostly property damage."

"Even with the logger getting hurt?"

"Yeah, it would be impossible to show intent. Bottom line, we're in a better position if we treat the incidents separately. Make the Bill Rossman case—if you can make it. If we bundle the cases and the feds screw it up or decide not to prosecute it or whatever, we could be left with nothing."

"Is Chief Murtaugh on board with this?"

"I already talked to him. He agrees."

"Just so you know, we don't think Lauren Wilcox had anything to do with attacking Bill Rossman, but maybe she hacked the Rossman Mining servers."

"Interesting. That sounds a little more her speed. What I'm saying is, use your time to collect as much evidence as you can before the FBI comes calling."

"Okay, Larry, thanks a lot." I ended the call and saw that I had a message from ten minutes before. It was headquarters.

"That call? When we were in Cheryl's living room? One of the admins: Bill Rossman's phone records are on our desks."

I headed out of the garage, handed the attendant his ticket and showed him my shield, then drove us back to headquarters.

We hustled back to the detectives' bullpen. "What are you seeing?" I said to Ryan, who was looking at his own copy of the phone records.

"Same thing you're seeing: what the heck is Bill Rossman talking to Nathan Kress about?"

I sank into my chair and studied the printout. A total of five calls between the two of them, the latest one from Nathan Kress to Bill Rossman around seven in the morning yesterday—the day the kid was attacked. "This making any sense to you?"

"Not yet," Ryan said. "I see five calls. The shortest, nine seconds; the longest, almost six minutes."

I picked up my phone and dialed the chief's office. "Margaret, the chief in?" She said yes. "Could you ask him to meet us in the incident room? We're heading over there now." She said she'd ask him.

When he got there, Ryan and I were sitting on office chairs, looking at the board. "Hey," the chief said. "What've you got?" He sat on the edge of a desk.

I stood up and walked over to the board. "Two things we want to tell you. See if you can figure them out. Ryan and I are just spinning our wheels."

"Go ahead."

I pointed to the photo of Cheryl Garrity. "We interviewed her this morning. She knows all about Bill Rossman being attacked. That makes sense."

"Florence told her," the chief said.

"So we ask her about her comment, from Monday, that Lauren Wilcox is an eco-terrorist, which we now know is true."

The chief nodded, like that was worth talking about.

"She tells us Lauren Wilcox hacked the Rossman Mining IT system, planted some kind of program to spy on them."

"She knows this how?"

"Her IT people traced it to her account at the university."

The chief looked skeptical. He turned to Ryan. "Isn't it possible that the hacker just made it look like it came from the university?"

Ryan said, "I wouldn't be surprised. We could ask Jorge about that."

"Plus," the chief said, "there's got to be hundreds of computers on campus an outsider could use to launch an attack from."

"Sure," Ryan said. "A student is checking her email, forgets to log off, walks away."

"What Cheryl Garrity seemed to be really pissed about was that Lauren Wilcox published some stuff about how cool Ho Chi Minh was."

The chief looked puzzled. "Ho Chi Minh? North Vietnam?"

"Seems Cheryl's father died in Vietnam."

The chief scratched at his cheek. "Cheryl Garrity might be looking for someone to blame her father's death on, and Lauren Wilcox might fit."

"Is there any crime that's been committed? I mean, the hacking?"

The chief shook his head. "Not until someone reports it."

"There's nothing we can do to see if it happened?"

"If you can tie it to the Lee Rossman murder or the attack on Bill Rossman—and show that the Bill Rossman attack was in our jurisdiction—then I can present it to Larry, and he'll get us a warrant to search the Rossman IT system. But I need probable cause. All we've got now is an employee saying her system was compromised."

The chief was right. We didn't know there was any hacking,

and if there was, we didn't know who did it. What did we know? We knew diddly.

"All right: one other thing." I walked over to the photo of Nathan Kress, the president of Rivers United. "This guy's talked to Bill Rossman five times in the last week. Most recently, he phoned Bill Rossman at seven AM yesterday, the day the kid was attacked."

"What do we know about Kress?"

"He's the well-behaved environmental guy in town. The one Lauren Wilcox thinks is too soft."

"He the one who had the sick kid you said Lee Rossman paid the medical bills for?"

"Yeah, that's him. He has a good alibi for killing Lee Rossman. We didn't think he had any connection to the Bill Rossman attack." I paused. "So we're not seeing what Kress and Bill Rossman were talking about. You see something Ryan and I are missing?"

He sat there on the edge of the desk, giving it some thought. "No," he said. "I'm not seeing anything." He paused. "I think I'd have another go at him. Squeeze him a little harder."

"Thanks, Chief."

He nodded and left. We went back to the bullpen, got our coats, and headed over to Nathan Kress' house, downtown. Knocked on the door. A middle-aged woman wearing a thick hand-knit sweater opened up.

"Good morning, ma'am. Detectives Seagate and Miner to see Nathan Kress. Is he in?"

"Yes, he is," she said. "Come in."

We waited in the entryway while his wife went upstairs to get him. I left my coat on in the chilly house.

"Detectives," Nathan Kress said, halfway down the stairs. "You have something to tell me about Lee Rossman?"

"Good morning, Mr. Kress," I said. "You have a minute to

speak with us?"

"Of course," he said, leading us to the sitting room where we had interviewed him the other day. He gestured for us to sit.

"Thank you," I said. "No, sorry. Nothing to report about Lee Rossman. We want to talk to you about his son."

"Bill Rossman?" He looked confused. "What about him?"

"Could you tell us what your relationship with Bill Rossman is?"

"I'm not sure I'd call it a relationship. I met him through Lee, of course. Lee had me and my wife and our son out to their house several times ... Have you ever been to their house? Overlooking the reservoir?" He smiled.

I didn't. "Yes, we have."

"It's spectacular, isn't it?" He was still smiling.

I said nothing and showed nothing. Finally, his smile faded.

"This was a couple of years ago. As I said, we talked. Bill is a very intelligent boy. Well, he must be a man, now."

"What did you talk about?"

"Well, any number of things. He's interested in the oil business—of course—but he's also quite knowledgeable about my side of the equation—"

"I'm sorry, I didn't ask the question clearly enough. What did you talk about yesterday morning, at 6:57 AM for six minutes?" I turned to Ryan, who was pulling the phone log out of his suit jacket pocket. "Would you like me to list the other calls between you and Bill Rossman?"

He shifted in his chair. "No, no. That won't be necessary. Yes, we have spoken on the phone a few times recently—"

"Yes, you have." I looked at him hard. "And I'm asking—for the last time—what did you talk about?"

"I don't understand what is going on. We talk about any number of things. Environmental things. Life out in Marshall ... I've never worked on an oil rig ..."

I stood and walked over to Nathan Kress, lowering myself onto my knees. I leaned in to look closely at his face. "You keep this house about forty goddamn degrees, and yet you seem to be sweating, Mr. Kress. Right above your upper lip. Are you okay?"

"Yes," he said, pulling back. "I'm just a little confused about why you're grilling me about a perfectly innocent friendship I've developed with Lee Rossman's son. You're scaring me, is all." His finger came up to his face and he wiped away the sweat. "What's going on?"

"What did you speak with Bill Rossman about yesterday morning, at 6:57, for six minutes?"

"I ... I don't remember specifically. About mining, I think."

"At 6:57 in the morning?"

"He must have been getting ready to begin a shift. That's when he called me."

Ryan said, "You called him."

"Yes, you're right." He smiled. "I was returning his call from the day before."

"Do you know where Bill Rossman is, right now?"

Nathan Kress furrowed his brows. "No, I don't. I imagine he's at the rig. Working."

"No, Mr. Kress," I said. "Bill Rossman is in the ICU at Rawlings Regional."

The color drained from Kress' face. "Oh, my God. What happened?"

I just looked at him. "He was attacked. Beaten, very badly. The doctors had to remove his spleen. And someone poured fracking wastewater down his throat."

Nathan Kress let out a cry of pain and slumped forward in his chair. He began to weep, out of control.

His wife rushed into the room. "What is happening in here?" she said.

I turned to her and waved her off. Ryan stood, walked over to her, and told her he was okay. He led her out of the room.

I leaned in, a foot away from his head. "The police tell us Bill Rossman was attacked right after you spoke with him at 6:57 for six minutes. Now, can you tell me what you were talking about?"

"Is he going to be all right?"

"I very much doubt that, Mr. Kress. What were you talking about?"

He shook his head.

I couldn't tell if he was saying he wasn't going to tell me or he couldn't talk. I didn't move.

After a minute, Kress began to pull himself together. He retrieved a tissue from his pants pocket and tried to dry his face. "He said he wanted to meet with me. Said he needed to talk with me."

"What about?"

"I asked him that. He wouldn't say."

"Where did he want to talk to you?"

"He said it didn't matter. In Marshall, here in Rawlings, somewhere in between."

"So what did you say?"

"I told him this wasn't a good time. I had some commitments here, with Rivers United, I mean. And with my family."

"So what did he say?"

"Just that it was important. That he needed to meet with me. I was the only person he could trust."

"About what?"

"I don't know. He wouldn't say. It was too dangerous to discuss on the phone. But that I had to meet him."

"So how did you leave it with him?"

"I said I'd get back to him later today. I needed to check my schedule and see what I could do."

"Mr. Kress, is there anyone who can vouch for where you were yesterday?"

A look of horror came over his face. "Do you think I might have had something to do with this?"

"Is that a no?"

"No, of course it's not. My wife—she knows I was here all day. I work right here, in the house."

"All right, Mr. Kress." I straightened up and stood. "If you can remember anything more specific—I mean, about what you and Bill Rossman talked about—I want you to get in touch with me." I handed him my card. "We're going to give this information to the Marshall Police Department. They don't know who attacked Bill Rossman. They might want to get in touch with you." I let that idea hang in the air.

Chapter 26

We were driving back to headquarters, somewhat down because Nathan Kress didn't tell us anything useful about what he and Bill Rossman chatted about on the phone, when I got a call from Detective Carpenter in Marshall.

"Hey, Detective," I said. "Good to hear from you. What's up?" I put the phone on Speaker.

"Calling to let you know we got the guys who beat up Bill Rossman."

"Talk to me."

"We tracked down Bill Rossman's roommate from the man camp. Guy named Andy Bellows. He was home for a two-week R&R. Anyways, he told us three roughnecks came to the room looking for Bill, the night before the attack. They were real pissed off, but he wasn't there. The roommate knew the guys, gave us their names. Turns out they're on the same crew as Bill Rossman."

"Why were they looking for him?"

"They saw him draining some wastewater out of the truck that hauls it away. They asked him what he was doing. He gave them some answer they didn't like. So next morning they confronted him again, beat the crap out of him. After he was unconscious, poured the wastewater down his throat."

"What did the guys think Bill was doing?"

"Not exactly sure, but they concluded it wasn't good. If you're pulling some dirty water out of the truck, they figure you're going to analyze it. Guess they thought Bill was working for someone who wants to prove that the wastewater is dirtier than the company admits."

"And if the wastewater is dirty, the rig could be shut down— at least temporarily."

"The three guys aren't the smartest boys in town, but that seems to be their thinking."

"Okay, so where do you stand with the three guys?"

"We separated them, offered them each a good deal for rolling on the others. Two of them wouldn't talk to us, but the third one says he didn't actually kick Bill Rossman or pour the shit down his throat. He's the one who talked to us. We're working with our prosecutor right now to figure out what charges to file on them. But I wanted you to know that we got it under control. The crime occurred right where we thought it did: on the drilling site."

"Excellent work, Detective. That's great news. Thanks for catching us up," I said and ended the call. "Shit."

"I understand the 'great news,'" Ryan said. "But why the 'Shit'?"

"'Shit' because the two cases are now in two jurisdictions, and it's gonna be harder for us to link them together." I kept driving toward headquarters.

"Talk me through that."

"Nathan Kress on the phone with Bill Rossman a couple minutes before he gets beat up. What do we do with that? Write it up, send it to Carpenter?"

"Well, yeah, we ought to do that, but that doesn't mean we can't use it on the Lee Rossman case."

"All right," I said. "We'll be at headquarters in five minutes. You're you; I'm the chief. Explain to me what we ought to do about Nathan Kress and how we link Bill Rossman and the dirty water to the murder of Lee Rossman. Remember, the crimes occurred in different jurisdictions. And were committed by different people."

He was silent. Finally, he said, "The key is to understand why the three guys beat up Bill Rossman. Right now, all the police in Marshall have is the one guy who says it's about dirty water."

"But that guy only made a statement. He wasn't deposed, wasn't testifying under oath. For all we know, he didn't even have an attorney present when he talked."

"All of which works in our favor," Ryan said. "If we can push Nathan Kress a little more and get a better idea of what Bill Rossman was up to, we might be able to link the dirty water to corporate."

"And if we can do that," I said, "there's the link to Lee Rossman. Which lets us investigate Cheryl Garrity, the number two in the company."

"Maybe," Ryan said. "But unless she's willing to formally report the hacking, how are we going to investigate her?"

"Like I said before, shit." I pulled the Charger into the parking area behind the headquarters, and we made it to our desks. I hung my coat over the back of my chair.

"How are we going to go after Lauren Wilcox if Cheryl Garrity doesn't report a crime?"

"If we could look at Lauren's account at the university, we might be able to tie her to Nathan Kress and Bill Rossman and link the two cases that way."

"You're thinking maybe Bill Rossman was working with both of them but he used phones with Nathan Kress and email with Lauren Wilcox?" Ryan said.

"I'm not sure what I'm thinking, but if Bill was attacked because of something at Rossman—"

"Not because he was snaking someone else's girl—"

"That's right, the two crimes have to be related. We're just not getting it yet. Why was Bill taking the dirty water? And how does that link up with his father's murder?"

"Let's take a walk down to the incident room," Ryan said. "I want to come at this a different way."

We left the detectives' bullpen and rushed to the incident room.

"We're not having any luck linking the two crimes. Let's see if we agree on who we still like?"

"For which crime?" I said.

"Doesn't matter. Let's just see who we think is clean, who isn't."

I waved at him to go ahead. I settled into a chair. Ryan walked over to the board. "Susan Warnock, Lee Rossman's girlfriend. Any evidence she's involved with either crime?"

"Not that I can put my finger on." I thought a second. "Put it this way: There's nothing we can use to push her harder."

"Agreed," Ryan said. "Ron Eberly, Florence's boyfriend."

"Except that he's a scumbag who stabbed his best friend in the back—"

"But there's no evidence he stabbed him in the front."

"Very nice," I said. "But yeah, nothing we can pursue unless some new evidence turns up."

"And it's the same with Florence." Ryan said. "We can come up with motives for almost everyone, but nothing that gives us probable cause to go looking for more."

"So unless Lee Rossman was stabbed by a hooker or a thief, we're left with only three players we can squeeze: Lauren Wilcox, Nathan Kress, and Cheryl Garrity. Am I leaving someone out?"

Ryan looked at the board again. "That's all there is." He stood there, hands on his hips.

"Of the three of them," I said, "the one who's gonna talk first is Nathan Kress. Obviously, Lauren Wilcox is gonna do everything she can not to cooperate, and Cheryl Garrity has lots of experience dealing with regulators and protesters. She's tough.

I say we go at Nathan again."

"How?"

"Drive back to his place. Put him in the cruiser, throw him in Interrogation, let him look at the bracelets on the table for twenty minutes, then we come at him hard. I don't believe him when he says he doesn't know what Bill Rossman wanted to talk about."

"You want to tell the chief?"

I thought a second. "No, it's just a follow-up interview."

We headed out, back to Nathan Kress's cold, dark house. Through the gate, up the walk. I rapped on the door, hard. Ryan looked at me. "It's all in the wrist."

The footsteps were rapid. Kress opened the door. "Detectives," he said, "you scared me."

"Sorry, Mr. Kress." There was no sorrow in my voice. "You need to come to the station with us, right now. Make a statement."

"I don't understand." His voice was high-pitched, his eyes wide. "We just spoke. I told you everything I know."

"You're gonna tell us again. Let's go."

"I need to tell my wife where I'm going."

"You have fifteen seconds. If you're not back in fifteen seconds, you wear handcuffs. Understand?"

He nodded and rushed back into the house.

"Easy does it," Ryan said.

"I'm tired of people jerking me around. Every damn thing he knows, I'm gonna get it. Now."

Nathan Kress hurried back to the front door, looking flush and out of breath. Ryan put him in the back seat, pushing his head down like they do on TV, to add to the atmosphere.

"What are you doing?" Kress said. "What do you think I'm not telling you?"

"We're bringing you in to make a statement. We'll turn the recorder on. That way, when it gets to court, there's no question about who said what. In the meantime, sit tight and do what we say."

"When what gets to court?"

I had no idea. So I didn't say anything.

We walked Kress in through the front entrance, with its lobby full of flags and photos of the president, the governor, and all the police chiefs. Then, inside the steel door, around the sergeant's desk, where a couple of uniforms were processing the misdemeanors and low-level felons wearing cuffs and sitting on the wooden benches. Coming through the front entrance gives you a clearer sense that we're cranking up the machine.

We put Kress in Interview 1, the room with handcuffs attached to a bar on the beat-up metal table. "Stay here," I said to him. Ryan and I left, walked through the door labeled Utility, and checked on him through the glass. He was squirming and sweating.

"He's not going to need twenty minutes," Ryan said.

"Okay, ten," I said. "I'm gonna hit the ladies'. See you back here in ten."

When I got back, Ryan was still looking through the window. Kress was sitting there with his head in his hands. It was time.

"Let's go," I said. I'd brought with me the dummy folder full of scrap paper with the words "Rossman, William" written in Sharpie on the tab. I dropped it on the table. Ryan walked over to the controls for the video recorder on the wall. He turned it on. I announced the date and time and who was in the room.

"Okay, Mr. Kress. You told us earlier that you were in communication with Bill Rossman early yesterday morning, before he went to the rig. You told us Rossman said he wanted to meet with you. That is what you told us, isn't it?"

"Yes." His voice was shaky. "Yes, that is the truth."

"And you said you didn't know why he wanted to meet with you. Is that correct?"

He tried to speak, but his throat seized up. He cleared it. "Yes."

"That's not true, Mr. Kress. You do know why Bill Rossman wanted to meet with you."

Nathan Kress looked terrified, which was what I was hoping for. I've done this at least a hundred times: accusing people of knowing shit they say they don't know. Their faces tell you what will happen next. If they really don't know, they look real confused about why you think they're not telling you everything. If they're hardasses, they look defiant, sometimes even confident, like you can bully them all you want, but they're not going to answer because there's nothing more to say and you can't prove there is. But when they look terrified like Kress did now, it's because they're thinking a few moves down the board, wondering how we got the information that's going to ruin their day.

"Best thing you can do right now, Mr. Kress, is tell us the truth. We don't think you're implicated in the attack on Bill Rossman, but if you withhold evidence, we have to re-think that. Bill Rossman told you why he wanted to meet, didn't he?"

Kress's eyes darted to the left, then back at me, then down to his hands on the table. He was about to tell me.

He lowered his head to the table and started to moan in agony. He started hyperventilating and crying, the snot and spit all over the scratched steel table. Ryan looked at me, as if he wanted to do something to help him or get help or something. I put up my palm to tell him not to move.

The three of us sat there, Kress falling apart, trying to get control of himself. After a couple of moments, he raised his head and looked at me, his face pale and wet and disgusting. "He was going to give me the sample of the waste water."

"Why was he going to do that?"

"I told him I could get it analyzed for him."

"What did he think you were gonna find out about it?"

"That it was dirtier than the company reported."

"Reported to who?"

"The EPA."

"Why did he come to you?"

"Said he trusted me."

"Why did he trust you?"

"I don't know. His father trusted me. I don't know."

"Why didn't you just tell us this?"

"It's illegal."

"What is?"

"The dirty water is sealed after it's pumped into the truck. Breaking the seal is a violation."

"So you were afraid you'd conspired to break the law?"

He looked at me, wiping his face with the palm of his hand. "I should have told him not to do it. Not to get mixed up in something like that. I should have known. The guys he worked with …" He started breaking down again.

"What about them?"

"What happened to Bill is my responsibility."

"What was Bill going to do with the information, the analysis? Who was he gonna tell?"

Nathan Kress shook his head, unable to speak.

"Did Bill Rossman say anything about Lauren Wilcox?"

He looked confused. "I don't know what you mean."

"Those times you talked to Bill Rossman on the phone, did he mention Lauren Wilcox? Did he say anything about going to her the way he was going to you?"

"No, he never mentioned Lauren Wilcox."

"And did you ever say anything about her? Anything about you working with her on analyzing the dirty water?"

He wiped at his nose. "No, I never did. Nobody ever said anything about Lauren Wilcox."

Chapter 27

"Chief, we want to get you up to speed on the Bill Rossman case." Ryan and I were sitting in his office. The chief had also invited Larry Klein, our prosecutor, because we needed his help.

"Go ahead," the chief said.

"Nathan Kress told us everything he knows about what happened with Bill Rossman out in Marshall. At least, we think he did. We came at him pretty hard. Bill Rossman was attacked because he grabbed some dirty water and was gonna take it to Nathan Kress, who offered to get it analyzed."

Larry Klein leaned forward in his chair. "Who attacked him?"

"Three of his buddies on the drilling rig. They thought he was trying to shut down the rig or something by showing that the wastewater was dirtier than the company said it was."

"Okay," the chief said. "The crime occurred in Marshall, right? It's their case, then."

"Yeah," I said, "but it's the key to the murder of Lee Rossman."

The chief shifted in his chair. "Explain."

"The attack on Bill Rossman was motivated by his actions on the drilling rig. It had something to do with company policy and operations."

Larry Klein spoke. "Not necessarily. That hasn't been established yet. That's what the three guys are asserting—"

"Actually," I said, "it's only one of the three guys—the one who wants to cop to a lesser charge."

Larry Klein waved his hand dismissively. "Worse yet."

"All right," I said. "I understand it's not proven, but at least it's evidence. It's the link we're looking for to tie it to Rossman Mining."

"Tell me the story." Larry Klein sat there in his black suit, his right leg folded beneath his left knee. His expression was beyond skeptical. Just this side of contemptuous. "What are the issues?"

"Cheryl Garrity says Lauren Wilcox hacked the Rossman Mining data system," I said, "planted some spy software on them."

"Has the company brought it to you?"

"No."

"Until she does that—or files it in civil court—it didn't happen. Next?"

"I want to look at Lauren Wilcox's email at the university."

"I want to be taller," Larry Klein said.

"If we can see that she did hack the company, that brings us one step closer to understanding what was going on at the company, which gets us one step closer to understanding why someone killed Lee Rossman."

"What's your rationale for asking for a warrant?"

"Terrorism."

"Unless it was a hooker and her boyfriend who killed Lee Rossman, in which case it's manslaughter. Tell me how you know it's terror."

"If Lauren Wilcox killed Lee Rossman to intimidate his company—to make them stop drilling—and someone attacked Bill Rossman to intimidate the company—remember, it's two guys named Rossman—that's terrorism, isn't it?" I said.

"You can't search a person because you might find what you hope to find, Karen. The Fourth Amendment says you can't."

Ryan said, "If we search her university email, that's not protected by the Fourth Amendment. She has no reasonable expectation of privacy."

Larry Klein shook his head. "Still need probable cause."

I said, "But she already has a federal warrant for terrorism."

"When was that case?"

"Nineteen eighty-six."

"Statute of limitations," Larry Klein said, frowning.

"Not on murder," I said. "The logger died."

"'Died' isn't murder. It's negligent homicide at best. And you don't even know if she was implicated in it."

"She talked it up in a newsletter."

"First Amendment."

The chief spoke. "Larry, does it go to pattern?"

"No, not close enough. The crimes are too different—first-degree murder and negligent homicide—and too distant from each other in time." He put up his hands in frustration. "You don't have probable cause. You have a fishing expedition. I'm not going to file for a warrant."

Over the years I've learned that when Larry begins a sentence with "I'm not going to …," that's the end of the discussion.

Ryan, who hadn't yet learned that, said, "Does the Patriot Act give you a pretext?"

"It might," Larry Klein said. "I'm not an expert on that. But my instinct is that things will go smoother if a federal prosecutor files the order—especially since there's already an outstanding federal warrant."

"Larry," the chief said, "how would you feel if we brought it to the FBI? Maybe they can figure out how to piggyback it on their terror warrant."

"Be my guest."

"I don't like it," I said.

Larry Klein turned to me. "What's not to like?"

"We have different goals. I want to find out if Lauren Wilcox killed Lee Rossman—or had his son beat up and poisoned. The feds want to clear a thirty-year-old terror case."

"Work it out with the FBI," Larry Klein said. "Make it a *quid pro quo*. They agree to your terms, you give them the lead."

"Will they screw me over?"

"If it's in their interest." He smiled. "But I don't see that you have a lot of other options."

"Would you help us?"

"What do you want?"

"Two things," I said. "First, we get access to the whole file they generate. Second, if they find something linking Lauren Wilcox to the murder of Lee Rossman or the attack on his son, you get to file charges first. Is that reasonable?"

"I'm not sure that's the right question to ask, but I don't mind trying."

I took out my phone and speed dialed Allen Pfeiffer. "Hey, Allen, Karen Seagate in Montana. I got my county prosecutor here with me. Name's Larry Klein. We've got some new information for you about Lauren Wilcox, but Larry wants to talk to you about how we can go forward with it. Can I put him on?" I listened to Allen for a moment. "Okay," I said, "here he is." I handed the phone to Larry Klein.

"Klein," he said. I reached over and hit the Speaker button. "Karen Seagate's got this lead that she thinks might help you with your terror case against Lauren Wilcox, but she'd like to reach an understanding with you about process."

"What does she want?"

"She'd like a copy of the file, and the first shot at Lauren Wilcox if you find out she's implicated in a felony murder or attempted murder here in Montana."

"Best I can offer her is I'll try."

Larry turned to me. "Good enough?" He was nodding his head, telling me to say yes.

I shook my head and whispered, "Not good enough."

Larry turned to the chief, who nodded his okay.

Larry talked into the phone. "She says that's fine. Here's the information you don't have. The Number Two at Rossman Mining says Lauren Wilcox hacked their data system. Plus, Rossman's son was beaten up out at the drilling rig. The guys who beat him say he was grabbing some dirty water and was going to have it analyzed to see if the company was lying about the pollution it was putting out."

"What does Karen want me to do?"

"She wants you to do a sneak-and-peek search of Lauren Wilcox's university email—it's Central Montana State University, they use Google—see if her fingerprints are on either of the two crimes in Montana. I told her I can't do it because there's no probable cause for the search."

Allen Pfeiffer was silent a moment. "You're right, that's not probable cause. But I might not need it. Since there's a federal warrant out on her already, I could pitch it to a federal magistrate in Montana."

Ryan was reading something on his tablet. He sprang out of his chair, rushed over to Larry Klein, and handed him the tablet, pointing to something on the screen.

Larry said, "Allen, I'm looking at the Patriot Act, Section 219: Single-jurisdiction search warrants for terrorism. You don't have to use the magistrate in the jurisdiction where the crime occurred. If you could get the magistrate who signed off on the original federal warrant to sign off on this one, that might be faster. Where was that warrant issued in 1986?"

"Here in D.C." Allen Pfeiffer said. "But he's probably long gone."

"You might not need the same guy. Maybe just the same district. It's worth a phone call."

"Let me give it a try. You want me to get back to you?"

"No," Larry Klein said, "I'd just as soon stay out of the loop on this one. You've got Karen Seagate's number, right?"

Allen Pfeiffer confirmed that he did, the two lawyers said some diplomatic lawyer crap, and they ended the call. Larry handed me back my phone. "Anything else I can do to help you suborn the Constitution?"

"Thanks, Larry," I said.

"I appreciate it." The chief stood and nodded to the prosecutor.

It was after seven-thirty that night when I got the call from Allen Pfeiffer. "Don't you go home at night?" I said to him.

"Some nights."

"Are you calling to tell me you can't crack Lauren Wilcox's email?"

"No, if that was it, I'd have waited till tomorrow. I'm calling to tell you it's done."

"Shit, you're kidding me. You got a warrant and went in?"

"We've got a lot of judges in D.C., and most of them want to get the terrorists."

"And Google?"

"We deal with them a lot."

"Okay," I said. "What did you get?"

"We can't tell if the Rossman Mining network has been hacked—"

"You'd need access to that network to see that."

"That's right. But we saw that two people were talking about hacking it."

"It's already happened?"

"Yeah, last week."

"Who's the other person, besides Lauren Wilcox?"

"We don't even know if it was Lauren Wilcox."

"Huh?"

"The conversations were on Lauren Wilcox's account, but they were never sent—and they were never signed."

"What do you mean?"

"You know how on Gmail you can write an email but not send it? It's called 'save as draft.' What they did was write back and forth to each other but not send anything. They'd log on and read the draft, then write on it."

"You mean Lauren Wilcox gave her login information to someone else?"

"Unless she has multiple personalities, yes."

"They're doing this so they don't leave any trail, right?"

"Bad guys have been doing this for a while."

"Does this mean you can't figure out who the other person is?"

"It means it will be a lot harder to figure out who the other person is. They leave fragments of metadata every time they log on to her account. We can sift through that data, but it's going to take us a while."

"Shit," I said. "Okay, what are the two saying?"

"One of them hacked the Rossman Mining system and planted some eavesdropping software, just like the person from the company said. And the hacker identified some email chatter about irregularities in the data—"

"What irregularities, what data?"

"Take a deep breath, Karen. I'm telling you everything we saw."

"Yeah, I'm sorry. I just want to get this woman."

"Well, you're not going to."

"What do you mean?"

"Like I was saying, there's email chatter about irregularities in the data—some internal reports with discrepancies, but that's as specific as they get. There's nothing about either of your two crimes in Montana."

"Goddamn it. Nothing on taking out Lee Rossman? Nothing on Bill Rossman?"

"There are no names at all. No names or code names or initials on the two people writing the emails, no identifying information on anyone in the company or outside the company."

"You didn't see the name Nathan Kress—or his initials?"

"No names, no initials."

"The fact that they're using the saved-drafts thing, whatever it's called, what does that tell you?

"It tells me they want to avoid leaving a phone record or an obvious email trail. That they know they're up to something they don't want anyone to overhear. And that they're not amateurs."

"Legally, where are you?"

"I'm right where I was a few hours ago: I know we have the right Lauren Atherton, but she hasn't done anything incriminating. In fact, she and this other person could be talking about taking out an airliner and I wouldn't have anything new on her. Because Google uses dynamic IP addresses—"

"What's that?"

"It's a little complicated, but every time someone goes to Google, their computer is assigned a different identifying address, rather than the same one. So we can't prove the communication comes from Lauren Atherton's own computer, or even from a computer in Montana. And since it's obvious there's two people involved in the communication—in fact, it could be more than two—she could always say it wasn't her saying anything about taking out an airliner. She could claim her account was hacked."

"That would take some balls, wouldn't it?"

"We've known for a long time that Lauren Atherton's got balls."

"All right, let me see if I've got what you're telling me. Lauren Wilcox and John Doe did hack Rossman Mining. You might learn who John Doe is, but it could take a while longer. And you didn't see anything that lets me arrest anyone for killing Lee Rossman or attacking his kid."

"You can bring them in for questioning, but you're not going to get any search warrants off of what I told you." He paused. "Sorry."

"So what are you going to do now?"

"I'm going to hold off one more day before we pick up Lauren Atherton on the outstanding terror charge."

"You don't have to inform her you did the search, do you?"

"Not right away. The law gives us a 'reasonable period' before informing her. Because she's a flight risk. We'll arrest her, then inform her."

"Can I get a look at the emails?"

"Yeah, I'm having them encrypted and sent to my guy in Billings. He'll hand deliver them to you."

"Allen, thanks a lot for doing this. I really appreciate it."

"No problem, Karen. Sorry I can't serve her up to you. If you're planning to arrest her, get moving. This case is on our radar now. I won't be able to slow it down much longer."

Chapter 28

Friday morning, a minute after eight, I was walking back to my desk from the break room, where I'd gotten a cup of coffee and a doughnut.

"Karen, look at this." Ryan was staring at his computer screen.

"Where are you?"

"The overnight. Item 4."

I pulled up the report. It showed everything that had happened in the most recent shifts. I read it. The body of a twenty-two-year-old white male was discovered in Allumbaugh Park. He'd been attacked by a mountain lion. There had been reports of sightings the last few days, scaring the shit out of all the old ladies with their little dogs. "Jesus, that's not how I want to go." I looked up at him.

He held my gaze for a moment. "You might want to look at the rest of the entry, Detective."

I read it. The guy's wallet said he was Kirk Hendrickson. "How do I know that name?"

"He's the guy arrested with Bill Rossman last year. Got in a fight, remember?"

"Shit, I do." I thought for a second. "You figure out who Kirk is. Call the university, whatever. I'll contact Pelton," I said, "see what he has." Pelton was listed as the night detective who had caught the case.

"Got it," Ryan said.

I called to see if Pelton was still at headquarters, but the sergeant told me he was gone. I phoned him on his cell. He picked up. I could hear the traffic noises faint on his phone.

"Pelton, Seagate. Sorry to get you off the clock."

"No problem."

"The case you caught last night—young guy named Hendrickson—what have you got on him?"

"Not much. Fish and Game were out looking for the mountain lion, and the tracks led them to the body. In Allumbaugh Park. Tell you this, you don't want to look at that poor bastard's face."

"Chewed up?"

"Just half of it."

"The mountain lion kill him?"

"Not sure," he said. "Robin's there now."

"You interviewed the first officer on scene?"

"Yeah, we did."

"Give me your best guess what happened."

"We logged the call from Fish and Game after eight. That's when the lions start moving around, they tell me. So it was after nine when we got there. I don't know if Robin's gonna find anything useful because the Fish and Game guys were tramping all over the scene. So, I don't know, maybe the guy was out there—jogging, homeless, whatever—and got jumped by the lion. Or someone killed him and dumped him there and the lion smelled him. It was cold enough he'd stay real fresh for the lion to chew on him. The body should make it to Harold soon, if it's not there already. He'll tell you what happened to the guy."

"Okay, thanks, Pelton." I hung up. I looked over at Ryan, who was writing in his skinny notebook.

He looked up. "What would you like to know about Mr. Hendrickson?"

"Whatever I ought to know."

"Kirk Hendrickson—if that's the victim—was a computer-science major at Central Montana State University. A junior with a 3.1 GPA: lots of A's, lots of C's. He was arrested in that scuffle with Bill Rossman, and he took Lauren Wilcox's water-pollution course with Bill."

"Any other charges on his sheet?"

"Couple minor traffic citations."

"Let's go brief the chief. I'll fill you in on the call I got from Allen Pfeiffer last night.'"

We walked down to the chief's office. He's usually at his desk by six. Says he can get a lot of work done in the first couple hours, before everyone else gets in. He waved us in and told us to sit.

"Two things, Chief," I said. "Last night, Allen Pfeiffer called me. Lauren Wilcox and another person have been using her email to talk about discrepancies related to the water-pollution data from some of the rigs around Marshall. Apparently, Lauren—or this other person—did hack Rossman Mining."

"Who's the other person?"

"FBI doesn't know, at least not yet. Way the two talked, they wrote an email, then saved the draft without sending it. They'd log on and add to the draft of the email."

"So there's nothing we can use on Lauren Wilcox in her emails?"

"That's right," I said. "You looked at the overnights?"

"I did. What about them?"

"The mountain lion attack? We think the vic is Kirk Hendrickson. That's what his ID reads. He's a classmate of Bill Rossman. They were arrested for a scuffle last year. He was a computer-science student. I think he might've been Lauren Wilcox's email buddy."

"That's quite a coincidence, don't you think?"

"No, Chief, I don't think anything in this case is a

coincidence."

"What do you want to do?"

"I haven't had a chance to talk it over with Ryan yet, but I think we should run out to the scene, talk with Robin, then swing back here and see what Harold's figured out. Then give you some options. How does that sound?"

He scratched at his cheek, then sat there, still. "I'm going to call Allen Pfeiffer, let him know where we are. He might want to put a detail on Lauren Wilcox in case she killed the boy and decides to run."

"Good idea. Thanks," I said. "We'll see you a little later." He nodded. Ryan and I left, got our coats, and headed to the cruiser for a trip to Allumbaugh Park. The temperature was about ten degrees, the sky overcast, the faces grim on the drivers headed off to work. We pulled into the park, about eighty acres of open space with access to the Rawlings River, four tennis courts, and a forlorn-looking kids' area with brightly painted play equipment that did little to make the place look inviting. I spotted Robin's old black-and-white Volkswagen Beetle.

The area was brush and untended grass, already taped off in yellow, and there was a tent set up to protect the area where the vic was found. Someone had already put down the steel steps leading to the tent so we wouldn't contaminate the scene. We crossed the tape and hop-scotched our way to the tent, where Robin was bent over, doing something in the dirt.

She was wearing a white plastic suit over her puffy down coat. She looked up when she heard us. "Hi, guys," she said, giving us a big, toothy smile. "You catch this one? I thought it was Pelton."

"It started out as Pelton's, but I'm afraid it's ours."

"Really? The old guy at the bar, with his fly down?"

"Yeah, we think so."

"Cool." Robin loved crime scenes. "Look at this." She pointed to a paw print. Kirk Hendrickson's remains had already been moved. "This kitty was a good hundred pounds."

"Just the one?"

"I think so."

"You saw the vic's body?"

"The parts that were left."

"Really?"

"Not an attractive look."

"You think the lion killed him?"

"I'd say no. Lions attack by biting into the back of your skull. To break your neck. The vic was lying on his back. The back of his neck was intact. The front of his face and his hands were exposed."

"That's what got chewed: the exposed parts?"

"Yup."

"So you think he was dumped here, already dead?"

"That's what I think. If the lion had attacked him, the area would be more torn up. What I'm seeing is tracks showing the lion sniffing him out, chewing on him for a while, then leaving."

Ryan said, "Cats will scavenge?"

"If they're hungry enough." Robin nodded. "Fact that the cat is here in town tells me maybe it was."

"The human footprints," I said, "they're the Fish and Game guys?"

"Yeah, they just walked in, crushed the vegetation a little. One of them blew lunch."

"So, no weapon? No shell casings?"

She raised an eyebrow.

"Thought I'd ask," I said. "All right, thanks, Robin."

"No, thank you," she said enthusiastically and turned back to her work.

We left and drove back to headquarters, then went down to Harold's lab in the basement.

"Hey, Karen, Ryan." Harold Breen looked up and greeted us

as he heard our footsteps clicking on his tile floor. It was barely eight-thirty, yet he looked washed out for the day. "I appreciate the job security," he said, "but I could've done without this young man."

"Yeah, we spoke to Robin."

"I'd stay over where you are if you want to sleep tonight," he said. The body was on a steel table, covered with a sheet. "I've got a set of photos for you to take with you."

"Give them to Ryan, will you? He got enough of a face to ID him as Kirk Hendrickson?"

"The height and weight on his driver's license match, but no, we're going to need dental records."

"Jesus Christ. Robin told us she didn't think the lion killed him because they bite you on the base of your skull."

"That sounds plausible." He shrugged his shoulders. "I don't know anything about big cats. But I think she's right. This gentleman was just a carcass when the lion came along."

"How do you know?"

"I x-rayed him. Right side of his body, the leg had a compound fracture, the hip was shattered, the ribcage all busted up. And his trunk was full of blood."

"The lion didn't do that?"

"No, his clothing was intact. I think he died of a massive trauma. Like he was dropped onto a slab of concrete from ten or fifteen feet. Or maybe hit by a car."

"When do you think you'll have a report?"

Harold Breen lumbered over to his desk and picked up a clipboard. "I've got two ahead of you. I'll try for the end of the day."

"Thanks, Harold," I said. "Cheer up. It's Friday, you know."

"I keep telling myself that."

Ryan and I left, went up to the detective's bullpen, hung up our coats, and swung by the chief's office. He invited us in, and we sat down.

"Ryan and I haven't had a chance to talk this through. We're hoping you can help us."

The chief smiled sadly. "I used to be a cop."

"Harold thinks—actually, both Harold and Robin—that the vic was killed and dumped in the park. Harold said there were massive internal injuries, like he was hit by a car or dropped or something. The lion just came along and chewed him up a little."

"So who killed him?"

I smiled. "Well, that's what we're going to figure out. Ryan, why would Lauren Wilcox kill him?"

Ryan frowned. "If Kirk was her email friend, either he or she hacked Rossman Mining—"

"Kirk was a computer-science major," I said for the chief's benefit. "It was him."

"Okay," Ryan said. "It was him. They were trying to find out about some bad recordkeeping at the company."

"I asked you why she killed him," I said.

"They found out something was wrong at the company but disagreed on what to do about it."

"Could you be more vague?"

"No." He smiled. "I don't think that's possible."

The chief said, "He found out she has a colorful past. She had to eliminate him."

"They conspired to kill Lee Rossman," I said. "Kirk was going to cut a deal, flip on her. She had to eliminate him."

"By the way, I put a lid on the case," the chief said. "The tent over in the park—we're just looking at paw prints."

"Good," I said. "Should we be thinking about Florence Rossman?"

The chief frowned. "What do you mean?"

"I don't really know. Just that her stepson gets beat up bad out at the rig. Kirk shows up dead, with massive internal trauma."

Ryan said, "Kirk didn't get stomped. It's a different kind of trauma."

"I realize that." I thought for a second. "But it has a kind of symmetry to it. Like it might've been payback."

"You see Florence doing something like that?" The chief was wearing a skeptical expression. It was clear he really didn't want to see her as a suspect.

"It didn't have to be her," Ryan said. "She didn't even have to know about it."

"Ron Eberly?" I said. "Explain why he did that."

"I don't know," Ryan said. "She's distraught about her stepson getting attacked, the poisons in the water. Ron can't un-do it, but he knows Bill Rossman had this run-in with Kirk."

The chief said, "Maybe Eberly found out that Bill was collecting the dirty water and working with Nathan Kress to shut down the drilling operation. Eberly knows he's out of a job if the operation shuts down."

"I like that better," I said. "Eberly's all about Eberly, not about doing something for Florence."

"Next?" the chief said.

"My turn," I said. "Cheryl Garrity. Kirk found out something from hacking the company. He threatened to give it to Lauren to publicize. Cheryl had to take him out before he contacted Lauren."

The chief was looking down at his desk. Ryan was tapping his stylus on the edge of his tablet. Neither spoke.

"Well?" I said.

"Did Cheryl kill Lee, too?" the chief said.

I shook my head. "I'm seeing her killing Kirk because he's threatening the company. I don't know what's going on with Lee Rossman."

The chief's phone buzzed. He got up from the soft chair and picked it up. "Yeah," he said, then listened. "Send him in."

Jorge, our IT guy, came in. He was about thirty, skinny, with gelled hair. He was wearing his usual uniform: Hawaiian shirt, cargo shorts, and flip flops. "Thought you might want to see this." He started to hand a piece of paper to the chief, who pointed to me.

I took the paper. "What is this?"

It was a list of outgoing calls Jorge pulled off Kirk Hendrickson's phone. I scanned it quickly, and I knew who killed him.

Chapter 29

"Anything you'd like to share, Karen?" the chief said as he returned to the soft chair.

I was holding the piece of paper with Kirk Hendrickson's call log from Wednesday night. Apparently, I was gazing at the wall over the chief's shoulder, not saying anything. Thinking but not saying anything—two activities not typical for me. "Sorry?"

"What's the piece of paper say?"

"Kirk called Cheryl Garrity three times Wednesday night, at her office. Last call was after nine-thirty. She killed him around nine-forty, in the garage, put him in the trunk of her car, and drove him to Allumbaugh Park, where she dumped his body."

"It says that on the paper?" Ryan said, with a hint of a smile.

"Not in so many words."

"Why'd she kill him?" the chief said, slowly and patiently.

I shook my head. "Not exactly sure. But Kirk represented a threat to her or the company—or both. Something to do with dirty water he found out about by hacking her."

"So Kirk Hendrickson and Cheryl Garrity were talking three times that night," the chief said. "They were negotiating?"

"That's right," I said.

"And negotiations broke down?"

"No, I don't think so. Cheryl Garrity got Kirk to come to the garage. He thought the negotiations were going well. He was ready to wrap up the deal."

"What was the deal?" the chief said.

"Not sure," I said. "She was gonna give him money or a job or something in exchange for his silence about what he found out."

"How did she kill him?"

"She ran him over, just like Harold said."

"Nobody saw this?"

"Not at nine-forty at night. Nobody saw it."

"Then she put him in her trunk and drove him to the park?" the chief said.

"That's right."

The chief turned to Ryan. "Is she strong enough to do that?"

"Yes, she is." Ryan nodded. "They're both about one-fifty. With the adrenaline, not a problem for her."

"Let's pick her up," I said.

"Wait a second." The chief was leaning forward, his head hanging down, his forearms on his thighs. "Nobody's picking anyone up till we get this worked out."

"What do you mean?"

"I mean I'd like to understand what the hell we're doing. You pick her up now, how are you going to come at her? With a theory? We don't have any CCTV of her killing him, no forensics putting Kirk in the truck of her car. We accuse her of the crime, all we do is give her time to clean up the trunk of her car and destroy any company records that would implicate her."

"So what do you want to do?" I said.

"First, I want to rule out the other suspects. Second, I want better forensics. Ryan, how do we rule out Ron Eberly?"

He thought for a second. "If he was in Marshall late Wednesday night, he probably didn't kill Kirk. Ask the Marshall PD to find out where Eberly was that night. We might be able to figure out where Florence was then, too."

"Karen, you okay with Ryan doing that?"

"Yeah."

"All right, good. Karen, how do we rule out Lauren Wilcox?"

"Ask her for an alibi." I paused. "Ryan, you have those photos of Kirk's body?"

"They're at my desk."

"Any that we could show Lauren that wouldn't make her puke?"

"There's a couple of his arms showing some tats. We could crop out his chewed-up hands."

"We show her the photos, we'll be able to tell if she knows he's dead."

"All right," the chief said. "Tell me how we can test out your theory that Cheryl Garrity killed Kirk in the garage."

"The way Harold described the trauma on his body, she hit him hard with her car. Look for rubber on the concrete."

"How do we know where she parked?"

Ryan said, "Rossman Mining has about ten or twelve spots. Lee Rossman and Cheryl Garrity have their names on their spots."

"We send Robin over there," I said. "She can take pictures of the concrete. There's gonna be rubber there. She can shoot the car, too, for damage."

"Go do it," the chief said.

I stood up. "And if all that lines up, then can I arrest her?" It was my way of telling him I liked his approach, it being smarter than mine.

"No." He smiled. "Then you can come talk to me." It was his way of telling me he was the chief of police. "But I appreciate your asking."

Ryan and I went back to the bullpen.

"I'm going to call Detective Carpenter," Ryan said, "see if he can run down where Ron Eberly was Wednesday night, okay?"

I thought for a second. "Is there some way to do this without tipping him off what we're up to?"

"We don't tell Carpenter what we're doing. So Carpenter can't tell Eberly. I'll just tell him it's the case we're working on. What's Eberly going to do: not tell Carpenter where he was that night?"

"Yeah, I guess," I said. "Yeah, call him, then we'll try to track down Lauren Wilcox."

I called Robin and told her to go over to the garage at Rossman Mining to see if she could get tire prints.

Ryan was done in a minute. "Carpenter says he'll get on it and get back to us as soon as he's got anything."

"Thanks," I said. "Let's find Lauren Wilcox." I walked over to get my coat. "Don't forget the photos."

"I got them," he said, pointing to his briefcase. "Wait a second. I want to see if there's a photo that doesn't show him all chewed up." He pulled the folder out of briefcase and started leafing through them. He settled on one and pulled a pair of scissors out of his desk drawer and trimmed it. "Not exactly professional-quality work, but it'll do."

We went out the back and I drove us to the Sciences Building. Into the elevator and up to the third floor. I looked in the window on the door of room 319. Couldn't see anyone. I knocked and walked in. A few seconds later, Lauren Wilcox emerged from a little office adjoining the lab.

"Detective Seagate," she said. "Detective Miner." Her face showed her impatience with the interruption.

"Professor Wilcox, we need a minute."

She nodded. Didn't invite us to sit at any of the round tables off to the side of her river machine, which was still.

We want to show you a photograph, see if you can help us identify a person. Will you do that?"

Again, a silent nod. Ryan handed her the photo of Kirk's right arm. On the bicep was a tattoo of three computer keys—Alt, Ctrl, and Del—with the Del key above the other two, making a triangle.

She smiled. "Oh, yes, I recognize this. It's one of my students: Kirk Hendrickson. When I saw it, last year, I asked him what it meant. He said it's the three keys you use to re-boot a Windows machine when it freezes up." She laughed. "I'm an Apple person, but he said it means sometimes you need to just start over. I thought it was really cute."

She looked at me and then at Ryan. When she noticed we didn't consider it really cute, the smile faded from her face. "Why are you showing me this? What's happening?"

"Professor Wilcox, we need to tell you that a body of a young man has been recovered. He was carrying a wallet with the ID of Kirk Hendrickson. This is a photo of his right arm."

Lauren Wilcox began to shriek and started to collapse. Ryan rushed over to her and grabbed her. He led her over to one of the round tables and helped her into a chair. She was shrieking and moaning. "No," she cried, over and over. She looked like a puppet with all the strings cut, her arms and legs limp, her head hanging down. It was a couple of minutes before she could talk in sentences.

"What happened to Kirk?" she said, tears still streaming down her cheeks.

"We're not sure. The body was discovered late last night. The autopsy hasn't been conducted yet."

"Where was he found?"

"In Allumbaugh Park."

"What was he doing there?" she said.

I shook my head. "Can you help us with that?"

"I have no idea."

"When did you last see Kirk?"

"He's not in any of my classes this semester. Maybe a couple of weeks ago."

"You haven't had any contact with him in the last few weeks?"

She thought for a minute. "No, I haven't." She tried to pull herself together. "Why did you show me the photo of Kirk's tattoo? Why didn't you show me his face?"

"His face sustained some damage in the attack. That's why we aren't sure it's Kirk Hendrickson. We'll need to check dental records. The photos of his face are very disturbing."

She swooned again, and Ryan had to grab her to keep her in the slippery plastic chair.

We sat with her there for a minute while she got her crying under control. Eventually, she put her hands on the table and began to sit upright. "This is unbelievable," Lauren Wilcox said. "I don't understand why anyone would want to hurt Kirk. He was such a nice young man. So bright."

"Tell us a little about him."

"Well, we weren't friends socially, of course, and he never shared anything with me about his personal life—girlfriends, whatever. But I do know, from the course he took with me, that he was passionately interested in protecting the environment."

"Was he one of your majors?"

"No, in fact, he was a computer-science major, I think. I tried more than once to get him to switch over, but he thought his talents lay more on the quantitative side of things. He thought data was the entry point for everything, and computing was the key to all data. We had many interesting discussions—in class, I mean—about how computer modeling was changing the way we understand how ecosystems evolve over time—you know, as new elements are added. I can tell you, as an old-fashioned ecologist with test tubes—like you saw the other day out at the river—I got a new appreciation of where the field is heading: data mining and data analysis. I think Kirk could have been an important person in that approach." She paused and wiped away a tear. "This is just such a huge loss."

"So you don't know if there was anyone had a grudge against

him? Anyone he might have had some conflicts with?"

"No," she said. "I don't know of anyone like that at all."

"To your knowledge, he wasn't involved in any—I don't know—inappropriate activities? Hanging around anyone who might have lured him into something he shouldn't have been into?"

She looked at me quizzically. "What do you mean? What kind of activities?"

I brushed it off with my hand. "Nothing in particular. Just a generic question we always ask: about people he was associating with. But, like you said, you didn't see him regularly now since he's not in any of your courses." I stood up, and Ryan did, too. "Do you want us to notify the department, see if they can send someone over to help you get home or whatever?"

"No, Detective." She pushed herself to her feet but kept one hand on the table for balance. "I'll be okay. Thank you for asking."

"All right, Professor Wilcox. Sorry to have to tell you this about Kirk, but we appreciate you helping us out with the information. If you think of anything that can help us with the investigation, would you give us a call?" I put my card on the table.

Ryan and I took the stairs down to the parking lot. Inside the Charger, I said, "She is a very good liar."

"She is, indeed."

"But she did not kill Kirk Hendrickson."

"No, she did not," Ryan said.

Chapter 30

We caught up with the chief in the incident room, where he was studying our board. He looked up when he heard us. "Any luck?"

"Lauren Wilcox ID'ed Kirk Hendrickson from his tat. She was the one working with him on hacking Rossman Mining, but she didn't kill him."

The chief glanced at Ryan to see if we were on the same page. Ryan nodded.

"I got a call from Florence Rossman." The chief walked over to one of the old desk chairs, sat down, and interlaced his fingers behind his head.

"Oh, yeah?" I sat down a few feet away. "What did she want?"

"She started off by asking where we were on Lee's murder. I told her it was our top priority, *et cetera*. Then she told me Bill's regained consciousness."

"That's good."

The chief nodded in agreement. "And he has a lot to say."

"Also good."

"The guys beat him up because he was grabbing some dirty water. But Bill explained why he was doing that. His father told him that he and Cheryl Garrity were arguing about what to do about the pollution levels in the wastewater. The DEQ analyst who oversees the data collection and reporting found discrepancies between what was in the dirty water and what the company said was in it."

"What did Cheryl want to do about these discrepancies?"

"Bill said Cheryl wanted to 'work with' the DEQ analyst to see if they could reconcile the discrepancies."

"As in bribery?" I said.

"That's how I'd interpret it."

"And Lee? What did he want to do?"

"Lee wanted to get to the bottom of it. If the company was reporting inaccurate information, find out how that was happening and fix it."

"So Bill was grabbing some dirty water to get it tested independently?"

"That's right." The creaky chair groaned as the chief shifted his weight. "Bill offered to get the water. Lee okayed it, telling him to get it to Nathan Kress."

"Not Lauren Wilcox."

"No, Lee trusted Nathan."

"Holy shit. That means Cheryl Garrity did kill Kirk Hendrickson."

The chief put up his palm. "Hold on. Let me tell you Florence's plan."

"Florence has a plan?"

"She wants to set up a meeting with Cheryl. She'll wear a wire. Cheryl will confess. Game over."

"I have a plan, too: Now that Bill Rossman's talking, we depose him. Game over."

The chief shook his head. "Getting Cheryl to confess, on tape, is stronger. Her lawyer could poke all kinds of holes in Bill's deposition."

"Such as?"

"One, it's hearsay. Bill wasn't present when Cheryl and Lee argued about what to do. So the lawyer says it was really Cheryl who wanted to do the right thing, and Lee wanted to bribe the DEQ analyst." The chief started sticking out fingers with every point he made. "Two, we don't have any evidence to support Bill's story. Three, Bill's a grieving son lying to protect his father's memory. Four, he's a moody high-school graduate who spends his time drinking beer and screwing women he doesn't know." He paused. "Get my point?"

"What about Kirk?" I said. "How do we get Cheryl to admit to that one?"

"I told Florence we could coach her on that."

Ryan said, "If Robin comes back from the garage and says she's got the rubber on the concrete, Florence tells her it's all on the CCTV."

"There is no CCTV." And immediately I felt the two sets of eyes looking at me. "Okay, I get it," I said. I could feel my face getting hot. "But how do we know Florence will stay on script?"

"I think she wants to make sure we've got the best shot of putting Cheryl away for killing her husband. And if she doesn't stay on script, then we go back to your plan: deposing Bill and getting as much evidence as we can on the two murders."

"So who was it came up this idea: Florence or you?"

"The basic idea came from her."

"Why do you think she suggested it? What does she know about the law?"

"She said she'd be able to get Cheryl to admit things we wouldn't be able to."

"For example?"

"She said we'd have to trust her."

"You willing to do that?"

The chief let out a long breath. "Yes, I am. If it blows up in our face, what does it cost us? Cheryl Garrity doesn't respect her local police department? Given that we have a backup, I think we should do it."

"What do we do next?"

"I wanted to bring it to you—you're the lead detective. It's your case. You have to sign off."

"Okay. Done."

"I'll call Florence." The chief stood up. "See if she can set it up at her house, tonight at nine. We'll go over at eight, wire her up, rehearse her. With any luck, we'll have this thing wrapped up by ten o'clock."

I stood. "Let me get in touch with Robin, see if there's rubber on the concrete. If I'm right about that, let's do it."

"Let me know," the chief said as he left the incident room.

Ryan and I went back to the bullpen, where I called her. "Hey, Robin, tell me what you see."

"DMV says Cheryl Garrity drives a 2014 Lexus RX350 SUV in dark red. I contacted the Lexus dealer here in town, and that model comes with Bridgestone all-weather tires. I got the tire patterns off their site. I looked up the track distance, you know, the side-to-side wheelbase? And you called it: There's rubber on the concrete that matches that model in tread design and track distance."

"Great."

"Couple other things. There's some dark red paint on the concrete pillar next to her space, like she turned the wheel abruptly and smashed the passenger side of the Lex into it. It lines up with one of the tire patterns on the floor. Plus, the car in her spot this morning is a rental. It's a Chevy Cruze."

"I need you to do me one other thing while you're there. Look around and tell me where you'd mount a CCTV camera so that it covers the Rossman Mining employee cars."

"Give me a second." I heard the soft squishing of her soles on the concrete as she walked around the area.

"Make it unobstrusive, so the Lexus woman could park there every day and not notice it."

"They use tube fluorescents in the ceiling for the main lighting, but there's flood lights mounted high up on the poles.

You could put a wide-angle lens in the pole marked Section M. That would do it."

"Section M. All right, thanks a lot, Robin." I ended the call and turned to Ryan. "Tell the chief to set it up, would you?"

I was jumpy the rest of the day, like I was getting prepared for some kind of performance. The truth was, I didn't have much of a role to play, but I really did want it to go smooth. If Florence was telling us the truth about what Bill Rossman said, his father was a good guy—and Cheryl Garrity definitely was bad business. But I had no confidence that Florence could pull off this performance. And my instinct, when someone says "Trust me," is to run for cover. Still, the chief was right in betting that Florence was being straight with us. After all, she wanted to get Lee's killer more than any of us cops did.

The chief took me and Ryan and Jorge out to an Italian place for dinner. It was a nice gesture, but it was obvious we were all having a crappy time. The silences stretched for minutes. I think everyone was trying to think through the angles, see if we had prepared everything as much as we could. Naturally, I was trying to imagine everything that could go wrong. After all, I used to go out with Murphy, right before he came up with his Law.

Back at headquarters, we checked and re-checked the recording device we were going to tape to Florence. Finally, at 7:30 we piled into the Charger and headed out to her place. We traveled east along the river, then took the winding road up to the foothills above the reservoir. Couple of times I spotted a set of still, shiny eyes in the brush along the road. We got closer to the Rossman house, and on one of the hairpin turns I could see down to the reservoir, a huge black hole with a necklace of dim lights.

As we got closer, the chief called Florence to tell her we were on our way and to ask her if there was someplace we could park the Charger out of sight. She told him they have an eight-car garage, and she'd leave one of the doors open.

We pulled into the big parking area with the garage built into the rock face. Florence had left a garage door open, like she said she would. I was wondering how you can have an eight-car garage. Not all that difficult, really: four doors, with each space two cars deep. In fact, it was closer to a twelve-car garage if you counted all the space along the back wall for the woodworking equipment, the wooden cabinets nicer than the ones I have in my kitchen, and the bay where you climb down a ladder to work under a car, like they have at those quick-lube places. Off to one side was a big metal frame holding a car engine on a set of chains. Lee Rossman apparently liked two-seater sports cars. I counted four of them, including a green Triumph with white racing stripes, from the sixties. The three guys I was with were all moon-eyed over a white coupe with a long hood. I didn't see a nameplate on it, just a yellow crest shape with a black horse rearing up.

As we left, the chief located the button on the wall and shut the garage door. We walked over to the wide double doors that led into the house. I knocked. Florence answered the door and invited us in. She gave us each brief smiles, including me, who she'd slapped pretty hard last time we were together. Then she leaned in and hugged the chief. I introduced Jorge, who looked like he was having a vertigo attack when he gazed through the tall window at the reservoir below.

"You'll be quite safe," Florence said to him, "I assure you." She led us into one of the conversation areas in the main public room and invited us to sit. The chief sat near her on a long leather couch. He opened with a few polite questions about how she was doing and thanked her for her willingness to do this. She answered with gracious but concise replies. It was clear she wanted to get this show going.

"Ms. Rossman, we believe Cheryl Garrity is responsible for two deaths: Lee, obviously, and a young man named Kirk Hendrickson. We think she killed him Wednesday night, after nine-thirty."

Florence Rossman looked deeply sad. "I don't know that name."

"He was a college student at Central Montana; he wasn't associated with the company," I said. "We know that he and Lauren Wilcox, the professor—you know who I'm talking about?"

"Yes, I do."

"Okay. He and Lauren Wilcox hacked Rossman Mining. We assume he was planning to publicize the data discrepancies that Bill told you about, in order to discredit the company and shut down its operations here in Montana. Cheryl lured him to the garage under Lee's office, where she hit him with her car. She transported him to Allumbaugh Park, where she dumped his body."

"How do you know this happened?"

"We have some circumstantial evidence—tire tracks, paint in the garage, and so forth. But here's the important point: We need you to tell her she was recorded on closed-circuit television in the garage."

"I didn't know there were cameras in there."

"There aren't. But she doesn't know that. You tell her there's a camera mounted on the pillar near the Rossman cars. It's on the pillar marked Section M. "M" as in mining. Tell her Lee had it installed. One of the employees' cars was vandalized about a year ago, and he just did it on his own. He didn't go through the building management. He thought it would be more effective if it was unobtrusive, so he had it attached to one of the floodlights. The pillar with Section M painted on it, if she asks. Can you do that?"

"Of course."

The chief said, "Cheryl won't have any way of knowing you're aware of the Hendrickson murder. His death hasn't yet been made public. But someone has shown you the footage from the garage. Earlier today we got Lauren Wilcox to identify Hendrickson by some tattoos in a photograph, but Detectives Seagate and Miner agree that she didn't know that he was murdered, or even that he was missing. And Nathan Kress was not involved in any way, either. And obviously, your stepson could have no way of knowing about it."

"Therefore anything I know about the murder in the garage should completely surprise Cheryl."

"That's our belief," the chief said. "It has to be the camera in the garage. We think that after Cheryl realizes that you know about the Hendrickson murder, she will realize that she has no alternative but to listen to anything you propose. At that point, it should be relatively easy for you to lead her into admitting that she killed him. Of course, it would be ideal if you could get her to confess to Lee's murder, as well. We haven't yet been able to gather sufficient forensic evidence to charge her with that crime, too." He paused. "Do you want to talk about strategies for getting her to admit her role in the crimes?"

"I have known Cheryl Garrity for over four years, Chief Murtaugh. And my late husband knew her for decades. I believe I will be able to lead her to the statements that will incriminate her."

The chief nodded. "Do you have any questions you want to ask us?"

"I do not," she said.

"Karen." The chief turned to me. "Would you like to go with Ms. Rossman and attach the wire?"

Chapter 31

Jorge busied himself with the recording equipment while Florence unbuttoned her blouse and I taped the receiver to her chest. She buttoned the blouse up, then turned to me, for a professional opinion, I guess. I thought the blouse was opaque enough to disguise the wire. She buttoned one more button, then walked up to her wood-framed dressing mirror. She frowned slightly, then went into a closet and came out with a cable-knit sweater. She put it on, looked at her image again, and was satisfied.

"Detective Seagate," she said, once we were done with the costume, "I want you to know how sorry I am that I slapped you the other day."

"I understand," I said. "Forget it."

"The beating that Bill took, on top of Lee's death—it's been an unbelievably stressful time. When I got that phone call from Ron—I realize now that you need to investigate the private lives of the people close to Lee—my emotions were just out of control. What I did was wrong, and I apologize."

She walked toward me and put her arms around me tightly, holding the hug for a few seconds. Then she stepped back. "Did you feel it?"

"Excuse me?"

"Did you feel the device?" She tapped the radio taped between her breasts.

"No," I said after a second. "Feel free to hug Cheryl Garrity."

I left the bedroom to tell the chief and Ryan we were ready.

When we got back, Florence was seated at a long mahogany makeup table with dozen of bottles and jars up against the big mirror, which was ringed with light bulbs. In the mirror I could see she was seated still, her eyes closed. Her expression was serene, with a hint of a smile, like she was meditating.

Jorge and the chief were off to the side in an area about twelve by fifteen, kind of a separate living room inside the bedroom. Jorge was sitting on a small upholstered chair, his equipment on a side table. The chief sat on a high-back chair with a floor lamp next to it. I sat on the edge of the king-size four-poster bed. Ryan sat on the long bench at the foot of the bed.

At two minutes to nine, the doorbell chimed. Florence Rossman stood up and walked with a model's gait to the bedroom door. She glanced back at the chief, who gave her an encouraging nod.

A few moments later, we heard the door open. Jorge adjusted a dial on the controls on his recorder. He turned to me and gave me a thumb's up.

"Cheryl, thank you so much for coming. Let me take your coat."

We heard the rustling of the fabric, then Cheryl Garrity said, "Thank you."

"I hope the roads weren't too bad."

"No, they were fine," Cheryl said brightly.

We heard the tapping of the shoes on the concrete floor, then silence as the women reached the carpeted area in the living room.

"Please sit," Florence said.

"Thank you."

"Let me start by telling you how much it has meant to me— your kind words over these last horrible days."

"They have been horrible," Cheryl said.

"It has been a real comfort to me to know that you have

everything under control—at the office, I mean."

"You know you will always be able to count on me for that," Cheryl said.

"I asked you to stop by this evening so that we could chat about the future of Rossman Mining. I never sought the position of president, of course, but the tragic events of this week have thrust me into that position. I am confident that with your considerable assistance, we will be able to ensure that the company continues to prosper for many, many years.

"I share that confidence, Florence," Cheryl said.

"It will take you some time to become comfortable with my style of management, having worked so long with Lee. I'm afraid I'll have to ask questions that Lee certainly never had to ask."

"About the operations? Yes, that will be fine. I will always be available to help you understand the business as we move forward."

"I'm so glad to hear that," Florence said. There was silence for a moment. "Let me start, then, with this question: Why did you kill Kirk Hendrickson?"

There was more silence. I glanced over at Jorge, who nodded his head to tell us the wire was still working.

"Excuse me?" Cheryl Garrity's voice was low and hesitant.

"I asked you why you killed Kirk Hendrickson."

"What ... what makes you think ... who is Kirk Hendrickson?"

"He was the young man who hacked into the company's data system. The young man you killed Wednesday night. Tell me about that."

"I really don't ... I have no idea what you're ... I don't know what you're referring to."

There was silence for a moment. "Cheryl, I need you to listen to me. I have a right to know what is going on in the company. Please don't pretend you don't know what I'm referring to. And don't be defensive. I'm not criticizing you. After everything that has passed between us? It's very likely I would have made the same decision you made. Start by telling me what you know about Kirk Hendrickson and why you decided to kill him."

There was another long pause. "Kirk Hendrickson was a student at the university. He was working with that professor, Lauren Wilcox. Lee told you about her, I think."

"Yes," Florence said. "Yes, he did. Now what exactly did Kirk do?"

"He hacked our system. He planted some spyware."

"Have you had that spyware removed?"

"Yes."

"That's good. Did he also discover any irregularities in our reports to the DEQ?"

"Yes," Cheryl Garrity said. "He did."

This time it was Florence who paused. "That was unfortunate. That should not have happened."

"I take responsibility for that. It won't happen again."

"Did you kill him before he had a chance to pass that information to the professor?"

"I don't know whether he did tell her—or whether he was ever planning to."

"I don't understand."

Cheryl Garrity spoke softly. "I decided to take action when he told me he was going to blackmail the company. He asked for one-hundred thousand dollars—he called that the first payment. If I did not give him that money, in cash, he said he would go to Lauren Wilcox with the information he had downloaded from our system. But I'm not sure he had fully worked out what he was going to do."

"I see."

"I didn't come to you. I thought ... I thought it was best if you didn't know. To insulate you from it."

"I appreciate that."

"How did you find out … how do you know what happened?"

"There's a camera in the garage. I have it on the tape." The leather on the couch rustled, as if Florence shifted her position. "What did you do with the body, after you hit him with the car?"

"Really, Florence, I don't think it's a good idea for me to talk about these details. The less you know, the better."

"If we are to work together, Cheryl, we need to create an environment of trust. As we go forth, each of us knows something about the other's background that cannot be divulged. I know, for example, that you are aware of my background, in St. Louis—"

"I never breathed a word of it to Lee. Never once."

"I know that," Florence said.

"I swear on my parents' graves that I never told a soul. No one."

"And that is why I know you will be honest with me now."

"I killed Kirk Hendrickson because he threatened everything that Lee worked so hard to build over the decades. Everything Lee and I built. I don't know whether he had already told Lauren Wilcox, but I felt it was necessary to eliminate him. If it turns out that Lauren Wilcox has that information, we will have to deal with that. She might be sufficiently intelligent to let it be, for her own welfare. Perhaps she realizes that I am fully prepared to act on behalf of our company, to protect your interests and mine, if there is an additional threat. I hope you believe that."

I looked over at the chief, who was smiling.

"I do, Cheryl. I do," Florence Rossman said. "Thank you for being frank with me. I know it's not easy to talk about these things. But you need to know that I will not repeat what you say here tonight."

"I cannot tell you how relieved I am to hear that."

"Now I need you to answer one more question."

"Anything." I could hear the relief in Cheryl's voice.

"Why did you kill Lee?"

It was silent in the living room. It was silent here in the bedroom.

"I had to." Cheryl's voice was barely a whisper now. Jorge was hunched over his equipment, fiddling with dials. "He was going to destroy the company."

"It was about the wastewater," Florence said softly.

"I begged him to let me take care of it."

"How were you going to do that?"

Cheryl let out a sad laugh. "I had already begun to solve the problem. In fact, the solution was in sight. The DEQ analyst. He's fifty-six years old. He wanted a little security for his retirement. He wanted a position with Rossman. I told him that wouldn't be a problem. And it wouldn't have been …"

"Except for Lee, you mean."

"Yes." Cheryl Garrity's voice was a whisper. "Except for Lee."

"Did you order the attack on my stepson?"

"Oh, my God, no. Never. I would never have done anything to hurt Billy." Cheryl Garrity started to moan. "When I learned what had happened to him, I was sick. Literally, sick. I love Billy, like a son. I held him in my arms the day he was born. I was there. Lee wasn't there that day. Lee wasn't there a lot of days. Of all the things I have done, the one thing that I will never forgive myself for is my role in the attack on Billy. But you must believe me that it was Lee's decision, not mine. Lee must have authorized Billy to take that water. I would never have let him do that. I would never have let him put himself in danger like that. I pray for Billy's recovery."

"I believe you, Cheryl. I believe you."

The leather sighed as the two women stood.

"I'm so glad we had this talk, Cheryl. Come here."

There was silence, then Florence said, "Robert, please come out now."

After a moment, Cheryl Garrity said, "What did you just say?"

The chief, Ryan, and I came out of the bedroom and arranged ourselves in a semicircle, facing Cheryl Garrity.

Florence Rossman unbuttoned the top two buttons on her Irish sweater, then the top button on her blouse, revealing the recorder taped to her chest. "It's over, Cheryl."

Cheryl Garrity stood there, motionless and uncomprehending, her bag hanging from her shoulder. "What have you done, Florence? What have you done?"

"I have done the right thing, Cheryl," Florence said, her voice steady and strong.

Cheryl Garrity's face hardened into an expressionless mask as she started edging backward, slowly. "No, Florence, you definitely have not done the right thing."

"It's your turn to do the right thing," Florence said. "You will get only one shot."

Ryan and I charged at Cheryl Garrity. She thrust her hand into her bag and pulled out a snub-nose revolver, barely visible in her palm. Ryan leapt at her, trying to tackle her around the waist, but he was a half-second too late. I got a hand on her right arm, but she pulled it free, raised the revolver to her mouth, and fired. The explosion was deafening in my ear. I felt the spray of blood on the side of my face and the back of my neck and saw it spatter onto the brown leather couch and a Native American rug. Her body crumpled to the floor, pinning my left hand under her shoulder.

I pulled my hand free. "You okay?" I said to Ryan, who had landed hard on the floor.

"Yeah, I'm fine," he said, lifting himself up and rubbing his elbow.

The chief was on the phone, calling for an ambulance.

Florence stood there, serene, as the action swirled around her.

I walked over to her. "You knew she was armed?"

"I had told her Lauren Wilcox would be coming later. I assumed she would bring a gun."

"How did you know she wasn't going to shoot you?"

"I didn't know."

Ryan and the chief were standing over Cheryl Garrity's body, which was still. Her eyes were half-closed. I said, "She gonna make it?"

"No," the chief said, turning away from the body.

I spoke to Florence Rossman. "Did you know she killed Lee?"

"Yes," she said. "I knew. Only Cheryl loved him enough to have done it."

"That's a strange way to show love," I said.

"I don't think so, Detective. When she said she never told Lee about my past? That was true. She never did. She knew it would destroy the marriage, which would have given her some satisfaction. But she didn't tell him because she thought it would hurt him too much. She was wrong about that, of course. She never understood the first thing about Lee. She didn't realize that he was incapable of real love, that he simply used women all his life. She forgave him for that—forgave him even for disposing of her and marrying a woman like me. Lee never experienced a great passion, but Cheryl did—she loved him completely. She was a great romantic. In that way, he was never worthy of her."

Chapter 32

A shooting seems to take just a few seconds, but really it takes hours. There is the ambulance, the medical examiner, the statements at headquarters. We weren't done until after two AM.

Right after the shooting, Florence Rossman drifted back into her bedroom. I let her be for a while, then I knocked and walked in to ask if she needed anything. She was sitting on a chair, gazing straight ahead. She looked a little startled when she saw me in the doorway.

"Could you come in, please?" she said and gestured for me to sit. She seemed to want to talk, and I was the only other live female in her house. "Am I going to be arrested?"

I thought for a second. "I'm not an attorney, but I don't see you've broken any laws. Nothing related to Cheryl's suicide, that's for sure."

She nodded but didn't say anything. We sat there for a few moments.

I said, "You want me to leave?"

"No." She looked at me, and for the first time I saw the loneliness in her eyes. "Stay."

"Have you thought about your plans?"

"I have thought about that, quite a bit, since Lee's death. I think I'll head back to St. Louis. That's where I'm from. It's where I belong."

I didn't know what, if anything, that last sentence meant. "And the company?"

"It's going to a real mess for a while. I'm sure there will be an investigation of the discrepancies about the wastewater. And about the DEQ analyst. It could go on for months, maybe longer." She paused. "I don't even know who can take over for Cheryl. Lee relied on her so much."

"And longer term?"

"I'm going to talk with Bill about that. If he continues to recover as he has, I'd like to sign it over to him. That is, if he wants it."

"I bet he will."

"Why do you say that?"

"I think he loved his father, and his father loved him. Lee trusted him to help him to get to the bottom of the problem with the dirty water. He didn't go to Ron Eberly." Florence Rossman looked at me, to see if I was making some sort of comment about her affair with him, which I wasn't. "He'd known Ron for thirty years, but he went to Bill. I think Bill is an honest guy, like his father was. Working out on the rig like he's doing, when he could take a desk job or just sit on his ass, waiting for an inheritance? No, I think he's still learning from his old man."

Florence Rossman smiled a little bit. "That's very kind of you to say. I think he is honest, too. But with all that's happened, Bill might decide to walk away. He might not be strong enough to stay. He might be like me."

"Tonight, after you got Cheryl to confess to the two murders, you could have said 'Excuse me' and left the room, let us walk out there and arrest her. But you stood there and told her to do the right thing. You knew she was armed. That took some courage."

She closed her eyes and kept them shut for a bit. Then she opened them. "That was more about not caring either way."

"What I'm saying is, the oil business isn't your life. It never was. But I bet it will be Bill's life."

"Well," she said, "he will have to decide. He can have it if he wants it."

The doorbell chimed. It was Harold, the medical examiner. "Excuse me," I said to Florence, and headed out to the front door to greet him and stand around while he called the official time of death.

The way things worked out—with Cheryl Garrity shooting herself—made it easy for me and Ryan. It was a simple suicide, with the confession on tape and four live witnesses. Suicides are always easier than officer-involved shootings, with their paperwork and mandatory leave and the other cops asking you if you're okay.

Still, it's hard not to think about how it ended and ask yourself if you could have handled things differently, if you could have prevented any of the deaths.

I thought a lot about Florence's comment that Cheryl was a great romantic, but I didn't buy it, and I still don't. I'm no psychiatrist, but it seems to me Cheryl Garrity was just a murderer. She didn't have anything going on in her life except Rossman Mining, so she did whatever she thought she had to do to protect it, including killing two people.

When she decided to kill herself rather than Florence with her one shot, I think she had decided she didn't want to go to prison for the rest of her life or take the needle. Florence told me it meant Cheryl was fundamentally a good person, that she understood that what she had done was wrong and she deserved to die for the two murders. I think Florence is a little bit more of a romantic that she realizes.

I was fine with how Florence got Cheryl to bring a weapon: telling her Lauren Wilcox would be there so she would think she might need to kill one more person. And I was fine with Cheryl killing herself like that. I don't see that it does anyone any good to put her on trial for a few weeks. It would sell a bunch of newspapers, especially if whatever Florence was into in St. Louis became public. But if the purpose of a trial is to discover the truth, there was no point in going through the motions. Cheryl had already confessed to both murders.

And I didn't see any reason to make Cheryl sit in prison forever and reflect on her actions. You're the kind of person decides to kill the boss because you doesn't like how he wants to solve this particular business problem, it doesn't seem all that likely reflecting is going to help you see anything clearer.

Maybe a priest or minister or a thoughtful normal person would think it's a real shame that Cheryl got so screwed up she started killing people, and how it was a real loss when one of God's children dies. I was willing to go along with the first part. Yeah, it would have been better if Cheryl Garrity hadn't gotten so twisted in the first place. But Sunday night, when she knifed Lee, she forced the rest of us to move on the next two questions: Who killed Lee Rossman, and what were we going to do to get that person off the street? The cop questions.

The point is, Florence did a damn good job taking care of the Cheryl Garrity problem. Of course, there's never only the one problem, and you never finish taking care of it. Bill Rossman is going to be shitting bricks for the rest of his life every time he coughs a couple times, wondering when he's going to start getting sick from the poison those idiots poured down his throat.

And Lauren Wilcox is done teaching, or at least teaching outside of a federal prison. She was picked up the day after Cheryl killed herself, and Allen Pfeiffer told me she would probably do the full ten years, or most of them. That will give her plenty of opportunity to think about whether she did right by Kirk Hendrickson. So far, we don't know if Cheryl Garrity was telling the truth that he was blackmailing her. After all, Cheryl was a pretty good liar, and maybe she just wanted to justify her decision to kill the kid. We did figure out that Kirk used Lauren Wilcox's university email account to hack into Rossman Mining. So it's clear he was a coward—about that, anyway. But that didn't mean he deserved to die, and it didn't let Lauren Wilcox off the hook for involving him in the hacking.

All in all, it was a long, tough week, but I didn't see how I could have prevented either of the murders or saved anybody any heartache. So, all things considered, I was doing fine.

Monday morning, Ryan and I were writing up all the files we had neglected while we were driving back and forth to the oil rigs. I heard a woman's voice behind me.

"Excuse me," she said. "I was told you're Detective Seagate." I turned around and looked up. It was Maureen McNamara, Mac's daughter. She looked confused. "Oh, I'm sorry, you're Eleanor, aren't you, the woman I met at the hospital? From Mac's AA group?"

I felt Ryan looking at me. After a moment, he stood up, said "Excuse me," and walked out of the bullpen.

"Sit down, Maureen," I said. She sat on the chair next to my desk. "I'm Karen Seagate."

"I'm sorry. You'll have to excuse me. I haven't gotten a lot of sleep lately."

"No, Maureen. We did talk that night at the hospital."

"Why didn't you tell me who you really were?"

I let out a long breath. "I don't know … sometimes I don't know what to say, so I lie. I thought maybe it would upset you if you knew who I really was. Your father was so banged up—and it was me did it to him. The fractured skull. It was just too complicated." I looked down at my desk. "I shouldn't have lied to you. I'm sorry."

The color drained from her face. "Oh, my God. I didn't know my father had attacked you."

"You never found out the name of the woman?"

"No," she said. "I knew he attacked a woman, and she defended herself. I knew she hit him, but I never found out her name. She didn't press charges. That was all I knew."

"It was me. He was drunk. He broke into my house. I didn't know it was him. I thought it was a rapist or something. I hit him." I stopped and tried to get myself under control. "Can I do something for you, Maureen?"

"Mac asked me to tell you he was sorry. I didn't know what he was talking about. The note just said, tell Karen I'm very sorry. I swear to you: I didn't know he attacked you. I'm so sorry."

"How is Mac doing?"

Maureen started to cry. She shook her head. "He walked out of the VA."

"You mean, they didn't discharge him?"

"No," she said. "He walked out, with the bandage still on his head. He made it back to my place. He had gotten his hands on some liquor." Her shoulders started to shake and her head sank onto her chest. "He tried to slit his wrists. He botched it, which isn't surprising. I came home and found him on the kitchen floor. I called 911."

I felt the warm tears gliding down my cheeks. I got out of my chair and went over to Maureen, put my arms around her.

"Where is he now?" I said after a minute.

"Back at the VA," she said. "All the note said was to tell Karen he was sorry. And that he would never do it again."

I managed to get Maureen taken care of, tell her I was sorry she'd had to go through all of that. And I asked her to tell her father that I knew he didn't mean to hurt me, that I wasn't mad at him or anything. That I was sorry I fractured his skull. That I wished him the best.

I didn't feel so good and went home after that. I don't remember exactly what happened the rest of that day. I'd had some episodes like that a few times before. This time, when I came to I contacted Sarah, the woman who runs my AA group, and she and a couple of others came right over. There was always someone with me the next week. I was smart enough this time to call in to headquarters and talk to the chief. He said he understood and would take care of the personal-leave paperwork. He did all I could have asked him to do, and he didn't make me feel guilty or ashamed. He didn't need to. I'd already done that to myself.

The next week I had it under control and came back into the office.

"Hey, good to see you back," Ryan said, giving me a big smile, like I'd just gotten back from a vacation. "I missed you," he said. I decided to believe him.

"I missed you, too." I knew I was telling the truth.

A little later that day, he said to me, "I found out about Florence Rossman. Her life in St. Louis that we didn't know about?"

"Yeah?"

"Guess what her secret was."

I thought a second. "Actually, Ryan, I don't think I want to know."

He looked puzzled. "You sure?"

"Yeah, thanks, anyway."

###

About the Author

Mike Markel is the author of the Detectives Seagate and Miner Mystery series:

    Big Sick Heart (Volume 1)
    Deviations (Volume 2)
    The Broken Saint (Volume 3)
    Three-Ways (Volume 4)
    Fractures (Volume 5)

He lives in Boise, Idaho, with his wife.

Thank you for taking time to read *Fractures: A Detectives Seagate and Miner Mystery*. If you enjoyed it, please consider telling your friends or posting a short review. Word of mouth is an author's best friend.

MikeMarkel.com

The Detectives Seagate and Miner Mystery Series

To sample or buy any of these titles, visit Mike Markel's author page on Amazon.

Visit MikeMarkel.com.

BIG SICK HEART (Volume 1)

Bad decisions have finally caught up with police detective Karen Seagate. Her drinking has destroyed her marriage and hurt her job performance, and the chief is looking for any excuse to fire her. Still, she and her new partner, a young Mormon guy who seems to have arrived from another century or another planet, intend to track down whoever killed Arlen Hagerty, the corrupt leader of Soul Savers. Clawing his way to the top, Hagerty created plenty of enemies, including his wife, his mistress, his debate partner, the organization's founder, and the politician he was blackmailing. When Seagate causes a car crash that sends a young girl to Intensive Care, the chief thinks he finally has his opportunity. But even the chief can't believe what Seagate does when she finally catches the killer.

DEVIATIONS (Volume 2)

Former police detective Karen Seagate is drinking herself to oblivion and having dangerous sex with losers from the bar when the new police chief tracks her down. The brutal rape and murder of a state senator by a lone-wolf extremist gives Seagate a chance to return to the department, but the new chief has set down some rules, and Seagate is not good with rules. At this point, she is just trying to stay alive. With nothing left to lose and nobody left to trust—not even her partner, Ryan—Seagate goes off the grid to find the killer. She doesn't care that she will be fired again. She has much bigger problems, now that she has been captured inside the neo-Nazi compound.

THE BROKEN SAINT (Volume 3)

Seagate and Miner investigate the murder of Maricel Salizar, a young Filipino exchange student at Central Montana State. The most obvious suspect is the boyfriend, who happens to have gang connections. And then there's Amber, a fellow student who's obviously incensed at Maricel for a sexual indiscretion involving Amber's boyfriend. But the evidence keeps leading Seagate and Miner back to the professor, an LDS bishop who hosted her in his dysfunctional home. Seagate takes it in stride that the professor can't seem to tell the truth about his relationship with the victim, but her devout partner, Ryan Miner, believes that a high-ranking fellow Mormon who violates a sacred trust deserves special punishment.

THREE-WAYS (Volume 4)

When grad student Austin Sulenka is found strangled, nude on his bed, the first question for Seagate and Miner is whether it was an auto-asphyxiation episode gone bad. Evidence strewn around his small apartment suggests that he spent his last night with three or four women, each of whom had a motive to kill him. Later, when one of the women is pulled from the reservoir with a bullet in her brain, Seagate and Miner wonder which victim was the prime target—and whether there will be more. As Seagate and her partner try to unravel the complicated couplings, she finds herself in a three-way relationship that threatens to destroy her own fragile sobriety.

FRACTURES (Volume 5)

The fracking boom in eastern Montana has minted a handful of new millionaires and one billionaire: Lee Rossman, the president of Rossman Mining and the leading philanthropist in the small city of Rawlings. Rossman is the last person Detectives Seagate and Miner expected to discover dead in the alley next to a strip club. Later, when Lee's son is found out at the rigs, with significant internal injuries, numerous broken bones, and a belly full of fracking liquid, the detectives know the two crimes are related but can't figure out how. In their toughest case yet, Seagate and Miner try to solve a mystery awash in enormous fortunes, thwarted ambitions, and grudges both old and new.

The Reveal: A Detectives Seagate and Miner Mystery

Following is the Prologue of *The Reveal*, Book 6 in the *Detectives Seagate and Miner Mystery* series.

He sat in his car, a hundred yards from her house, thinking about what had happened. For the past four days now, that was all he had thought about. What she had done. At first, it had made him furious, but by the second day the fury had cooled into determination and begun to assume a shape. He had molded that shape, kneading it, pressing and forming it, and now he was ready to act.

Nobody would notice his car parked among all the others on her quiet street in the original residential neighborhood in Rawlings, Montana. The houses were old—fifty years, even a hundred—two stories set on narrow lots separated by fences. Running alongside the fences were driveways of broken concrete or pea gravel or tire ruts on grass leading to one-car detached garages in the back.

He cracked the window to let out the cigarette smoke. One leg tapping rapidly, he was oblivious to the sweet aroma of the turned soil from the gardens that edged the front porches up and down the block. In the purple twilight of a mild late April evening, he did not notice the white, pink, and yellow petals of the daffodils, chrysanthemums, peonies, and tulips all around him.

Here on Harkins Street, there were no light poles. Porch

lights on the close-set houses, some only ten or fifteen feet apart, provided ample illumination. He glanced at the house sitting back from the curb to his right. On one side of the large spruce tree in the front yard was a metal swing set; on the other, a trampoline with netting around it to keep the kids from tumbling out. He looked up at the second story. It was dark; the kids must be asleep. An indistinct yellow glow came from the side of the house, near the rear on the main floor. He guessed it was the kitchen. That would be the parents, sitting at the table, exhausted after getting the kids to bed. They wouldn't hear anything.

He looked down the street toward her house. The last car had left more than fifteen minutes ago. He pulled his phone from his jacket pocket to check the time: 10:03 PM. He lowered his window halfway and flicked his cigarette out, watching it bounce once and then roll a few inches and come to rest on the pavement, the grey smoke snaking into the night air and then disappearing.

He got out of the car and closed the door softly. The lock didn't catch. He leaned his hip into the door and it clicked almost silently. For a moment he stood there, looking up and down the block and listening. A pickup truck approached. The driver saw him and steered out into the middle of the street to give him room. As the bright twin cones from the truck's headlights swung away from him, he turned back toward his car, as if he had forgotten something on the front seat.

After the pickup rumbled past, he looked and listened again. He picked out the tiny scratching sounds of two squirrels chasing each other around the base of an oak tree in a yard across the street. He heard the rustling of new leaves on a quaking aspen twenty yards in front of him on the narrow strip of grass between the street and the sidewalk. But he saw no one and heard nothing to cause him any concern. He was alone on the street.

He walked around the front of his car, his finger tracing a line in the fine layer of dust on the warm hood; then he crossed the grass strip, and stood on the sidewalk. His hands in his pockets and his head bowed slightly, he walked toward her place. A gentle breeze carried the sound of recorded music from the top floor of a boxy, ugly tan-brick house. In the next house, blue and red lights from a widescreen flickered across a front room.

He stopped, her house now just across the street. Although the eight or ten cars that had been parked in her driveway and along the curb were gone, the house was still lit brightly on both floors. He looked around one more time but saw no one. He stepped between two parked cars, crossed the street, and approached her waist-high wooden fence. He pushed the gate open, the spring creaking softly. He followed the flagstone path, then climbed the five concrete steps to the painted wooden porch.

He opened the dented white aluminum storm door and stepped up to the window in the navy blue wooden door. He peered inside, then glanced over his shoulder once more. Seeing no one on the street, he tried the knob. He smiled, relieved to find it unlocked. He opened the front door slowly, stepped into the house, and gently closed the door behind him.

He stood on a worn oval-shaped braided wool rug, the blue, green, yellow, and red braids faded with time and use. He closed his eyes and breathed in the air, still moist from all the students, still heavy with the scents of their sweet lotions and perfumes and the cheeses, dips, coffee, and wines.

He opened his eyes. Before him was the wide staircase, made of sturdy, dark wood ornately turned. The balusters were polished, but the handrail was dull, the surface scratched and nicked. His eyes followed the worn stairs to the second floor, which was lit by a single bulb in the hallway.

He glanced to his left, into the living room. The inside wall was dominated by a wide brick fireplace, painted white but stained grey above the firebox by decades of smoke. The room was crammed with mismatched furniture: sofas, loveseats, armchairs, and cherry dining-room chairs. Side tables, hassocks, and metal TV trays were scattered about, all of them covered with glasses, cups, china dishes, and plates.

To his right was the dining room, with a cut-glass chandelier from another era and a heavy, dark dining table with thick legs. At the far end of the dining room was the doorway to the kitchen. He heard the sound of running water.

He walked into the dining room, over the old carpet with floral patterns and ragged fringes around the four sides, past the large table. He paused in the entryway to the kitchen, glanced behind him, and listened. He was confident they were the only two in the house.

She was washing dishes, her back to him. Her hair was wavy, grey mixed with brown. She wore a grey wool blazer over a red turtleneck knit top. Her jeans were black, her socks red. She wore no shoes.

She did not hear him.

When he stepped onto the old linoleum in the kitchen, it creaked, startling her. She turned to face him, her eyes wide.

It took him a moment to realize that she was weeping. She turned off the faucet and faced him again. "You scared me." She wiped at her eyes with a finger. "What are you doing here?"

He did not respond.

She gathered herself and stood up straight, her posture defiant. "What do you want?"

His voice was soft and unforced. "To give you one more chance to fix this."

She raised her chin. "And if I don't?"

He held her gaze. "What you did was wrong."

She shrugged, becoming more comfortable in a familiar role. "Wrong?" She almost smiled. "That wouldn't be the first time."

"I don't think you realize what is happening here."

She tilted her head slightly. "Tell me what is happening here." Her jaw was high. "Explain it to me."

His expression was solemn. "We're way past that now." He paused. "I explained it all before. No more talking. It's time for you to make it right."

She shifted her weight and asked again. "And if I don't?"

"Then I have no choice."

"You always have a choice. You could, for example, take responsibility for your actions. You could move on." She shook her head, as if arguing with him were futile. "But I imagine that isn't your style. That would be a foreign concept to someone like you."

He advanced a few steps. She stepped back until she bumped into the counter, which was covered with dirty dishes and glasses. Her eyes fixed on his, she moved her right hand tentatively across the countertop. Her fingers wrapped around the black wooden handle of a long bread knife.

When he saw the blade coming at him, his left hand came up quickly. Grabbing her wrist, he stopped her tentative thrust. He twisted her wrist, pulling her trunk and head downward. She cried out and the knife fell to the floor.

"You shouldn't have done that." His voice was threatening now.

"You're going to kill me? Over this?" She lost her composure and began to weep again, out of control.

He maintained his grip on her wrist, then twisted it sharply. She cried out once more, her upper body bowed over.

"You didn't get back to me," he said.

Through the pain and the fear, her speech was high-pitched and halting. "You know ... very well why I didn't."

He tightened his grip again and twisted her wrist once more. Something in the wrist gave way.

She screamed in pain. "Do it, then."

"Last chance," he said.

"Fuck you."

As he twisted her wrist again to draw her arm behind her and spin her around to face the counter, her left hand came up quickly and she scratched his neck. He flinched, more in surprise and indignation than in pain. He drew his right hand up to his neck and inspected it for blood, but the scratches were too shallow. He drew the hand back and hit her hard across the side of her face. She recoiled, her body sending glasses and plates crashing onto the linoleum. Then she fell forward and sank to the floor.

Still conscious, she reached out, grabbing at his leg, but her hands had no strength. He pulled his leg back, breaking her grip easily. He bent down and lifted her, her legs swinging weakly in the air. Gathering her up, encircling her arms, he hoisted her onto his hip and carried her out of the kitchen and into the dining room.

She tried to kick him, but her legs bumped harmlessly against the dark table. He stood in the foyer, looking up the staircase. He shifted her body, her legs still swinging but slower now, and tightened his grip on her waist. He stepped onto the staircase.

He heard her breathing, faint and shallow, as he climbed the stairs. She didn't scream but moaned softly as he paused briefly on each of the thirteen steps. Finally, his breathing labored, he stood on the pale green carpet in the hallway. He lowered her to the floor and looked at her, but her eyes, half-shut, did not focus on him.

He looked down the staircase toward the foyer and the front door, then reached down and picked her up again from her waist. He tried to get her to stand but her knees buckled. He took a deep breath, gathering his strength. Reaching under her armpits from behind her, he pulled her up to her full height, her toes barely touching the carpet. He adjusted her position so that she was centered over the broad staircase.

He grunted as he pushed her off the landing. When her face first hit a step, he heard a single cry of pain, but then she made no more sounds, except for the rumbling and slapping as her limbs and her head thumped against each of the steps. She came to rest with her face and shoulders on the braided rug in the foyer.

He walked down the steps, careful not to touch the handrail or the wall. He stepped over her legs, which extended up to the fourth step. Lifting her blazer, he saw her chest rise and fall softly beneath her red turtleneck and smelled the faint aroma of fresh perspiration.

He picked her up again by the waist. It was easier this time because now her limbs did not move at all. Once again he carried her up the thirteen steps and lifted her to her full height. Her head was slumped forward, her chin on her chest, her arms and legs limp. Once more he thrust her out over the staircase. Her head hit the steps with a muffled thud and she tumbled down. This time, her body came to rest on the staircase. She looked like she was swimming down the stairs, her right arm dangling over a step, her left arm behind her, by her hip.

Again he walked down the staircase, stepping carefully around the body. Standing on the braided rug, he placed two fingers on her neck. There was no pulse. He waited another moment, studying her red turtleneck, which now did not move. He lowered himself to one knee and placed his ear to her mouth. He felt no breath.

He stood up straight and walked to the front door. Using his jacket to turn the doorknob, he opened the wooden door, then shouldered the screen door, which had not clicked shut when he entered the house three minutes ago. He wiped the doorknob with his jacket as he secured the wooden door, then pushed the screen door shut, the air hissing as it escaped from the pitted aluminum closer. He rubbed at the push knob with his jacket, then turned and descended the five concrete steps. He followed the flagstone path, opened the gate, and walked down the block toward his car, his hands in his pockets and his head slightly bowed. He heard no unusual noises and saw no one.

###

www.ingramcontent.com/pod-product-compliance
Lightning Source LLC
Chambersburg PA
CBHW060537180626
46817CB00002B/612